IS THERE A CABLE CAR KILLER?

It could be . . .

Dunbar Oates

Celia's high society decorator, who shows up uninvited on Maggie's doorstep, full of explanations . . .

Henry Sloan

Celia's husband, who was slightly mistaken about his place in his wife's will . . .

Mark Sloan

The son who seems bent on self-destruction by drink, an expensive proposition . . .

Lindy Sloan

The college girl who was scheduled to take Celia for a little mother-daughter psychiatric counseling on the day of her death . . .

Mary P. Lewis

Celia's best friend, who Maggie discovers lurking around the back door of the Sloan mansion . . .

Also by Elizabeth Atwood Taylor:

A Maggie Elliott Mystery

MURDER AT VASSAR

THE
CABLE CAR
MURDERS

Elizabeth Atwood Taylor

IVY BOOKS • NEW YORK

Ivy Books
Published by Ballantine Books
Copyright © 1981 by Elizabeth Atwood Taylor

Library of Congress Catalog Card Number: 81-5809

ISBN - 0-8041-0281-3

This edition published by arrangement with St. Martin's Press, Inc.

Manufactured in the United States of America

First Ballantine Books Edition: December 1988

To the Atwood sisters:
Stella, Margaret, and in memory of Lib

ACKNOWLEDGMENTS

(pp.37,59) "Something to Think About" (Willie Nelson)
© 1966 Tree Publishing Co., Inc.

(pp.69,70) "Long Black Veil" (Wilkin & Dill)
© 1959 Cedarwood Publishing Company, Inc.
All Rights Reserved—International Copyright Secured

(p.88,89) "When I'm Sixty Four" (John Lennon and Paul McCartney)
Copyright © 1967 Northern Songs Limited
All rights for the U.S.A., Mexico and the Philippines controlled by
Maclen Music, Inc.
Used by permission. All rights reserved.

(p.123) "Those Were the Days"
Words and Music by Gene Raskin
TRO © Copyright 1962 and 1968 Essex Music, Inc., New York, N.Y.
Used by Permission

(p.166) "Them There Eyes"
By Maceo Pinkard/William Tracy/Doris Tauber
© Copright 1930 by Bourne Co.
Copyright Renewed   All Rights Reserved
International Copyright Secured

PART ONE

ONE

THE DECEMBER STREETS WERE SLIPPERY FROM THE RAIN THAT had been coming down hard most of the day. It had stopped, but the fog was beginning to move in now, over the bridge and across the bay and into the city, adding to the misery of the crowd waiting to catch the next downhill cable car.

It was a large crowd for a weekday, abnormally swollen as by disease with Christmas shoppers come down to the water-front street-artist stalls, the boutiques and specialty and import houses to find, they didn't know what. Something different, from India perhaps, or Japan or Nepal or Easter Island, or anywhere but industrial America. Something colorful, something handmade, something unusual for the relatives back in Des Moines and Buffalo, Dallas and Denver and Clinton Corners. Something special sent back from the black-sheep restless and wandering ones who'd ended up in this quiet, beautiful city on the western rim of the continent, stopped at last, perhaps, only by the wide cold Pacific Ocean.

And as always there were tourists, shopping today not only for Christmas but simply because they were tourists, then waiting to ride the cable car so they could say they'd done it.

All with lists in their pockets or heads, most of them feeling cross, and angry, and impatient, and worried about money, and tired, and getting cold now with the fog moving in so fast. Burdened down with bags and packages that kept trying to get away and fall in a jumble onto the dirty wet streets, arms sore with the effort of keeping them all together. Heads sore with the worries of how to get done everything they had to, or thought they had to, before the miserable day itself arrived.

Fathers who didn't live with their children anymore, struggling to do something really special with Santa Claus and the presents this year, whether they could afford it or not, because

3

they'd left that unhappy home, or it had fallen out from under them. And then, what a depressing prospect: January and Master Charge and Visa; dark short days and long cold nights; the mailbox full of bills and broke. Alone, too, more often than not. The girls they got at Henry Africa's didn't last very long, usually.

Mothers who did still live with their children, simply at their wits' end.

A discontented-looking lot, no sign of brotherly love or Christmas spirit, whatever these might be, in the entire crowd that straggled up the side of the hill like a lost cause waiting for something to come along and save it. So observed Richard Patrick O'Reagan, himself a homeless father, standing across the narrow street. A worried-looking woman halfway up the hill caught his attention; she was middle-aged and a little heavy, but her eyes—he noticed them even from across the street—were extraordinary, a curious rich green and clear, he thought, clear as mountain lakes. And bright; too bright? With tears? No packages. Expensive clothes; a good tweed; carrying not wearing her raincoat; soft rich leather handbag—what's that color, he asked himself, purply, soft, mauve?

His mind ticked off the details. He was an ex-policeman, trained in precise observation, and he was also an artist of sorts. Part-time, liked to draw, always had. And paint, when the energy was right and he had the time. So mauve, yes, and shoes to match.

The problem isn't money apparently, he mused. But she looked worried. Her children probably, on drugs or flunked out of school, or getting married, or not getting married . . .

Garish-looking blonde to one side, a little behind her uphill. The showy sort, he judged, raincoat open in spite of the cold, bright pink nylon blouse with her tits showing through—big ones. Dark tinted glasses on this gray day, trying to look like some TV star? Farrah? Fat chance. Still wearing a rainhat, day-glo pink and lime-colored bubbles on clear plastic. Ugly creature, garish, he thought again, really calls attention to herself. Why do they do it, these ugly ones? Women!

And where were all the cable cars? He looked around: Beach Street, Hyde Street, the worried-looking woman with the green eyes, the peroxide number, several men in sunglasses this sunless day . . . and now a drab-looking woman in a loose brown uniform of some sort, moving along in front of the crowd. Shaking and ringing a little tambourine kind of plate with money in it, gabbling in a singsong; he could just hear some of the pitch:

"Give mumble blah madam, mumble Cripple Children mumble blah give blah, nickel mumble dollar help mumble mumble homeless . . ."

O'Reagan watched, feeling cynical . . . although she had the big Christmas Charity ID pinned to her flat brown chest. . . . He heard the rumble of the cable car and looked to his right. The car had crossed the top of the steep hill and was coming down fast. A derelict, skin and bones, clothes too thin for the season and too big for the alcohol-abused body, shuffled aimlessly into the street, past noticing—or more likely past caring about—the approaching car. It would soon be upon him, but O'Reagan clamped a big hand onto the fragile shoulder and pulled the man back, a reflex from the time his job had been to keep the citizens alive whether they liked it or not.

"Come on, Admiral, watch where you're going, for Chrissake—" An odd sort of motion across the street, from the corner of his eye; he turned. "No!" he yelled, "no, aaah, *Christ!*"

The crowds on both sides of the street pulled back; there were screams, confusion. The woman with the green eyes had somehow lurched out in front of the cable car and then gone down underneath its wheels. O'Reagan had to shove against the people on his side of the street, some of them now pushing forward toward the woman, or, rather, toward the body. For it was immediately clear there was no chance of life there; she'd been practically cut in half between the steel wheels of the cable car and the steel tracks.

The brakes screeched, and the cable car finally stopped down at the end of the block. O'Reagan pulled out the police whistle he still carried and blew it, several times, loud, loud, shouted to the people in his fiercest voice, hoarse with shock at the sight he'd seen and was still seeing: "Move back, *move* back, keep this area clear, goddammit!"

The derelict he'd been pulling back, been concentrating on when it happened—O'Reagan saw him bending over the body now, then straightening and hurrying off, clutching something under the loosely flapping raincoat. Then he was across the street, moving quickly with his head down and then bumping, thump, into the ugly peroxide blonde, who was also leaving.

The collision knocked off her hat and sunglasses, and she grabbed for them. The tramp stopped and looked her in the face. O'Reagan could see only her back. The pair seemed for a moment frozen, timeless.

"Hey there! You! Admiral! Stop!"

The drunk turned and ran off around the corner, leaving the blonde still standing there looking after him. Then she grabbed up her hat and ran off in the same direction. They didn't seem worth pursuing, O'Reagan thought, and anyway it wasn't his job anymore . . .

He pulled his attention back to the grisly scene in front of him. People in the crowd were talking to each other in low voices, shifting their weight around, some of them looking away from, some of them staring at, the horrible object which had been, until a few moments before, a worried-looking middle-aged woman with beautiful green eyes, standing with no packages in a crowd of Christmas shoppers.

Now the body was twisted horribly, the top half thrown out on O'Reagan's side of the tracks, the arms outflung, the eyes gaping, no longer beautiful, an expression on the face of—was it surprise? Anger? The neck in an impossible position, obviously broken, and below that, a horrible mangled mass of—flesh and blood, he thought, flesh and blood and . . . *stop* it, he told himself and again forced his attention back to the scene before him.

He'd seen bodies before: dead ones, mangled ones, bloody ones. But this was worse, the rainy, peacetime Christmas streets, he himself only a moment before speculating about her troubles and admiring the fine eyes. . . .

A few others in the crowd were pushing toward the edges now, wanting to get away, wanting not to be involved. The driver of the cable car had got out and was leaning against its side.

"Oh, my God," he was saying, over and over. "Oh, my God."

A blue and white squad car pulled to a skidding stop on the cross street below, in front of the cable car. Another cop who'd heard the whistle came running from around the corner, took in the scene, and stopped and stared.

The Crippled Children's woman was holding her thin sides, clutching the tambourine and money across her little round stomach, laughing loudly. Another woman, an earthy type in a long rainbow-colored skirt, one of the street artists, walked over and slapped her. She looked surprised, and stopped.

The driver of the squad car could be heard in the sudden silence calling on his radio for assistance, for an ambulance, for all those needed at the scene of the death to record it, investigate it, and finally clear it away. Then he got out of the car and started over toward O'Reagan, whom he had known slightly when they were fellow policemen.

In an hour or so, O'Reagan was thinking, this will be just another street corner, with bigger than usual crowds down for the Christmas shopping. He and the squad car cop talked; then the other cop joined them, and O'Reagan described briefly what had happened as far as he knew it. They walked over to the mangled body.

By now the crowd, even in this short time, had swollen to monster proportions. The smell of blood, O'Reagan thought, draws them like a bunch of sharks. The body all mangled. The legs twisted, sticking out across the other side of the tracks; at first they'd twitched, jerked horribly, one slim purply shoe fallen off, but now the legs, thank God, were still. Two little rivers of blood, mixing and diluting with the dirty rainwater, ran slowly downhill alongside the metal car tracks. More blood, lots of it, splattered all around both sides of the tracks. And little bits of, skin and guts, it must be, and cloth.

With an almost physical effort, O'Reagan dragged his attention away from the horrible sight. He saw with satisfaction that other cops were beginning to close off the area so no one who hadn't already left could go until they'd made a statement. The woman who'd been collecting for the crippled children seemed to have disappeared, he noticed. He looked at his watch; it was twelve-thirty. So it had happened, then, he noted to himself, at approximately twelve-fifteen. No more than fifteen minutes could have passed. At the most.

Why did this woman die this way? he wondered to himself, curiously formal. And that damn tramp took her purse, he thought, that soft purple purse—must've looked like a whole goddam gold mine. Her ID would be in it. Maybe the guy dumped it in the trash, maybe he won't be hard to find, maybe someone here knows her . . . and it's not my job anymore, he reminded himself, thank God.

The cop from the squad car blew his whistle now—three times, a long and two short ones—and held up a hand for silence.

"May I have your attention, please," he began. The crowd quieted; it was staring, avid, eager for the next installment.

TWO

I WAS HAVING A HARD TIME KEEPING THE PACKAGES I WAS carrying from crashing down to the ground. I'd been shopping, I was trying to unlock my front door, and the key was sticking the way it always does in wet weather. Finally I eased one bag down along the wall, got a hand free, grabbed another bag, put it down, gave my full attention to the sticking key . . . and heard my telephone ringing.

I opened the door in a hurry and shooed the dogs up ahead of me, but by the time I got upstairs the phone had stopped. So I went back down, brought up the groceries I'd left on the stoop, and started putting them away.

Then I remembered by friend Kelly was supposed to call about going for a run in the park. It was now almost five o'clock and nearly dark, so I went back to the front room and called her. I hadn't really wanted to go running—it was something I did sometimes with the idea that it was good for me—but mostly it seemed a dreary sort of effort, the way most things did at that particular time in my life. When Kelly's phone didn't answer, after a fair but not enthusiastic six rings, I went back and finished putting away the groceries and made myself a cup of tea.

I have one of those big, long San Francisco apartments that take a while to walk from one end to the other of, high-ceilinged and a little cold most of the year, a bit ramshackle and still quite cheap in spite of the rents rising like cakes all around me. From time to time I had fits of worry that the landlords would double or triple the rent and I'd have to move, but they didn't, and the fits passed. Other worries generally came to fill up the space they'd left, though. If there was nothing specific, I could usually count on a general sense of impending doom to come in and fill the gap.

It was the time of day when for a good many years I used to sit down with a nice stiff drink, preferably gin, but not any-more—not for a few months now. Three months and seventeen days, when I stopped to think about it. Which was most of the time. I wasn't so crazy about afternoon tea, but alcohol was out, and coffee after five o'clock kept me awake all night, and, any-way, too much of it made me more nervous than I already was, which was plenty.

After I drank the tea and smoked about ten cigarettes, I took my dogs out for a walk. It started to rain so I cut it short, and when I got back the phone was ringing again. I remember all these details, probably, because I had to go over them several times later on for the police. In fact, there's a formal statement somewhere covering all this—indeed, a whole collection of them—buried away in some official cellar. Microfilmed by now, I suppose.

I ran back upstairs to answer the phone and was surprised to hear the voice of my niece, Lindy.

"Maggie?"

"Margaret," I corrected automatically. I was trying to change my image at the time. "How nice to hear your voice."

Actually I loathed the telephone and didn't much like the sound of anyone's voice, on the phone or off, but I'd always liked Lindy in spite of her mother and father and felt willing to make an effort to sound friendly.

"How are you? Are you home from school?"

"Yes, I'm fine, thanks, Mag—Margaret, sorry. I got in Wednesday. Listen, is Mother there by any chance?"

"Celia? I don't think I've seen her in a year, Lindy. Since around this time last year, Christmas, in fact. Why?"

Celia was my half sister, but I saw her only occasionally, and then as briefly as possible. We had never been very close, and when she and I ended up living in the same city our paths had little reason to cross. She was ten years older than I, for one thing, and I believe always rather resented the fact that our mother had married my father only a few months after her own father had been killed—and resented me as well when I came along a year or so later. She never admitted that, though, and was always a conscientious "big sister" to me. Rather too much so, bossy, in fact. And meddling and rigidly conventional she seemed to me while I was growing up, and what I saw of her later gave me little reason to change my mind. In any case, given my attitude toward Celia then, I seemed an unlikely place to be looking for her.

I asked Lindy again: "Why? Is she missing?"

"I don't *know.* I mean, of course not. But she was supposed to meet me here at three-thirty—I'm at home—so we could go together to my shrink; we'd arranged last summer for a joint session at the beginning of this vacation. . . . And she never showed up. Which isn't *like* her . . . And Cook's wanting to know about dinner. She says Mother was supposed to bring her some ducks from Petrini's and never did, and that's not like her either—you know how dinner is always ready on time come hell or high water. I went on to the shrink's, and when I got back, there was still no sign of her, nor had she telephoned."

Lindy, who was nineteen and back East in her second year of college, had had the kind of education starting with kindergarten that insists on words like "nor" even in times of extreme stress, the upper-class British model and the stiff upper lip instilled to prevail no matter what the circumstances. . . . I brought my mind back from Lindy's language patterns to her present concern.

"Well. Where was she earlier? What was she doing? Do you know?"

"Just she was going downtown somewhere, because she was saying at breakfast how awful it'd be down there this time of year. She didn't say if she was meeting anyone, and if she did it probably wasn't anyone I know or she would have said. Because you know how she's always trying to hook me into her world, her friends, her—oh, skip it, I'm sorry. Anyway, she just said she'd meet me here at three-thirty sharp—and I was here, and she wasn't."

"Oh well, then. I was downtown myself earlier, and it's a mess. Christmas shoppers, and rain most of the day, and buses broken down, and godawful traffic. Maybe she ran into someone she knew and had lunch. Maybe they decided to get off the streets and go to a movie or something."

"She hates movies."

"Well, but it's Friday. People are never themselves on Fridays. Especially this time of year. She took her car, I'd imagine?"

The thought of Celia on a bus was like the thought of the Queen of England on her hands and knees, crawling, so the question was more rhetorical than actual.

"Yes. Actually, Daddy's got her car. He's gone off north somewhere, some Buddhist place."

"Buddhist? Henry?"

"I know, but it's some new technique he's been wanting to learn so he can use it on his patients. He was talking about it at breakfast. He was supposed to go up yesterday but put it off because of some party last night. Anyway, they decided he should take the Mercedes because it's better for a long trip like that. But his Porsche is gone too, so presumably Mother took that. At least Mark's here, so he's not in it. Daddy won't let him drive it anyway; he totaled another car last week, so it must be Mother—"

"Lindy! Is Mark all right?"

"Oh, sure, he wasn't hurt, he never is—"

"Was he drinking?"

"He *says* not, but who knows? Anyway, he wasn't drunk because he walked away from it without being arrested for drunk driving this time. No one else was hurt, luckily. But listen, about Mother—"

"All right, I'm listening."

Mark is Celia's son, a couple of years older than Lindy. He'd been kicked out of two colleges by his junior year, and both times drinking was involved. Celia had been worried enough about him when I'd seen her the year before to talk to me about it, though I was not her usual choice of a confidante, and she hadn't realized the kind of drinking I was doing myself then.

She'd come by my apartment to bring me a Christmas present, I remembered, which she never missed doing no matter what the state of relations between us. It was always something for the flat; that year it was a Stieff crystal owl about eight inches high. After she had gone, ignoring her instructions not to open it before Christmas, I unwrapped the package and looked at the owl, then put it away in a bottom drawer. I didn't want it around looking at me; so cold, I thought, and superior. Somewhat like Celia in fact. Anyway, when she stopped by with the present, I'd offered her a drink, which she, surprisingly, accepted. She let loose for a couple of hours that day on what had been happening in her family, especially with Mark.

"First Princeton and now Berkeley. He can reapply in a year, but *will* he? I'm thinking of cutting off his money supply—do you think that would help? We've had him to an excellent man Henry knows; he recommended a group, though I had wanted something more intensive. . . ."

Celia's husband Henry Sloan is a shrink. They'd always had a lot of trouble with Mark, but I thought it must have hurt at least their pride to admit defeat and "seek outside help." But they'd done it finally. A bit late, perhaps.

Celia said that day that she was obsessed (she'd picked up a lot of expressions like "obsessed" since she'd married Henry) that Mark was following in the footsteps of a great uncle of ours, J.C. As a child I'd been half in love with the image of J.C., an orphaned cousin of our mother's brought up by my grandparents. I'd loved the family stories of his wild and rebel doings: pawning his dead mother's jewels for money to go drinking and gambling and woman chasing, biting the thermometers in half when they finally had him tied down to a hospital bed before his death from TB and what the aunts called "extreme dissipation" at the age of twenty-one. But Celia had always hated those J.C. stories, and, with Mark a year away from twenty-one, she had been really frightened he'd be dead within the year "just like that awful J.C.," if somebody didn't do something—and who better than his mother?—to prevent it.

The trouble was, she'd tried everything she could think of over the past few years, and he only, she said, got worse. At the time I tended to discount what she was saying, partly because I considered Celia too conservative and stuffy to think much of any judgment of hers, but also because I was in the last of several years of increasingly heavy drinking myself and was therefore prone to dismiss allegations of excessive drinking as exaggerated. And unlike J.C., Mark did not suffer from tuberculosis, as I pointed out to Celia several times. . . . I brought my mind back to my niece, who was saying: ". . . don't know what to do; the answering service had just the usual social junk; it just isn't *like* her."

"Did you try any of her friends?"

"Yes," she said glumly. "They were mostly all together at

some Crippled Children's luncheon until the middle of the afternoon and then went home to sleep it off. Mother was going but canceled out at the last minute. She didn't say why, according to Mary P. Lewis, who was expecting to go with her. I don't know who else to try. I just thought of you as a kind of last resort," she added ingenuously. "Do you think I should try and get in touch with Daddy?"

"No, I don't. What's so important about tracking her down, anyway? It's only about six-thirty. Probably she ran into someone, stopped for a drink and forgot the time."

But as I said it, I didn't believe it. Celia had never been a drinker; she made a face over the occasional social sherry, and I'd never known her to forget an appointment in her life.

"Well, all these people are coming to dinner, didn't I say? And there isn't any. Dinner. And it isn't *like* her, and I'm worried." There was a long quiet space on the phone, and then I heard a sigh and a sniffing sound.

I made my voice as cheerful and confident-sounding as I could. "Whatever's happened—which is probably nothing, in the middle of the day, downtown—I can see why you're worried, but I can't believe anything very bad has happened. Take some deep breaths, first of all."

Lindy didn't cry or get emotional easily—all that British modeling in the expensive schools had had its effect—and she did as she was told. Also, she was a good kid, basically.

"I'm sorry, Maggie, I mean Margaret, but I really—"

"That's OK, now listen. I'm going to hang up and make a few phone calls, just to check out if there have been any accidents. You stay there, and I'll call you back. Don't worry if it's not for a while; this'll probably take some time. Go fix yourself a drink."

"I already have. But I can call, if you'll tell me where; I guess you know from when David—are you sure you don't mind doing this? I didn't mean to stir all that up for you. I should have thought. I'm sorry."

"That's all right, Lindy, really, I mean it. I know where to call, and I'll be glad to do it. Go fix yourself another drink, or go figure out something with Cook about dinner. I'll call you back. It may be an hour or so, though."

I knew where to call because I'd done it before. And in spite of what I'd said to Lindy, I was feeling very shaky at the thought of going through those phone calls all over again, partly apprehensive about Celia and partly jarred by the reminder of the death of my husband David five years before. Scared that feelings I'd tried to cancel out with drinking and pill taking might reemerge. Dead, and no chance anymore to iron out the wrinkles, make up for the mistakes, get back or forward to the real clarity and—the word's one I hate to use, but there's no other— the love, still alive somehow beneath the accumulated junk of a sometimes troubled relationship . . .

They did come back, the old feelings, stronger than they'd been in a long time because there weren't any chemicals in me to muffle them. I sat there and felt them, hit the point of "OK, I've had enough," and still I sat there. With my hand on the telephone, not wanting to pick it up, as I had not wanted to that other time.

It was the end of August; David had gone up to our cabin in the Trinty Mountains, and I'd stayed home. He always liked driving back in daylight when he was on the motorcycle, but the end of the day came, and he didn't, and night did, and he still didn't come, and if he'd had trouble with the bike he would have called. I waited several hundred years more, and then I called the police. They gave me another number to call, and finally there was the voice that said, yes, there's been a bad accident. . . .

I dreaded picking up the phone and making those calls again. In spite of the way I'd felt about Celia, her money and her society life, and what I had called in a sneering tone her "values," I suddenly realized I had some long-buried feelings, if not of love at least of affection, for her. I remembered a serious Celia dividing a piece of her birthday cake into exactly equal portions, her face stiff with concentration, the green eyes, like mine, like our mother's, measuring out the amounts. It was important to Celia to be fair, always. And I remembered when she fell in love for the first time, at sixteen, awkwardly, ridiculously . . . she was a late bloomer, was Celia; late for Texas, anyway. . . .

I tried to pull my thoughts together and made a conscious effort to stay out of the past. I hoped to God there wasn't going to be a voice on the telephone again saying, yes, there's been a bad accident. . . . How could there be? And if there had been, I told myself, someone was there always—servants—they would have notified Celia's home, surely? I lit the last cigarette in a pack that had been half full when Lindy called and picked up the telephone, dialing five-three-three . . .

THREE

AFTER I HAD IDENTIFIED CELIA'S BODY, THE POLICEMAN who seemed to be in charge, a Detective Simmons, said I could leave to go and break the news to Lindy and Mark. And I could find out where to reach Celia's husband, Henry Sloan, and break the news to him, too. I felt very sick and tired after what I'd seen in the morgue, and wished I could just go home and forget all about it, or leave it to someone else. But there wasn't anyone else.

Simmons also said that while Celia's death had presumably been an accident, the police would want to talk with all of us a little later.

"I said *presumably* an accident, Mrs. Elliott." A large man with a beefy red face and matching red-brown hair and eyes, he had no discernible bedside manner.

"You see, we can't be one hundred percent sure at this point"—he stretched the big lips in what he perhaps imagined to be a smile—"and one hundred percent is what we like to have. In all cases of unexplained death. If you see what I mean."

His suit was brown, too.

I didn't mention any of this to Lindy or Mark, although they'd have to be warned eventually to expect . . . what? I realized I didn't know myself what Simmons had in mind.

"Oh! I *knew* it! I *knew* something terrible had happened!"

Lindy burst abruptly into the tears she'd been holding back for the last several hours.

Mark's face turned so suddenly white he looked for a moment as much a corpse as Celia had, down in the morgue. Then he said slowly, sounding bewildered: "What? How could she be? What happened?"

They'd both been at the front door when I arrived and wanted to know what I'd found out, so I'd handed the news over right away without the benefit of any cushioning preparations. I put an arm around Lindy, who was just standing there in the front hall very still with the tears running down her face. It was blotchy already, and her nose was getting red. Mark turned suddenly and headed for the library. I pushed Lindy gently along after him. He was over at the bar, not surprisingly, fixing himself a drink with shaking hands. I almost told him to fix me one, too, but stopped myself in time, dug a cigarette out of my purse instead, took a deep, long drag, coughed, and asked Mark to fix something for Lindy.

"Scotch?" he asked her and when she didn't respond filled a tall glass half full from the bottle of J&B he was holding. He walked over and told her to drink it.

"But I don't want—"

"Drink it anyway. Don't argue, just drink it."

Lindy shrugged and downed it. "Satisfied?"

Good lord, I thought, are they going to get into a fight now? They'd never gotten along particularly well. But Mark merely said: "Perfectly. Give me the glass and I'll fix you another. You look like you need it, kid." He held out his hand.

"No," Lindy ignored the hand and put the glass down on a coaster on the table beside her. She was sitting at one end of the long couch placed perpendicular to the fireplace, and I was at the other. Mark paced up and down, drink in one hand, bottle in the other.

"I thought you were having guests for dinner? I didn't expect to find you two here alone."

"I canceled them. After I talked to you," Lindy said and, after a pause, added, "thank God."

Nobody said anything for a while. The fire made hissing noises. It was raining again outside, hard, and I thought some water was probably being blown down the chimney. Lindy sniffled intermittently; Mark drank. Outdoors, an ambulance went screaming by a street or two away, then faded out again in the distance. As if it had never been, I thought, and wondered if Celia would be like that to all of us soon. As if she had never been. David was starting to become like that to me, I realized; whether I wanted him to or not, he was slipping farther and deeper into the past.

I looked around the expensive, comfortable room, filled with things that had belonged to Celia, and found it hard to believe she wouldn't walk in the door any minute now and tell us, in the Texas accent that had only grown stronger in California, that of course she was all right. Of course it was all just an absurd mistake. "And don't you love my Renoir; isn't it delightful?" she'd ask, the way she always did. She liked words like "absurd" and "delightful" and "ghastly" . . . then I remembered the thing I'd seen in the morgue and hurriedly pulled my thoughts back from Celia to her children.

I told them, without hurrying, what I knew about the accident, which wasn't much. Then Lindy and I started talking about what arrangements would need to be made and decided they could wait until morning, until after we'd gotten in touch with their father.

Lindy suddenly interjected, "But it's so crazy. People don't just fall in front of cable cars."

Mark still said nothing. He just sat silently in a big chair over by the bar, drinking glass after glass from the bottle of scotch he'd put on the table beside him. He didn't seem to be bothering with ice or water, although when his sister asked him to fix her another drink, he did so competently enough. With his thin, white face, pitch-black eyes, and slightly wild dark hair, he looked like some suffering nineteenth-century romantic poet. Lindy, neatly blonde and green-eyed like Celia, looked in contrast almost serene. Except for the blotchy face and the bewildered eyes.

Finally, I started trying to find Henry. He'd given up his private practice about a year and a half before and had gone to work in a clinic. It was now well after the clinic's closing hours, and Lindy couldn't find a number for the Buddhist place on Celia's desk or in any of the telephone tables.

"Didn't he say the name of the place, Lindy? Think back."

"I don't *think* so, just some 'Buddhist place,' he said, 'up north.' In the mountains near Redding."

"Lassen? Shasta? Bullychoop?"

"I don't remember; I don't know," Lindy said miserably.

"It's all right. We'll leave it until morning. Maybe the clinic, but it will be Saturday . . ."

Mark sank farther down into his corner chair. Lindy went upstairs to bed. I didn't want to stay; I wanted to go home, but I knew I'd feel like a louse if I did. Not that I felt I was accomplishing anything by being there. I eyed the fine array of bottles across the room, the polished glasses. I was actually starting to tell myself "just one won't hurt" when the telephone rang. It was on the table next to me, and I jumped about a foot.

"Celia?"

"No, Celia's—who is this please?"

Silence.

"Hello?" I repeated, "Hello?"

There was a small click as the receiver was replaced gently in its cradle at the other end. A man's voice—slightly familiar, I thought—but I couldn't place it. I got up, made a wide berth around the bar, and climbed the stairs to one of the second-floor guest rooms. I threw my clothes in a heap on a big stuffed chair and crawled between cool linen sheets. I slept through the rest of that night like one of the dead myself.

The next morning I gave Henry's clinic twenty rings, just in case someone was there but was busy interviewing; then I tried again, and then I called Simmons.

"No, I don't know the name of the place, but it's about five hours north of here—and how many Buddhist monasteries can there be up there?"

"Those crummy places are all over the place! I bump into one of the damn things every time I turn around!" Simmons yelled unhappily.

"But maybe the Redding police would know? Wouldn't they have a list or something?"

"Yeah, they'd have a list or something," he agreed sarcastically. There was a fuming silence from his end. I lit a cigarette. "Will you have Henry notified, then? I mean, Dr. Sloan?"

"Yeah. We'll find him."

It sounded like a threat. Perhaps it was.

* * *

Mark and I were in the library when Henry arrived home a little past noon. Mark gave his father a kind of smoldering look and then got up and left the room without a word. Henry didn't seem to notice. He had an odd expression on his face, I thought, along with the tiredness, but I couldn't place it. Could it possibly be relief? Had he had enough, in the end, of Celia's constant managing? Whatever it was, he told me that he would handle the funeral arrangements, and he made it pretty clear that he didn't want any help. I was glad to hear this, although I found his manner a little grating. But then I had always found Henry too stiff and cold to like, and I decided that he was worse than usual, probably, because of the shock of Celia's death.

Simmons telephoned and arranged to see me at home later in the afternoon for what he called background information. I assumed the interview was mostly a formality and thought that it would be better for him to get whatever information he needed from me than to be bothering Celia's family right then. But as the interview progressed, I was not so sure. He was accompanied by another man he introduced as Lieutenant Casey, but Simmons himself did all the talking.

"Like I told you last night, Mrs. Elliott," he began, "almost certainly your sister's death was an accident, caused probably by somebody in the crowd behind her pushing to get in line for that cable car coming down the hill. She didn't have to be pushed that hard, maybe—the streets were slippery from the rain earlier, and maybe her mind was on something else. Which wouldn't have mattered ninety-nine times out of a hundred, only this time the cable car was just coming. That's probably what happened. But we can't rule out, at this point, that it's also possible she might have been pushed out there. On purpose, I mean. Or thrown herself out there. On purpose. Suicide's not particularly our business, but we like to be sure what happened."

"Oh, no! If you'd known Celia, you'd never suggest that in a million years," I said without thinking, really surprised. Then I stopped to try to consider his ideas but found them just inconceivable. "Not suicide—not Celia! I could believe she was pushed before I could believe that. And I really can't imagine her being pushed, either. She's always been so—so respectable, Celia."

He winced at this, and in retrospect I can't say that I blame him.

"Quite respectable people do get"—he paused, looked down at his cigar, and tapped the ash into the ashtray, barely making it—"get murdered from time to time, Mrs. Elliot. In fact, often when they are respectable, as you call it, they are also quite wealthy. Your sister, for instance, was quite wealthy. Wasn't she?"

"Well—yes. She was. Certainly. But I can't imagine anyone wanting to murder her, all the same." I remembered the curious expression I'd noticed on Henry's face. Relief, if that had been what I'd seen, was understandable, knowing Celia. And hardly in the same category as murder. It was the first time that word had come into the discussion, and I totally rejected it. I added, "And Celia and suicide don't make any kind of sense either, believe me."

"Yes, well, we have the statement of a former police officer who was standing across the street just before the accident. He happened to notice her particularly and says that she was looking very worried, very upset. Had she anything special to be worried about, do you know? Had she, as far as you could tell, been in a cheerful state of mind lately? Or had she seemed not herself in any way?"

"You'd have to ask her family about that. I haven't actually seen Celia in about a year," I admitted. "But—"

"Mrs. Sloan moved here with her husband and two children from Texas," he interrupted, "about fifteen years ago, I believe you said last night? And you have been living here for the past six years? And you last saw your sister a year ago?"

"Half-sister; yes, that's right, but we were never especially close, you see, Celia and I. She is . . . she was ten years older, for one thing, and we had, oh, different interests—values I guess you could call it—very different, uh, life-styles."

What I was starting to think of as Simmons' hatchet face was quite stony and expressionless, yet it managed somehow to express a kind of extreme disapproval. His partner Casey's face remained the blank it had been throughout, with no feeling expressed of any kind. I was beginning to feel not only annoyed and frustrated but also extremely uneasy. I started over.

"Celia was only my half-sister—we have different fathers. Hers left her a great deal of money when he died; she was away at school a lot. We didn't see that much of each other because we didn't have much in common." I paused to take a breath, picked up a fresh pack of Marlboros from the coffee table, and opened it. "It was just chance that we both ended up living out here. In the same city." I lit my cigarette and took several deep drags; the last one went down the wrong way and started off a small coughing fit.

"I see," Simmons said, looking as if he saw all sorts of things, none of them pleasant. "When exactly was the last time you saw your—half-sister? Alive."

"I'm not sure of the exact date. Last December sometime. She came by to bring me a Christmas present and stayed to talk for a while. About her son, mainly; she was quite worried about him." As soon as the words were out of my mouth I regretted them, thinking they might somehow cause trouble for Mark. I quickly hurried on. "You know how mothers are. But what I was trying—what I wanted to say—was, Celia just wasn't the type to kill herself, no matter what her frame of mind. She was much a dutiful kind of person. About her life, I mean. And also a bit unimaginative. I don't think she was capable of that kind of . . . of . . . despair. That you'd have to have to throw yourself out in front of a street—of a cable car."

I thought of Anna Karenina, romantic and suffering and desperate. Celia hadn't been like that at all. "And besides, if there's one thing Celia thought about at all times, no matter what else was happening, it was appearances. How things looked. Am I—do you see what I'm saying at all? Celia just wouldn't have done that to herself. Or to her family."

"I hear you. And you'd be surprised at the people who kill themselves. Or try to, when they come up against something they can't take or don't want to. People love death."

Any philosophy sat awkwardly on Simmons, I thought, but if there was going to be any, it would be that.

He went on: "Although that wasn't necessarily the case here, it's a possibility, that's all, that we have to check out in every case of unexplained death. As your sister's is. I'm sure you can understand that, Mrs. Elliot? If you try?"

He frowned and dug around in the brown jacket pocket for

another cigar, bit off the end, and then looked around for a place to put it. I got up and emptied the ashtray we'd been using into the fireplace. Simmons lit the cigar and continued. "So. What I want from you is general background information on your sister, whatever you can tell me about her family, her friends. What was the trouble with the son you mentioned?"

By the time they left, I felt like I'd been rolled over and flattened by some giant machine. I wanted a drink, ten drinks, twenty. Martinis, dry, straight up, standing in an orderly row on my kitchen table. I wanted to sit there and drink them one by one, alone, then get into bed and never get out again. An old familiar feeling.

I went over and sat with my exhaustion in the bay window instead, smoking innumerable cigarettes and looking out at the nearly matching gray-blue sky and blue-gray bay, separated by the buildings and hills of Berkeley and Oakland, turning darker and darker into an early winter night. Streetlights, then flying lights of helicopters and airplanes from the airport twenty miles south, and finally the lights of stars came on in bunches as I did in another pack of Marlboros.

Finally I got up and took a bath as hot as I could stand it and went to bed. I dreamed of horses, a white and a black, fighting.

I woke up at six and wrote down what I could remember of the dream, something I like to do with the ones that seem especially puzzling or numinous. This one felt a little of both. Outside my bedroom window the sun, big and round and orange, had just cleared the tops of the dark blue Oakland hills across the bay, the air and water were soft and shimmery, and birds were singing in the big eucalyptus trees in the backyard next door. It looked like a beautiful new day coming up, but I was still tired, and while trying to meditate on the dream and getting only images of Celia and of Henry, I fell back to sleep. When I woke up again the doorbell was ringing.

The sky had clouded over, and the ugly beige plastic clock by my bed said eight-thirty. I put on a heavy wool bathrobe—without the sun the house felt very cold—and went and stuck my head out the front window to see who was there.

It was an elegantly dressed man, tastefully hip even at what seemed to me in those days like the crack of dawn, with thick, wavy blond hair. I yelled hello with a question mark, and when he looked up I recognized a protégé of Celia's, Dunbar Oates. He'd been her interior decorator for years, and she'd mothered his career along with almost as much devotion as she had Henry's. He'd also been instrumental in helping her buy several very valuable paintings over the past few years. She'd been very proud of them. The most recent was a Renoir, supposedly: "The Woman in the Garden." Celia had been especially taken with that one because the woman looked very much the way she herself had about twenty years ago. I'd passed the time of day with Dunbar at Celia's a few times, but I certainly wasn't on eight-thirty A.M. calling terms with him. What the hell did he want?

I yelled down to him to wait a minute, went downstairs to let him in and told him to follow me back to the kitchen, where I put on some water for coffee.

"How nice to see you, Dunbar," I said untruthfully, and waited to hear what he had come for.

"I heard about Celia," he began, "and of course I'm *dreadfully upset*. I just felt I had to talk with someone else who was close to her and thought immediately of you. I hope you don't mind?"

Since Dunbar knew perfectly well that Celia and I had been anything but close, I found this statement impossible to believe.

"When did you hear it?" I countered. "How did you hear?"

"My dear, it was on the *radio* this morning, my clock radio. It woke me up, it was *horrible*. I couldn't *believe* it. I felt *so upset* I just threw on any old clothes, good heavens, they don't even match!" He looked deprecatingly down at the soft fawn and chocolate combination that looked all right to me, if a little on the fancy side, and repeated: "I felt *so upset* I just came right over."

He fluttered a graceful white hand across his forehead and sighed. Dunbar had a number of mannerisms that would have led you to believe he was a cliché sort of homosexual. But apparently this wasn't so. He had a wife of several years' standing whom he treated abominably (according to Celia, who had always sounded quite pleased at the fact while pretending not to be), and he also had passionate and short-lived affairs with many of his rich women clients (also according to Celia, who had sounded less pleased).

Usually Dunbar was a very good-looking man, the magazine type; an interesting combination of blond, clean-cut, and big. But he looked quite haggard now; he looked old, and he seemed to be in a state of advanced anxiety.

When he didn't say anything more, I said, "You do seem to be very upset, Dunbar."

"Yes," he agreed immediately, sighing again and looking confusedly around the room. "Could I have a glass of water?"

When I brought it, he gulped down a handful of small yellow pills that I recognized as ten-milligram Valiums. He shuddered, put the glass down on the table, and smiled a sort of sick-looking smile.

"What is it exactly that's bothering you so much?"

"Oh, the shock. Celia's death has been just a *terrible* shock. We were friends for so long; we go way back, you know, Celia and I." He didn't say anything more for a while, then asked, "Had you talked to Celia recently?"

"No." Then I suddenly remembered that Celia *had* telephoned me, a week or so before she was killed. "Yes," I amended. It hadn't seemed important at the time, but now that I thought of it she'd said something about Dunbar. I hadn't been paying much attention and couldn't remember what it was.

"Did she happen to mention me? When did you talk to her?"

"About a week ago. I think she did just mention you, but I'm sorry, I can't remember what she said. Why? Is it important?"

He seemed suddenly calmer, and I wondered if the Valium could already be starting to work.

"Not really. I just wondered. She had a big project she wanted me to do, redoing the attics into an art studio. She was going to take up painting. Pretty involved—"

"Painting? Celia?"

"Yes, it involved ripping out some of the walls, of course, and skylights, to get the light right. Now I guess the work won't be wanted?"

"You could check with Henry. He's hanging out with Buddhists these days, so anything's possible."

"Yes. Well. Maybe I'll do that. Thanks."

He tossed out a few more platitudes about how much he'd cared for Celia, sounding almost like a lover, and left. After he'd gone, I fixed myself some breakfast, bacon and eggs because it was Sunday, and another pot of coffee. I sat there a long time, looking out the window at the gray water, the gray sky, thinking about Dunbar and what he'd said. I wondered again what he'd wanted. To make me think he'd been Celia's lover? That didn't make any sense, but I was pretty sure he'd been putting on an act about something.

Perhaps it was the way he looked me so straight and steadily in the eye, which I've heard is a good sign that a person is lying. Perhaps it was the handful of Valiums. Perhaps it was a sense, from what I knew of Dunbar's character, that he wouldn't call on me at eight-thirty in the morning without a pretty good reason. I couldn't see Celia taking up painting, but I hadn't an inkling what that reason might be.

FOUR

CELIA'S FUNERAL WAS WELL ATTENDED. IT WAS A SOCIETY funeral, as her life had been a society life, and it was hard for me to relate much to it. But then, it had been hard for me to relate much to Celia. In fact, I thought, for a long time it had been hard for me to relate much, period. To anything.

Henry had engaged the city's oldest, most discreet, and most expensive funeral specialists, and the problem of the mangled condition of the body was gotten around by having the coffin closed except for the upper part. The face was made up beautifully, with just the right sort of very faint smile, quite spiritual, with the green eyes looking off at a slight angle. Into the ethereal hereafter, presumably. The coffin was lined with an emerald silk that went well with the sightless eyes.

I don't like funerals, society or otherwise. There is always such a gap between the flimsy words spoken by some nice minister man, in this case Episcopalian, and the mysterious hard fact of death itself. I see the need for rituals, I believe in ceremonies, and I think that to acknowledge death is to value life, but in these mortician-arranged affairs the old archetypes are so covered over with false fronts, they're just one more shuck job to be got through as quickly as possible, as far as I'm concerned.

Such were my somewhat grandiose thoughts as I entered for whatever ritual or ceremony might be provided for Celia. A tall and sort of battered, tough-looking man was standing just inside the door. Lindy and I had seen him at the funeral parlor where Celia's body had been on display, so to speak, over the weekend, and had wondered who he was. I learned later that he was the ex-policeman who had witnessed the accident.

At the funeral he was in a good position to have a look at everyone who came in without being conspicuous about it. He looked me over briefly as I passed, as poker-faced as he'd been the day before. I nodded for some reason, and he nodded back, his eyes gray and cold. I walked on down a side aisle and joined Henry, Lindy, and Mark in the front row, all looking horrible in their different ways. We were the only relatives.

"A good and upright woman," the minister was saying, "a pillar of our community and a help to a very great many in need."

My thoughts wandered away from this polite mumbo jumbo and settled on Henry, sitting next to me. I looked over at him cautiously, wondering if he would still have that curious look of relief about him, but whatever feelings were there today, none of them were showing. He only looked tired and rather grim. Perhaps he didn't have any feelings, I thought, shifting around on the hard, uncomfortable seat and already longing for a cigarette.

I haven't said much about Henry Sloan. I'd never known, really, what to make of him. He and Celia had met at a debutante party in Texas, where he was going to medical school. She had started divorce proceedings against her first husband—no simple matter in those days—and was just beginning to go out again socially. Practically over our mother's dead body, as I recall. But Celia was twenty-three by that time, had her own money and her own household, and there wasn't much our mother could do about it. I remember a lot of arguments and recriminations, though.

Anyway, they met and fell in love, Celia and Henry. Quietly, discreetly. I'd seen them together around the country club but hadn't taken much notice. Celia was going out with—to my thirteen-year-old mind—some much better-looking, more exciting, and friendlier men than the medical student from out of town—California someplace—and I was surprised when my mother told me they were going to be married at the end of the summer.

Not that Henry wasn't presentable. He was good-looking enough in a stiff sort of way, he had gone to all the right schools, and he was surprisingly good in social situations. But he was basically a cold person even then, a thinking type, which I would never have thought would have appealed to Celia.

He was, however, almost a pure opposite to her first husband. Number one had been glamorous, gorgeous, a top-ranked tennis player for the few years he bothered, but mainly a playboy. And not a very faithful husband, as it turned out. He finally ran off altogether with a woman ten years older than he, leaving Celia with Mark, two years old, and Lindy, just born. After a year passed and nothing further was heard from him, she sued for divorce.

After they married, Henry went on to specialize in psychiatry, which, in the world of our family and their friends, was considered the next worse thing to being crazy yourself. And which may be why, after Henry finished medical school, they moved to his hometown of San Francisco, where he soon built up a large society practice.

Not that they needed the money, heaven knows; Celia had tons of the stuff. But she was quite determined that Henry should do well in his career, as she called it, and she worked hard in social ways to help him. Celia's mentality was locked right into the 1950s, even before the fifties came along, and after. One's husband worked—not necessarily primarily for money, but it was important to be successful and keep going up the ladder—and the wife helped with dinner parties, the right volunteer work, and so forth. Then, in the year before Celia's death, Henry had become increasingly interested in various Eastern head and body trips, and had pretty much given up the private practice in favor of low-paying work in a public day clinic where he could experiment with the new techniques he'd become so interested in. Or so Celia had said when I'd last seen her.

"Not a fancy clinic at all, Maggie, run by the state or the city or something; quite *drab*—the kind of place you'd approve of."

She wrinkled up her nose in fastidious distaste. "But Henry just loves it there—can barely tear himself away to see the poor few private patients he did keep . . . Thursdays. He's even dropped his teaching down to one course, which I also think is a mistake . . . And it pays practically nothing. Of course, the money isn't important, only it *is* an indication of what you're worth, let's face it! But he's happy as a clam with what he's doing, which is all I care about, really." She slowly sipped her sherry and looked anything but happy.

Sitting there a year later at her funeral, I remembered how after she'd left I'd swallowed down the remaining alcohol in her glass, which was almost full, and had then polished off the rest of the bottle, which was one she'd brought and a better grade of stuff than I was drinking at the time. I'd thought vaguely about what she'd said and not said. Through the hazy warmth of the alcohol I'd realized quite well that, in spite of what Celia said about only wanting Henry to be happy, she didn't at all like the new direction his famous career was taking.

And from what I knew of Celia, she would probably be putting pressure on Henry in various ruthless and ladylike ways to prod him back to the work she thought he should be doing. In a way, I believe she thought of it as being as much her career that was being dumped as his. Which, in a way, it was. And I didn't think she was about to see it permanently abandoned for low-paying, unprestigious work in a world where she did not belong and could not follow. Not at least without a considerable struggle; Celia could be very charming, but she had a will of iron. And if she was not to spend her days keeping up the social fabric of Henry's career, I'd wondered foggily that day, then what *was* she to do with herself? Have Dunbar Oates redecorate her house for the fiftieth time? Play more bridge? She'd developed no work of her own, and her children were nearly grown. She'd been forty-two that Christmas, young enough to start something of her own, but psychologically she wasn't the type—didn't have, I thought, the capacity. Because she didn't have the desire. She still lived in a world where women didn't work unless they had been unable to get some man to support them and had no money of their own.

I think she knew all this, at least dimly, and I think these were her real concerns that day as she talked of Henry's changing work, of Mark's increasingly drunken, messed-up life. But she didn't mention them directly, and neither did I. I wish now I had, of course. Looking back, I think I sensed at the time that she was almost glad to have Mark's problems to distract her from her own, and perhaps it was partly this that made it hard for me to take her fears for him very seriously.

In any case, I hadn't passed on any of Celia's left-handed complaints about Henry to hatchet-faced Detective Simmons. I'd given him a brief and conventional picture of the family as I'd known it before Celia's Christmas visit: the family more or less as Celia had wanted it to be seen. It had seemed the least I could do for her. I looked over at Henry again, his face quite expressionless still, his eyes glazed, and I doubted very much if he were taking in any more of the funeral service than I was.

"We cannot know," the minister was saying now with considerable fervor, "no, we cannot know what the reasons are, what are the causes . . ."

I wondered where Henry's thoughts, so clearly not here, were. Simmons had seemed to think I was holding out on him. But if Henry and Celia had not been entirely happy the past year or so, it was mostly speculation on my part that said so, and in any case it was none of my business. Nor did I see any reason to set Henry up, though I'd never particularly liked him, for trouble with that cold, suspicious policeman. I really didn't think there was any possibility at all the Celia had been murdered, any more than I could imagine her choosing a cable car as an instrument of suicide.

My thoughts wandered then to Dunbar Oates. Celia's lover? I'd noticed him as I came in, sitting in the second row over on the left and looking the picture of proper mourning, armband and all. I glanced back at him now and saw that there were actually a few tears running down his suntanned cheeks. He took a handkerchief and patted them delicately away.

My wandering thoughts about my sister's interior decorator, her husband and her marriage were interrupted then by the arrival of her principal lawyer, Temple Ferguson. He sat down beside me just at the end of a lengthy prayer being offered by the insipid fellow in charge.

"Amen," the minister concluded, and "Amen, amen," the spectators agreed. The organ ground out

> *Rock of ages*
> *cleft for me*
> *let me hide*
> *myself . . .*

Celia's lawyers were located where her money was, in Houston, and Temple had been her financial guardian since before my first memory. I'd finally reached him on Sunday at a lodge in North Carolina, where he'd gone for a weekend of hunting. He was not unused to sudden tragedy and, after asking how it had happened, simply said he would fly out and come directly to the funeral from the airport.

> *hide myself*
> *in thee*
> *A-*
> *men*

the organ concluded. The funeral was over; people were collecting their coats, getting up, and leaving.

FIVE

TEMPLE AND I WALKED OUT TOGETHER, MY BACK STIFF FROM sitting still so long on the hard wood pew. He was thinner, I noticed, and his hair had gone quite white, but the black eyes still snapped with pleasure to see me.

"God!" I said. "That was dreary enough for two funerals! It's pitiful! Why can't they do them better?"

"People want to do the right thing, you know Margaret," he said gently. "It's just that they mostly don't know what that is."

The sardonic smile, more like the Temple I remembered than the quiet opening, brightened his face like a scythe.

"Not superior folk, like us?" It was an old joke we had, and he laughed.

"That's right, Margaret honey"—he was the only person from my childhood who always called me by my full name, rather like assigning me the status of a full person, I had always felt— "and your very superior person is a fine sight for these old eyes. But I wouldn't," he added somberly, "have expected to lay them on you at a funeral for Celia, by God! I never would." He sighed. We were quiet, thinking back over the years, the French dinners, and, in his case, all the financial things . . .

"Her father was only thirty-five when that fancy little plane of his crashed, and now Celia, too. And now," he repeated, "Celia, too. Forty-three." He sighed again, then shook his head abruptly. "Well. In the midst of life, as that pretty young fellow up there was saying. How are the children managing? And Henry? And what about you?"

"I'm all right, thanks. More tired than anything else right now. It's hard to tell about the others. Mark's been drinking a lot the past few years. I know he's only twenty-one, but it has been years. I can't really tell how much of this has even gotten through to him, how much there is left of him to feel anything. It's depressing."

"I thought he looked pretty bad. Hoped it was his mother's death, but I was afraid there was more to it. What about Lindy?"

"Well—she was very upset, cried a lot at first. But now she's put herself into some kind of stiff-upper-lip, iron-control trip. Unfortunately, in my opinion. I guess it's what she thinks is expected of her, poor thing—like what you said, people wanting to do the right thing and not knowing how. She goes around pale and grim, smiling bravely from time to time when she remembers to. I hope she'll get more real after a little time has passed . . ."

"She and Celia never got along very well, did they? That makes it worse, or I would think so. What about Henry?"

"You know he never says much anytime—except perhaps at parties. Now he's all buttoned down except for, oh, making arrangements, things like that. I haven't any idea what he's feeling. But then, I never have had. It would be easier to be around them all if they'd just let down and cry or something. Of course, we were all taught not to do that . . .''

"Were we not," he agreed, putting an arm around me as we walked over to the shiny limousine. "I was very sorry to hear about David, you know, Margaret. I tried to call you. Many times. But the phone was never answered."

"I know, Temple. And I'm sorry I never answered your letter, either. For a long time I just sat and drank. There were several years where I pretty much gave up answering the phone, too. But it meant a lot to me, your letter. I hope you'll forgive me for staying out of touch so long. I'm finished with the drinking now, for good, I hope—I've been going to AA. I like it, amazingly enough. But I'll tell you about all that later. It feels like a hundred years at least since I've seen you; goodness, it's good to see you!''

And it was. I had known Temple most of my life and had always, I guess the word is, loved him. When Celia's father was killed—in one of those fast little planes that the rich in Texas like so much to go rushing around the state in—Temple was left in charge of the giant fortune to be inherited by Celia when she turned eighteen. He had been a friend of Celia's father as well as his lawyer, and he used to come once a month and take us both out for a sophisticated (to us at least) and expensive dinner in the one good French restaurant in town. Dressed in our best clothes, we felt very grown up, beautiful, special.

I remembered Temple from those early years as a very tall man with bristly black hair and scratchy whiskers, his scrawny monkey face made beautiful by his gleeful smile and frequent, exuberant laughter. He smelled, always, of Havana tobacco and bourbon. When I was little, there was candy for me in the pockets of the big coat he wore. Later it was little oddities, a bell or a shell, or once, I remember, a hinged walnut with a perfectly carved miniature bride and groom inside, the bride's white net and the groom's black jacket impeccably tailored.

"Made by prisoners of another kind," he said, enigmatically to my childish mind, but Celia had smiled a superior little smile, so I'd smiled, too, pretending to understand.

It was reassuring to have Temple's tough-old-rooster brand of strength available again. It was needed, I thought, not only by me, but especially by Lindy and Mark. Though Henry had acted in all ways as their father, had in fact legally adopted them soon after he and Celia were married, his heart, or whatever Henry used for one, seemed mostly to have been left somewhere else—with his work, perhaps, with his patients. There was going to be a lot of money now—a good deal of it, I believed, left out-right to the children—and I was glad Temple was still around to help them manage it.

Although Mark had been looking, I thought, like someone beyond help. He was standing now by the door of the chapel like a wooden Indian, stiffly shaking hands. But at least he was standing. I wondered what effect all that money would have on him. I wondered if Celia had put it into a trust after she became so worried about the drinking. I wondered what, if anything, Celia had left me.

Henry and Lindy and Mark finally finished shaking hands and joined Temple and me at the limousine. It was about four o'clock in the afternoon and almost dark already. It was December twenty-first, I realized, looking out the window as we left the cemetery city of Colma and hit the freeway. The next-to-longest night of the year. It's always a relief to me when the winter solstice arrives and I know that every day from then on the light will last just a little longer. But that wasn't for two more days, and now and tomorrow were the darkest times of the year. A weary year, for me; the last dregs of the drinking times, the first fragile months of sobriety. I'd be glad to see it gone, this year.

The last year of all, for my sister Celia.

Back at her house—hers until Tuesday, when the will was read—Cook had put a lot of food out in the library. Ling So, the Chinese gardener, was serving drinks from a temporary bar set up in the wide hallway, much as when Henry and Celia gave a party. The room was quickly filling up with people, couples mostly, who'd come back to the house with us. All the lights were on, and the lights and a big fire in the huge fireplace at the far end made the room warm and welcoming after the cool and prissy chapel and the cold winter dark outside.

Lindy sat pale on the yellow silk couch by the fire, and Mark was standing, drinking steadily again, over by the bar. A lot of scotch was being consumed, it being December, and respectable amounts of gin as well. People put thin slices of ham on little homemade rolls, remembering this, remembering that about

Celia. When they had first known her. Things she had done for them. Country houses she'd had where they'd visited, in Jamaica one year, Nantucket another.

Temple had known her longer than anyone else there: "Since before she was born and your mother, Margaret, just a beautiful child herself. And none too pleased at the prospect of motherhood, as I recall."

I saw Dunbar Oates over at the other end of the room talking earnestly with Henry, who looked a little harassed at the deluge of whatever Dunbar was pouring over him. Finally Henry nodded over in Temple's direction, said a few words, and walked off, heading for the bar. Mark apparently saw him coming, held out a hand to Ling So who put a bottle in it, then turned and made his way through the clumps of people to the side door and left the room. Dunbar was moving sideways, crablike, through the crowded room toward Temple. Then a gushy Junior League friend of Celia's came over and started talking at me nonstop about all the wonderful things Celia had done in the League over the years, and I lost track of all three of them.

Finally a few people started drifting off, and I drifted with them, instead of staying through to the bitter end the way I probably should have. I was bone tired and not a little depressed; it was nine o'clock at night after a long, hard day—a long, hard several days—and I was supposed to be back at the house at ten sharp the next morning for the reading of the will. Celia had told me some years before that she'd put me down for a "memory legacy," as she called it, of twenty thousand dollars—"to do something fun with and remember me while you're doing it."

At this state of my finances, it would be something fun like eating.

Driving home, I thought how Celia was the sort who should have lived to be a hundred, one of the ones who would smugly attribute their long life to clean living, moderation with alcohol, and abstinence from cigarettes. With just as much conviction as those other centenarians who gleefully attribute their longevity to a bottle of bourbon a day and, often enough, a good chunk of tobacco in one form or another as well. She should have lived, I thought again, well into an opinionated, dictatorial old age, barring accident.

But there she was, so surprisingly dead at forty-three. I'd never doubted, the past few years of my own depressions and suicide binges, that I'd be dead and buried long before Celia, so I'd never given much thought to that twenty thousand dollars. Since David's death I'd been living at a more or less subsistence level off the money from selling our cabin in the mountains, which had given me sufficient leisure for full-time drinking. With no desire for the future, any future, I'd assumed that I'd surely be dead or something or other long before that money ran out. But alcoholism turns out to be a very slow death, and now here I was, three months sober, in better health than I'd been in, in probably ten years, with the house money due to run out quite soon. If Celia really had left me the money, I concluded, lying in my bed at last, it would certainly come in handy.

An interesting thought, but not enticing enough to keep me awake thinking about it. I was too used to being depressed and not really interested in anything, and I was tired. I felt like a stone sinking into a deep pool of warm water. Soon I came to rest on the bottom, and slept. I dreamed of Mexican jumping beans in a circle, jumping with no pattern, breaking the circle. A large walnut was in the center. Something was wrong with it, though; I didn't know what.

I realized the next morning when I woke up and wrote the dream down that there were no bride and groom inside this walnut, it was quite empty.

SIX

It WAS HARD TO GET UP THAT DAY. MY BED WAS WARM, THE house cold. And it was hard to cut short my slow morning routine of breakfast, coffee drinking, cigarette smoking, reading that I used in those days to ease myself into one more day in a real world I'd as soon have not been in. I'd begun on Carl Jung about then, I remember, and didn't at all feel like leaving *Memories, Dreams, and Reflections* for Pacific Heights and the reading of Celia's will.

By the time I hit the last steep hill up to her house, though, I noticed faint stirrings of curiosity in myself, even anticipation. I parked my car in back and went in through a side door which was usually open in the daytime. I found everyone in the library, and they all looked hung over—whether from alcohol, sorrow, or the sheer horror of funerals, I couldn't tell. Even Temple was drooping and subdued, the black eyes flat and expressionless, lighting only momentarily when I came in just after ten.

Henry and Mark were sitting in brown velvet chairs near the fireplace, not looking at each other. Lindy was sitting at one end of the long yellow couch, looking as if she hadn't moved from there since the night before; I walked over and sat down at the other end of it. The couch and chairs had been rearranged to form a sort of semicircle facing Temple, who was standing beside one of the straight-back wooden chairs usually kept over against the far wall. I had the impression he was not looking forward to the next few minutes and wondered why. Or did lawyers always expect the worst where families and wills were concerned?

We exchanged rather pallid hellos. They all had cups of coffee. I got some for myself, sat down again, and waited for whatever it was to begin.

Temple cleared his throat and started: "What I want to do

now is to read through Celia's will completely, to begin at the beginning and go right on through to the end—without any interruptions." He paused and looked around at us severely. "After that we can go into the particulars, what it means to each of you, answer questions and so forth. All right?"

We all knew Temple well enough to know that he would handle this exactly however the hell he wanted to, whether anyone objected or not. No one did.

After a short wait he sat down and took a pair of heavy black-rimmed glasses out of his jacket pocket and put them on. I hadn't known him to wear glasses before. Then he picked up a bunch of papers from the table next to him, shuffled them around a bit, and finally started reading.

I don't remember all the details now. There were a lot of smallish bequests in the beginning to the servants, and quite a large one to Cook. Then some stuff concerning various charities Celia had been involved in, the Crippled Children's Society, the Matlock Girl's Orphanage . . . my mind wandered off at that one into images of orphaned girls in pinafores and bright new dresses with puffed sleeves and little round collars, all courtesy of Celia. In the middle of this unlikely reverie, the sound of my own name brought me back to the library.

"—Elliott," I heard, and then, my attention fully back, "one hundred thousand dollars."

I felt surprised and, I remember, mildly pleased that I could stop worrying about what I was going to do when the money I'd got from selling my house ran out. Mildy, not because I was above such sordid things as money, but because nothing ever penetrated very far into the fog of depression and self-pity that I'd surrounded myself with for the past five years or so. Still, there were stirrings. At that mention of one hundred thousand dollars, there were definite stirrings.

> Well that's something
> to think
> about
>
>
> and I've already
> begun . . .

The somber country-western twang of Willie Nelson wound its way through my mind. I hadn't any idea what I might want to do with the financial freedom suddenly sent my way, but it was something to think about, all right. . . .

I think it was the silence that brought me back to the library again; anyway, my attention came back once more to Henry, Lindy, and Mark, sitting there with very peculiar expressions on their faces and Temple with no expression at all. The feeling in the room was strange, too. I couldn't quite put my finger on what the feeling was, but it wasn't joy, that was clear.

Temple, expressionless still, started droning on again, some technical stuff about trust funds, and I wondered what on earth was the matter. Finally he came to the end and stopped. He put the papers back on the table beside him and took a swallow of what must have been, by then, very cold coffee.

There was a long silence, and then Temple said, "Now, I imagine you all have a lot of questions, so let's get started on them. First, though, let me say that Celia had me draw up this will last August to replace the one she made shortly after you and she were married, Henry. She said that she hadn't discussed these rather major changes with you but that she was going to." He paused.

"She mentioned changing some things," Henry said in a low monotone, looking down at his hands, "but she didn't go into details. She merely said she'd changed it around so that the main part of the estate would ultimately go to the children. If she should die before I did. Which we both considered unlikely, actually. I assumed she'd done something fancy with trust funds. But," he added slowly, thinking back, "I was rather busy at the time and frankly, not paying that much attention. I wasn't even sure . . . well. It doesn't matter. Now."

"You can have half my part, Daddy," Lindy said quickly, with some embarrassment. "It isn't fair! It doesn't make any sense. It's rotten!"

"Don't be ridiculous, Lindy; it was your mother's money, and she disposed of it as she saw fit," Henry said stiffly. He was not known for graciousness.

"You won't have your share for another four years, Lindy," Temple interjected mildly. "You may want to make some arrangement with your father at that time, but there is nothing you can do right now."

I noticed Mark wasn't offering out shares in his part. He was looking down into his coffee cup as if something interesting were going on inside it.

"From what you read, Temple," Henry said, "I'm not clear, what does it really mean? I am supposed to clear any . . . . 'requests' was the term, I think . . . any 'requests' in the estate through my own children? Or you? Or what?" I suddenly realized that Henry was very angry.

"Not exactly—let me summarize in layman's terms, Henry. What it boils down to is this: The estate—about fifteen million dollars after the smaller bequests are paid—is divided into two equal trusts for Mark and Linden. Out of these is to be paid—let me read this part over again," he picked up one of the papers—" 'such money as required or requested, not to exceed thirty thousand dollars per year' to you. This situation is to continue until the trusts are turned over to the children outright, four years from now on Mark's twenty-fifth birthday. This house, meanwhile, which was in Celia's name, is to be maintained for use by the three of you from additional funds—over and above your thirty thousand, Henry—until the trusts are dissolved; then the house becomes yours outright."

"But not the money to maintain it?"

"That's right. At that time, though, the sum of twenty thousand dollars is to be paid to you each year, from principal that will revert to the estates of the two children upon your death." He swallowed down the last of the cold coffee and continued. "I don't know how much Celia said about it to any of you, but she was quite upset when her mother's estate was left outright to her stepfather—Margaret's father, that is. When he remarried—a woman considerably younger than himself—and proceeded to have other children, Celia felt an injustice had been done, particularly to Margaret. She said that she wanted to make sure no such catastrophe could happen to her own children, if for instance she should die and you, Henry, should remarry."

Temple put the papers down on the table beside his chair and gave Henry an appraising look. "That was some of the thinking that prompted these changes, if that's of any help."

"Who is executor? You?" Henry asked quietly, coldly.

"I am, yes. Actually, it is my firm, but in this case that means me."

"I need some money to buy a car," Mark said suddenly. "Do

I get that from you? Sir?'' He lit a cigarette, his hands shaking so badly that the picture of his driving again was not a pleasant one.

"I thought you were supposed to go to court next week." Lindy gave her brother a disgusted look. "Where they're probably going to take away your license, so you're not going to be needing a car. Unless you're planning to drive without one?"

"I told you, you are *not* to drive until you get this court thing cleared up, Mark. And you are *certainly* not to drive without a license. I absolutely forbid it." Henry glared at his son.

"Ah, yes, you're so law-abiding, aren't you?" Mark snarled back. "I'm twenty-one, and I'll do what I want."

"You'll leave this house, then."

"Fine! I wouldn't care to stay here, anyway." He turned from his father back to Temple. "Do I talk to you then, sir, about getting some money so I can leave this place? This so-called home?"

"Any special needs over and above your allowance, which for the present remain the same," Temple replied smoothly, "should be discussed with me, yes. Any more questions for the moment?"

He looked around at each of us briefly, a token pause that did not encourage response. "If not, I'd like to break this meeting up now and let you all digest this information. I suggest we meet here again about three o'clock—that will give us another hour or so before I leave for the airport. I have a court case beginning tomorrow that I wasn't able to postpone."

Mark got up and started fixing himself a drink. Henry left the room abruptly. Lindy smiled weakly at Temple and then at me, and went out after her father.

"I don't think I'll stick around for your afternoon session, Temple. There's nothing special I need to know, is there?"

"No, honey. I'd rather not be there myself if this morning is any example. You should be aware, though, that you can get an advance on the money Celia left you. If you want it."

"I don't know—how long will it take to clear everything up?"

"About a year. Most of the assets are in High Plains Oil, so it shouldn't be too complicated."

"I guess I do then. Want an advance. I'll be running out of money in a couple of months."

"How much do you want? I can get you up to twenty thousand very easily."

"No. Maybe—five thousand?"

"I'll put it through and send you a check next week. Now, tell me what's been going on with you these past"—he stopped to think—"these past five years or so."

We sat in the brown chairs by the fire and had a long visit; it was the first time we'd really been together for any length of time since I'd gone back to live in New York after I finished college. Which had been against my parents' wishes and which Temple had helped me to do in spite of that. They'd wanted me in the South, my parents, settled down in Texas, married to a rich man and taking my children to the country club for their swimming lessons on summer mornings, playing bridge or golf with the friends I'd grown up with in the afternoons. A peaceful, safe life, as they saw it. But I hadn't wanted it, and my life had not been like that. It hadn't necessarily been so wonderful up to that point, but it had certainly been different from the way my parents planned it. Well, it was my life.

I told Temple a little about David's death and the years of drinking, which had mostly amounted to one long depression interspersed with little short breaks of feeling barely all right. And about AA, and how that seemed to have made the difference.

"I still have the depressions, but they don't last as long," I smiled in conclusion. "I'm not all right yet, but I'm going to be."

"You're fine to me right now; you always have been, and you always will be."

I felt the tears, which came so easily to me that year, about to fill my eyes and spill down my face. I didn't want to cry, so I got up and gave Temple a hug and said good-bye. He was getting to be an old man, and I realized I might not see him again.

From the hall on my way out I saw Henry sitting by himself in the living room, a room that wasn't used, usually, except for parties. He was staring at a wall. I pretended I didn't see him and kept on going, down the hall and out the side door.

Driving home, up and down the steep Gough Street hills, I wondered how much trouble the new will was going to cause in Celia's family, and I wondered why she'd set it up the way she had. As a weapon to force Henry back to private practice? If so, she must have told him about it in more detail than he'd admitted. In any case, it hadn't worked. Which wasn't surprising; Henry had always done pretty much what he wanted to. It just hadn't conflicted that much, before, with what Celia wanted.

Well, it had this time. I wondered if he would find it difficult to adjust to not being a multimillionaire. I couldn't believe Celia had really intended him to, either. Unless she was angrier than I'd realized? Maybe their relationship had been ending, and the new will was straight and really intended what it said? Although no one had expected her to die so soon. Especially Celia.

I wondered what I would end up doing with my hundred thousand dollars.

And I wondered what Detective Simmons, old hatchet-face, would make of this surprising will.

SEVEN

THE FUNERAL WAS ON MONDAY, TEMPLE BROKE THE NEWS OF the will on Tuesday, and there was an inquest scheduled for Thursday. On Wednesday Simmons held lengthy interviews with Henry and with me, and shorter ones with Lindy, Mark, and the servants. He'd questioned us all before, of course, looking for anything that would hint at suicide or murder. But on Wednesday he really went at it; he had us all downtown, saw us separately, made us go over everything we'd already said. And over it and over it. He also grilled (as Lindy put it) Mary P. Lewis, Celia's best friend, although not at headquarters. Lindy knew because Mary P. had promptly telephoned and told her all about it.

"Mainly," Lindy said vexedly, "to try to find out more about what's going on so she could spread it around among her bridge set."

Lindy judged her mother's friends as "shallow," as she had her mother. And she generally put the least charitable interpretation on whatever they did, as she had with her mother. As I had, too.

On Wednesday, anyway, spurred on perhaps by Celia's will, Simmons was pursuing his suspicions with great enthusiasm. If that's a word that can be rightly used in connection with a nature as sour as his. He took formal, signed statements about where we'd been when Celia died. Our alibis, in other words. Or lack of them.

I had admittedly been downtown. This and the money left to me, combined with Simmons' spontaneous dislike, put me second in line after Henry as favorite suspect. Or so it seemed to me.

Second to Henry because he, in addition to being the husband and therefore automatically first, had no alibi. He had not been up north, safely vouched for by several score Buddhists and would-be Buddhists, as we'd all thought. He'd also been downtown at the time of Celia's death. He hadn't mentioned this to begin with, he said, because he hadn't thought it important.

He was downtown at the crucial time instead of well on his way north on 101, it turned out, because when he started off in Celia's car that Friday morning, the second gear was grinding. He said his own car needed some work and he didn't want to take it on a long trip, so he drove the Mercedes downtown to the garage Celia used, in just the first gear, he said, and third. The garage was in the wharf area where Celia was killed. Henry said he dropped the car off about ten o'clock and then just walked around. In the rain, thinking. He'd also bought a couple of Christmas presents from street artists. One of them had been located and remembered Henry but couldn't say what time he'd been at her stall. The other one hadn't been found yet. And no, Henry said, he hadn't known his wife was in the area that morning, and he certainly hadn't seen her. He'd picked up the car about twelve and left the city for the Buddhists', arriving about six-thirty Friday evening.

Lindy, Mark, and Cook didn't have alibis for the exact time, either, but Simmons didn't seem to be as interested in any of them. They all claimed to have been at home but couldn't verify that by each other, as they'd been doing solitary things—Lindy in her room, writing letters; Mark in his, reading a Ross McDonald mystery. Although he couldn't remember anything about the plot when Simmons asked him.

Cook had been with the family since before they came from Texas, had known both children since they were born, and would have lied without batting an eyelash to give either of them an alibi. Unfortunately, she'd already said she'd seen nobody all afternoon before she knew there was any question of an alibi being wanted. She'd been in the kitchen, making up the huge batches of decorated cookies Celia always gave the Crippled Children's charity for their party the weekend before Christmas.

At the inquest, the judge inquired why a four-hour drive had taken Henry six.

"I wasn't hurrying," he answered, "since I was going to be late, anyway. I was just taking my time, thinking some things over. Personal matters," he added haughtily. "And I stopped to eat along the way, one of those roadside places."

"No, I don't remember where it was exactly. Somewhere around Willets, I think."

Asked if he knew of any reason why his wife would take her own life, he replied firmly, "No, I do not. I'm certain she did no such thing." He said equally firmly that he knew of no one who would wish his wife harm.

"Thank you, Dr. Sloan. That will be all."

From Detective Simmons' point of view, I thought, watching Henry leave the stand, Celia could have been pushed in front of that cable car easily enough by Henry or by any of the rest of us. Husband, son, daughter, old devoted family servant, or not-so-devoted half sister. Me. What a choice. But people usually are murdered by the people closest to them, I reflected. According to the murder fiction I read so much of, anyway. According to the real cases in the newspapers, too. Usually for reasons having to do with money—which Celia had tons of—or passion, which it was hard to think of in connection with Celia. Dunbar Oates? Husband, son, daughter, old servant, sister?

I wondered whether Simmons had picked up any hints of Celia and Henry not getting along so well the past year or so. Her changed will would tell him something of that. When Henry claimed he hadn't known the extent of those changes, was he lying? And he hadn't admitted, as far as I knew, to any trouble between himself and Celia. Naturally not.

Mark was on the stand next, saying in a voice so low it could barely be heard that his mother had been in good spirits and had no enemies that he knew of. He looked angry and sounded like he was lying. If the way he got along with his father was any indication of his relationship with his mother, he was quite a likely prospect, too, I reflected. From Simmons' point of view.

I saw Dunbar Oates sitting toward the back of the courtroom. He had supposedly been having lunch with a friend downtown at the crucial time and so had an alibi. But knowing my Agatha Christie, I knew that didn't necessarily mean very much. He was not called to testify.

Apparently Simmons had found nothing very tangible to support his murder and suicide theories, though, because the state put forward no special evidence other than the testimony of the police doctor and of the tall, tough-looking ex-policeman who had witnessed the accident. He stated his name as Richard Patrick O'Reagan, his occupation as printer, and he merely described the accident as he had seen it.

"Thank you, Mr. O'Reagan. I understand that at one time you were a member of the San Jose police force, with the rank of detective."

"Yes."

"Would you look around the room, please, and tell the court whether you see anyone whom you recognize as being part of the crowd surrounding Mrs. Sloan before her death?"

"Yes," O'Reagan answered, and there was an excited flutter among the spectators. "The woman sitting in the front row, left, wearing the red hat, and the gentleman seated next to her—he was the driver of the cable car—and I think, in fact, all the individuals sitting in that row."

"Do you see anyone *else* here who was present?"

O'Reagan looked slowly around the courtroom, particularly at the family, and then said simply: "No. I do not."

The crowd, which had sat up and started to look interested at O'Reagan's initial affirmative, settled back with a palpable sigh of disappointment. The woman in the hat and several of the others from the scene of the death then testified that they had noticed nothing out of the way preceding what they one and all termed "the accident."

Finally, a verdict was brought in of accidental death. I was glad to think that Celia and the rest of us could now be left in peace. Or whatever facsimile of peace we could contrive, I amended, thinking of Mark, of Henry, of Lindy, of myself.

I was also glad to think that I was seeing my last of old hatchet-face, Detective Simmons.

The next day, Friday, was Christmas Eve. Now that the distraction of Simmons and his questions and suspicions was over with, I returned to my usual depressed preoccupation with myself, magnified considerably by Christmas. Alone, without lover, children, family. After a while I forced myself out of the house and over to Mission Street, where I went to a pet shop and bought ten dollars' worth of Christmas bones and toys for the dogs. Which only served to emphasize my lack of a—human—family of my own. On the way back to the car I stopped in at a Chicano art gallery called La Raza and bought four small woodblock prints, simple primitive scenes of big, simple people doing things in a countryside so far back in time it had never known pollution. I was having dinner that night with Henry and the children, and the prints were presents for the three of them and Cook. At the last minute I bought one for myself, too, a starstrewn lake surrounded by fat, round dogs and squat, energetic pine trees, with a bunch of rather bulky angels flying around in the dark night sky above.

Then I drove back home. The traffic was bad and the drivers crazier than usual that day, but I managed to neither get killed nor have my car bashed in. The way I felt I wouldn't have minded getting killed, but I didn't want to be maimed particularly, and if I was going to be alive on the planet I wanted it to be with a car, and mine wasn't insured. Although now that I'd have some money again, I thought listlessly, maybe I'd get some.

I hated Christmas.

In the late afternoon, cold and gray and still, I drove over the nearly deserted freeway that ends so abruptly in the middle of town, then up Franklin to Pacific Heights. Dinner was every bit as depressing as I'd expected, and then some. Mark was supposed to be there but wasn't; no one knew where he'd gone or when he'd be back, and Henry was furious at him.

"I hope you will excuse the very inconsiderate behavior of my son, Maggie," he said for the second time during the first five minutes we were at the table. His smoldering anger put an added pall over an already heavy dinner. Finally, while we were having dessert and coffee, Mark came wandering in, subdued and only moderately drunk.

"Where have *you* been?" Henry asked unpleasantly, banging down the fragile old coffee cup so hard I was surprised it didn't break.

"Out," Mark snapped back unoriginally. He poured himself a cup of coffee and sat down.

Henry immediately got up, though Lindy was still eating her chocolate mousse. "I'll be in the living room when you're all *ready* to open the *Christmas* presents," he said angrily and stalked out.

None of us said anything. There didn't seem to be anything to say. I was thinking that I'd never seen this spoiled-brat side of Henry, though maybe, without thinking about it, I'd always suspected its existence, and it was part of why I'd instinctively never liked him much. Even if he had been under a strain. So had the rest of us, I thought. Especially Lindy, especially Mark.

When we went into the living room, there was a huge, over-decorated Christmas tree with all its lights going and an over-abundance of presents underneath. The room felt too hot, and I longed to leave. Henry was sitting near the tree in a big blue-and-white striped chair, glumly sipping a yellow drink. An odd time for Pernod, I thought, but somehow it fitted in with his fit of the sulks.

Most of the presents had been wrapped and addressed by Celia. She was the kind who had everything ready for Christmas way ahead of time, I remembered, though to give her credit I think it was a time she truly enjoyed and not just something she did for show. There were several presents for each of the children, some labeled "from Mummy" and some "from Dad," and some "to Dad from Mark" and "to Dad from Lindy," but all in the neat backhand script Celia and I had learned all those years ago at Miss Prescott's School in Texas.

My present was a sort of wall hanging, East Indian fabric with an embroidered design of peacocks in turquoise, red, and gold, "from Celia and Henry." Ungratefully, I thought how much it reminded me of both of them and wondered who I knew who might like it. It had obviously been expensive.

I handed around the prints I'd bought that afternoon—I'd given Cook hers before dinner—and Mark and Lindy seemed to like theirs, and Henry didn't seem to like his, although, of course, he was perfectly polite. Then Mark opened a large box which turned out to contain one of those stationary exercise bicycles.

It was from his father, and Mark gave him a disgusted look and put it to one side as if he hoped never to see it again.

"You never get any exercise, the way you live. I thought you might just be able to manage this," Henry said in response.

"I'm sure you really care about my health. Sir. Or care about looking like you do," Mark said mysteriously.

"If you cannot behave yourself you can leave the room," Henry said coldly. "I've had quite enough of these innuendos of yours. These childish innuendos. You may be upset over your mother's death, but by God, so am I! Now. At once!"

Mark stared back at Henry in what I must admit was a very insolent, hateful way; started to say something, then changed his mind. He gave the exercise bicycle a sudden, violent kick that knocked it over and left the room.

Lindy, who had been opening another present from her mother—something silky and yellow—stated crying, put the package down, and walked quickly out of the room, too.

I left after that, telling Henry I wanted to get to an AA meeting on the way home. I was tempted to find Mark and ask if he wouldn't like to join me, but with the way everyone's eyes always glaze over at the mention of AA and the way they never ask anything about it, I restrained myself and left.

Even after the heavy, gloomy dinner, I felt about ten pounds lighter driving back downtown just to be out of that quarrelsome house. At the AA meeting the subject for discussion was Christmas, and most people were talking about their families.

"I had to learn to stop trying to get pizza from a Chinese restaurant," an older woman said, talking about her relationship with her parents.

EIGHT

CHRISTMAS MORNING I PUT SOME SWISS CHEESE, SOURdough bread, oranges and coffee, the dogs, the morning newspaper, and myself into the car and headed down the coast to a beach near Pescadero. It was cool and a little windy, I remember, but not cold. For the first time in weeks it was sunny and very clear. It's often clean like that after a rainy spell, with all the smog washed away and the world looking as if it were just freshly created. This only lasts a day or so before the brown murk creeps back and leaches the color out of what was, until quite recently, one of the most beautiful places on earth. But they're wonderful days, these washed ones, or can be, if the set of your mind isn't hopeless, gray, and dirty with its own smog of might-have-beens, haven't-gots, etceteras.

As it was in my case. The world around me was shiny and new, but I felt old and lonely and dark. Also, I had a panicky feeling that being alive and living my particular life wasn't a reasonable thing to try to do. That I'd put the pieces back together again one too many times to really believe in the possibility of their not just falling apart again. That not drinking, and AA, would turn out to be just another Band-Aid. That thirty-three was too late to set off for anywhere . . .

> *Humpty Dumpty*
> *sat on a wall*
> *Humpty Dumpty*
> *had a great fall*
> *and all the king's horses*
> *and all the king's men* . . .

I chanted to myself with gloomy satisfaction, thinking of my shrinks . . .

49

couldn't put Humpty Dumpty
together again . . .

I walked a long way down the beach, empty except for sea-birds, driftwood, a dead seal. Orphan, the white terrier, lagged behind. Diana, part shepherd and part coyote, black and thin and big-eared, ran ahead, circled back, chased birds and imaginary creatures, galloped and pranced with joy. A man and a woman were coming down the beach from a long way off, walking slowly, arms around each other's waists, happy, in love. Or so I imagined. I walked back to the cliffs and sat down with my back against them and cried. My hundred thousand dollars, I thought, wasn't making me very happy.

I ate some cheese and peeled an orange and looked through the newspaper, but I couldn't get interested. A plane with three hundred people had crashed in Chicago, killing them all; a type of plane that had been crashing a lot lately. The manufacturers and the airlines both denied any connection or responsibility. All as usual. Another school bomb explosion in Boston. Some oil company crookedness, some mess over a retirement fund locally. It was the world as usual, and all seemed very remote.

My thoughts wandered away from the news in the Christmas-day paper, back to Celia's death. I thought of Henry, newly poor and angry about it, or about something. I wondered how Celia would have felt to see him actually cast adrift in relative poverty at the tender age of forty-six. Speculation on what Henry would do with the rest of his life brought to mind the unpleasant question of what I would do with my own.

Just about then, luckily, the wind whipped up and started driving particles of sand like needles along the beach. They stung, and I gathered up my things in a hurry and raced Diana back to the car. We waited for Orphan to catch up, then drove back to the city on a Highway One deserted for Christmas. I stopped off at an early AA meeting on the way home and was in bed by nine o'clock, still feeling terrible. But it was getting more physical; my throat hurt, and I realized I was probably coming down with something.

"A fine Christmas," I thought, "a *fine* Christmas." Now who said that? Is it in Dickens? No. "A *fine* Christmas." *The Wind in the Willows?*

I kept waking up in the night, the phrase still with me until I thought I'd drive myself crazy—or, crazier. A *fine* Christmas. Celia run over by a cable car and the rest of us suspected of murdering her. Mark and his father at each other's throats. Myself alone and sick—ah, yes a *fine* Christmas, but who said it?

Finally I woke up again about three A.M. with the answer: Mrs. Prothero, when they had the fire, and the firemen came and sprayed water all over the living room. Or was it Mr. Prothero? I couldn't get back to sleep, so I finally got up and went to the living room, got out my record of *A Child's Christmas in Wales* and listened to Dylan Thomas reading the poem that ends:

> time held me green
> and dying . . .

That was me, all right, green and dying. I thought of Celia as I'd seen her in the morgue; not green, and not dying. White and battered and dead. I thought of Dunbar Oates and wondered what had really happened between him and Celia. My attention went back to the record; the Christmas fire in the living room was coming up, and yes, it was Mr. Prothero who said it: "a *fine* Christmas!" Celia killed in a freak accident and—stop it, I told myself. I felt horribly tired thinking about Celia and her family, but I couldn't seem to stop. The record continued:

> And Miss Prothero, Jim's aunt, said to
> the tall and handsome fireman—she
> said the right thing, always—"would
> you like anything to read?"

I took the record off and went back to the kitchen and made some hot chocolate, which felt wonderful sliding down my aching throat, took four aspirin, and went back to bed.

When I woke up my temperature was a hundred and one, about the same as the number of my aches and pains, and my throat was so sore it was interfering with my smoking. I called my doctor, who said something named "the Christmas flu" was going around and that he'd have my drugstore send some tetracycline over.

I always feel much better when I have some medicine to take. In fact, all in all, I must admit I have always secretly liked getting sick, or, rather, the first realization that that's what's going on. Not only does it pinpoint what the matter is, it also tells me that the misery I'm feeling probably won't last forever. That it's not some psychosis come down on my innocent or guilty head; a permanent depression; or some obscure, wasting, and incredibly painful disease they can't identify yet so that I'll be stuck with it until it slowly kills me off (quickly; I wouldn't have minded in those days).

I believe this is called hypochondria by some people. Not by me.

"OK, I'm sick," I said to myself. And not unhappily concentrated on bed rest, tetracycline, and a liquid diet of mostly Coca Cola.

And continued to think obsessively, off and on, of Celia, Dunbar, Mark, Henry. I decided it was a part of my illness, but that didn't make it go away. I only got free of thinking about them for any length of time when I slept. I slept as much as I could.

Lindy called and then came by, bringing more Cokes and a bushel of oranges she'd bought from a street truck outside Golden Gate Park.

"My God, Maggie, you look awful!"

I was pleased to hear this and smiled.

"Maybe you should come," she went on, "and be sick at our house."

"No, thanks."

"Really. Cook's been going around like a wounded duck, some old ancient platypus. You'd be just what she needs; you look worse than she does. Come home with me, how about it?"

"No. I mean, thank you and all that. But I'm quite content right where I am, in my own miserable way. And with all these Cokes and oranges I can last it out for quite a while; there's really nothing more I need."

Except love, I thought mournfully; I'd been feeling especially alone and neglected. I always do when I'm sick. But the thought of Celia's big gloomy house and a miserable Cook did not strike me as an improvement.

"All right. Actually you're probably right; it's pretty depressing over there. I'll be glad to get away, even though it's just back to school."

"Can't say I blame you, if Christmas Eve was anything to go by. When are you going?"

"Sunday. Around eleven, I think it is. Daddy got the reservation ages ago, last summer. It was originally for me and Mother, in fact; she had some board meeting and was going to fly back with me. I'd just as soon have changed it and gone back earlier at this point—but of course that's impossible this time of year. Anyway, I'll be able to get over to Grand Central in time to catch an eight o'clock for New Haven, so I'll have Monday to get reorganized.''

"Classes start Tuesday?''

"Yes. Tuesday.''

"Early this year.''

"Umm. I'd expected to hate going back, dark and dreary old Connecticut and exams in a few weeks—now I'm looking forward to it.''

"It's been a horrible Christmas, hasn't it? How are you doing with clearing up Celia's things?''

"Not so good. In fact I was wondering—I was going to ask you to help me, but you got sick. I've hardly gotten started on it is the truth. Could you finish it up, do you think? Would you mind?''

"I don't know about minding, but I'd be willing to, as they say in AA. I was going to offer, actually, before I got sick. Only you should be sure you've skimmed through for anything you want. Do I just pack up everything that nobody wants and send it off to the Goodwill, or what?''

"The Goodwill, yes, or anywhere you want, for that matter, I was going to check the Crippled Children's; Mother was always so involved with them. That's a *huge* load off my mind, Maggie, you're an angel! Thanks *so* much,'' she smiled. It was a rather dim smile, but at least she was trying. "The jewelry's already gone to the safe deposit; Daddy said that has to be part of the estate settlement. I thought about keeping some of the clothes, but then I realized, I don't want to. Too depressing. You should keep anything you want, though. Mother would have wanted you to.''

"All right. Also I'll check with Cook and, I suppose, the maids. What're their names?''

"Laurie and Eva. And Ling So might want something. Did you know he has a huge family in Chinatown? Not a wife and children, I mean, a mother and father, sisters, brothers, a whole bunch of them. Although most of Mother's things'd be too big, I'd think. For Chinese.''

"I'll ask. You might tell your father what I'll be doing, to be sure he has no objection."

"He won't. He mainly doesn't want to have to go near the stuff himself; that's why I started doing it. But I'll tell him. He'll be delighted, believe me."

I was getting tired, so Lindy left, saying she'd try to get by again before she left town.

When she telephoned a few days later I was feeling a lot better and offered to drive her to the airport.

"That would be *great!* Are you sure you're well enough? Daddy's gone back up to those Buddhists, and Mark's been, well, sick. Of course, he's not supposed to be driving anyway. Ling So was going to take me but I'd rather have you. Are you sure you're well enough?"

"I'm well enough. What's the matter with Mark? Flu like mine?"

"No. Actually, he was passed out—for almost two days, so I finally called the doctor. I was supposed to be out of town, in fact; it's a good thing I wasn't. Apparently he took a lot of sleeping pills along with his booze the other night and nearly killed himself."

"Do you mean intentionally?"

"No. I don't think so. He says he doesn't remember taking the pills—just taking what he calls a drink or two from a bottle of scotch he had in his room. Which in fact was empty. He sounds like he's telling the truth about the pills, though. That he doesn't remember anything about them, I mean. I can usually tell when he's lying. Mother never could. But it's all been pretty weird."

"I can imagine. Especially after what you've all been through with Celia. Is he all right now? If he was drinking, he probably took the pills in a blackout. Scary."

"Yes. I can't talk to him at all anymore."

"I can't, either."

"I thought of not going back to school, but I decided it wouldn't help."

"No, I don't think it would."

We were quiet for a while, thinking of Mark, his drinking, his anger. And now some sort of unconscious suicide attempt? Could I do anything? I resolved at least to try to talk with him as soon as I could.

"When's your plane—did you say eleven? Do you have your ticket?"

"Yes to both; the plane leaves at eleven, and I have my ticket."

"What kind of plane is it? Not the same as the one that crashed in Chicago last week, I hope."

"No. Well, I don't know, but it's a different airline so I don't think so. It couldn't possibly matter; those things never happen so close together."

NINE

I'VE HEARD BUSY PLACES DESCRIBED AS MADHOUSES OFTEN enough, but the San Francisco airport that Sunday was a lot worse than any madhouse I've ever seen, on film or off. All flights had been canceled because of fog, but by the time we got out there at around ten o'clock the fog was lifting, and Lindy's plane was supposed to take off more or less on time.

We'd had to almost hack our way through the jungle of people between the entrance and her airline's desk—difficult without machetes. There was a mixture of rage, frustration, and severe anxiety in the air, thick as a peasant soup. Too many people in too small a space were in too much of a hurry. Hurry to leave and end the holidays. Most of them suffering from what I call the Common Christmas Relapse. I'd noticed that I'm not the only one who seems to fall apart during those days of supposed family togetherness, of ending one year and beginning another. Bringing up questions of measurement, and meaning.

"Mr. Archibald Brown, to a white courtesy telephone, please," intoned a female loudspeaker voice in a singsong. "Miss Ellen Soames, to a white courtesy telephone, please."

"Is there another flight we could take?" a thin woman in the next luggage line asked a sick-looking man behind her.

"Baltimore."

"Just bring me a hot dog, a Coke and a hot dog," pleaded a woman in front of us holding a small child.

"I want a coke," whined the child. "I want a Coke, I want a Coke, I want—"

The harassed-looking father hurried off.

"Also, passengers who might have difficulty in walking," the loudspeaker voice came on again, "who might need assistance, please check with the desk."

A fat woman with beady eyes fixed intently on a candy machine to my left nearly knocked me over, then dragged her suitcase right over my toes as I stood there too angry to speak and too civilized to slug her. Or more likely just too slow to react as the thick, boiling crowd closed up across her wake like swamp water. I pushed off after and bought a paperback mystery at a gift shop, then pushed my way back. Finally Lindy's turn came.

The pale, distraught clerk checked her luggage through, and we were free to shove our way out and head for the departure area. We soon were stopped by the metal-detector line, which was long and very slow. Every second or third person was being taken aside and their purses and briefcases searched through.

"I used to think I'd rather be hijacked to Cuba than go back to school," I said. "Especially when it was boarding school."

"Now it's Arabs, and they're more likely to shoot you, I think—"

"Your bags, please," interrupted the thin, bored voice of a uniformed man sitting behind the metal-detector monitor. "Just put the books down with them and your coat, miss."

Lindy's hand luggage and my purse went through without challenge, and we walked on toward the departure area behind a group of people who'd gone through just before us.

"Twelve-thirty now, supposedly," one of them was saying.

"DC Eleven?"

"DC Ten, same flight. They're switching planes; our plane never made it."

I was just starting to worry that they were talking about Lindy's flight when we came to the gate we wanted and they kept on going.

"Thank God that's over. Now all we have to do is sit and wait," Lindy said and smiled the first real smile I'd seen on her face the whole horrible holiday. "Want a cigarette?"

"I sure do," I said, helping myself from a crumpled pack of

Kents she dug out of her coat pocket. "Ah, wonderful," I added after the first deep, long drag of smoke that I'd had for at least twenty minutes. "Wonderful."

There were still a few chairs vacant. I sank down into one gratefully, while Lindy sat with better posture in another. We smoked for a while in companionable silence.

"God!" she said finally. "Am I ready to leave! I did as you asked, by the way. Told Daddy you'd agreed to finish up going through Mother's things for me."

"What'd he say?"

"Nothing much, just that it was nice of you. Which it is."

"Ho hum," I replied.

The area was starting to fill up now. All the chairs were taken, and a number of people were standing, waiting for the flight to be called.

"Do you know Dunbar Oates?" Lindy asked suddenly. "He was Mother's decorator, sort of. . . ."

"Sure. I know Dunbar. Why?"

"He came by to see me a few days ago."

"He did that to me, too. What did he want, anyway?"

"I'm not sure. To offer his respects and say how much my mother had meant to him. That sort of thing. It didn't seem very real, somehow—I don't know how to explain what I mean."

"A feeling that he was really there for something else?"

"Maybe . . ."

"I felt that. I can't imagine what else, though. At your place, was he left alone?"

"Cook brought him right in, I think. I was in the library working on something for school, Roger van der Weyden. We talked; he left."

"Did you see him out?"

"No. He said he knew the way and not to bother."

"Maybe he came to steal something! He's always seemed pretty slick to me. But that wouldn't explain him coming to see me. . . . Say, isn't that that congressman over there? What's his name? Holcomb?"

"Holmes," Lindy said, looking over at a group of men entering in a hurry with a lot of bustle and importance. "Charles Holmes. They're friends of—they were friends of Mother and Daddy's, sort of. Burlingame. Hideously conservative."

"Why all the fuss, I wonder?"

"He's just made some big statement about invading the Arabs or something. It was on TV, but I wasn't paying much attention—invading Israel it would probably be in his case, come to think of it. He said he was flying to Washington today. . . ."

"Speaking of Arabs, how's Mark?"

"OK, I guess. He seems recovered physically, anyway. Very quiet. Daddy's furious with him. For being what he called 'so inconsiderate' by taking the pills. Can you believe it? Luckily, Daddy's gone back to that Buddhist place, which will put a little space between them. They both have such horrible tempers. . . ."

"Didn't Mark have an apartment somewhere?"

"North Beach. He says he sublet it and the rent's way overdue, and he's not sure if he can get it back. He wants to leave our house."

"Doesn't he have a huge allowance?"

"Yes, but you know he drinks so much—I think he goes to bars and buys for everybody in the place until the money runs out. That's what happened once when I was with him, anyway. It's pathetic. He's home now because his money's run out and it's a free place to live. And of course there's an endless supply of booze there; you know how Mother was about having plenty of everything."

"Well, I'll try to keep in touch with him. If I can restrain myself from nagging him about AA. I know it doesn't do any good. But I'll try. If you'll do me a favor?"

"What?"

"Go on back to school and concentrate on living your own life for a while. I'll let you know if I think there's anything you can do for your brother. Will you do that?"

"I'll try." She smiled feebly. "I'll try," she repeated, "but really, he's been acting so strangely I almost wonder—"

"Flight three seventeen to Washington and New York," the loudspeaker interrupted, "now boarding gate eleven—"

"Here," I said, helping Lindy gather up her things, "don't forget your books. Maybe I'll come to see you, meet you in New York in the spring. Last time I was in New Haven, everyone looked so young I don't know if I'm up to that—but I'd love to have some time in New York again."

"Great, let me know," Lindy smiled and turned her attention to the stewardess taking tickets.

Some people pushing from behind sent her on through the door. I waited and watched her walk into the tunnel, a slim figure carrying the standard beaver coat, blond hair shining long and straight as Celia's had once, a long time ago. . . .

I walked back almost to the main terminal and was digging around in my purse for some matches to light a cigarette when I realized I didn't have the paperback I'd bought while Lindy was checking in. I'd been looking forward to a quiet time at home reading it; it was an early one by a Swedish couple I like a lot, so I struggled back through the mobs to see if I'd left it in the departure area. The gate-eleven space was already empty except for an old, hunched-over man with a limp and a big, countrified-looking cane coming back through the door from the outside. A passenger who changed his mind—or had he been allowed on the plane to see someone off? Some little old lady in worse shape even than he was? He looked old and sick enough for special privileges, I thought, as he tottered on off up the hallway.

I felt down underneath the seat of the chair I'd been sitting in and found my book. A stewardess came through from the outside. Out the window I could see Lindy's plane still standing on the runway, the men just starting to take away the steps. The stewardess hurried off past me and then past the old man, still creeping slowly up the hall. She'd had big dark sunglasses and longish blond hair in a pageboy cut. Probably dyed, I thought sourly.

There was something about the sight of a stewardess that tended to bring out the sour in me. Probably sexual jealousy, I thought, busily muttering to myself something contemptuous like "shallow creature." And maybe no more shallow, than, say, one Margaret Linden Elliott.

> Well that's
> something
> to think about . . .

The gloomy tones of early Willie Nelson appeared in my head once again. When I stopped to think about it, there were plenty of times I'd traded on looks, so-called charm, even body, for something or someone I'd wanted. On a more sophisticated level, of course. Less out front, in other words. So who was I to sneer at airline stewardesses?

TEN

LATE THAT AFTERNOON I WAS COMFORTABLY SETTLED IN MY living room with dinner on a tray and *The Locked Room* open at page forty-three when the telephone rang. It was Mark, who asked in a small, tight-sounding voice: "Coast Airways Flight three seventeen to Washington/New York—Maggie, was that Lindy's flight?"

"I think so; why? What's the matter?"

"It's crashed," he said flatly. "It was on the five-thirty news. I just happened to be watching it. Are you sure—Flight three seventeen?"

"Oh, my God." I sat down. "I think it was. Were there—did anyone—were there any survivors?"

"No. There were no survivors. According to the news. Maybe they're wrong."

"Maybe I'm wrong." But I could hear as clearly as if it were in the room with me now, the loudspeaker voice repeating, "Flight three seventeen now boarding gate eleven . . ."

"What happened? Do they know? That was the flight number, I'm pretty sure. And I watched her get on the plane—what happened?"

"They don't know yet." His voice continued to be flat and expressionless. "They say it just exploded up in the air. In Kansas somewhere. They say it might have been a bomb. But there isn't—"

"A bomb? In this day and age? I thought that was impossible anymore. With all the electronic checking they do. Everyone went through those detectors—I was there, I saw them."

"They don't check the baggage, though. Just the carry-on stuff."

"Well, what the hell good is that?" I said angrily; then realized it was no good yelling at Mark. "I'm sorry. I just can't believe it, I didn't see the plane take off; maybe there's some chance—I'll call the airlines. Is your father home? No, of course not."

"I'll call them. He's out of town. I'll call you back."

He hung up. I remained sitting on the straight-back chair that belonged in the kitchen but for some reason happened to be in the front room by the telephone, smoking cigarettes and waiting. My legs didn't seem to feel like taking me anywhere more comfortable. I was having a hard time getting any feeling of reality; the things in the room, under the lamplight of early winter dark, had a kind of haze over them, but I hardly saw them, anyway. My brain was too busy with images of a plane, in silent slow motion, flying, blowing up, all the pieces falling very slowly down out of the sky. The brown tweed suit and the beaver coat, separate now, the long blond hair and the clear green eyes—like Celia's, like mine—wide, clear, blank, blind.

All coming to rest, very slowly, gently, with only a little ragdoll sort of bump, on the earth. Kansas earth: wheat, flat, a small farmhouse in the far distance, no trees. Wreckage, a faint breeze stirring bits of it, fanning the flames of the small fires. Little specks on the huge horizon, getting bigger; cars, people gathering. My brain spun out the pictures and I sat there and watched them, while I waited and smoked.

"CONGRESSMAN KILLED IN AIR CRASH" the headlines and the television blared. "No Survivors from Coast Airways Flight of 83 Passengers and 11 Crew" and "Bomb Thought Likely by FAA" were subheadings on the front page of *The New York Times*, delivered the next day promptly at eleven, as always, to Celia's front door. Eventually to be Henry's front door, I reminded myself, remembering that strange will . . .

He and Mark and I were in the library. Mark was drinking scotch neat, and Henry wasn't even glaring at him. Henry's face was a kind of putty color, and he looked exhausted and bewildered. Once more, he'd been notified of sudden death and had flown back home from the Buddhist monastery up north.

Early that morning, the airlines had officially confirmed Lindy's presence on the plane, the plane that had crashed with no survivors. The fact that Congressman Charles Holmes, billed as a "conservative statesman from San Mateo county," had been killed in the crash had already been on the late news Sunday night. Which I'd known anyway, having seen him board the plane behind Lindy.

The three of us were in a state of shock. To have Lindy killed in a plane crash just two weeks after Celia was killed by a cable car—with us suspected for a while of murdering her—was more than we could take in right away. Not to mention Mark's drinking and pill binge the week before, I thought, looking at him. He was very pale and quiet, and looked as exhausted and confused as his father. At least they weren't sniping at each other.

We watched the twelve o'clock news. A young man who looked like he ought to be modeling Arrow shirts excitedly informed us of a tape delivered to KTSF, the local "radical" radio station.

In the tape, a group calling itself the California Coalition claimed credit for blowing up the plane. It was a relatively short tape for that sort of thing, after the standards set by the Patty Hearst tapes, anyway. It simply stated that the "execution" of Congressman Holmes, along with other "bourgeois enemies of the people," was just the start of an entire "vigorous and relentless program" now launched by the California Coalition—which no one had ever heard of. "Fellow travelers must suffer destruction," it went on; "the fallout of justice now begun will carry us to total victory!"

The voice seemed to be that of a male heavily disguised. "Onward to total victory!" it concluded, somewhat redundantly.

"Local authorities," continued the Arrow-shirt model, "immediately called in the FBI, who say that they have no hard information" [that, I thought, undoubtedly meant they had none at all] "on this so-called California Coalition. The FAA refused to comment on preliminary results from the examination of debris from the crash. Usually reliable sources, however, have indicated the possibility that a new plastic explosive recently developed by Grabbon may have been responsible for the explosion. Grabbon denies the existence of such a substance, which, according to our sources, is not readily detected by bomb-surveillance mechanisms because it has no metal parts."

The image changed to a jowly-faced man who looked as if he hadn't had much sleep lately and was cross about that or about something. He stretched his big lips in a palpably false smile to indicate his good will and honest nature, and made the routine denials for Grabbon. His image alone was enough to confirm the report of the plastic explosive pretty thoroughly. You'd think they might have learned something from the Nixon debacle, but clearly they hadn't. Then it occurred to me that one reason I recognized the falseness of the grimace so readily was because that's how I myself smile when I want to lie and hope to get away with it but fear that I won't. The smile of a crocodile lacking any real self-confidence.

"In Minneapolis, meanwhile, snow continues to pile up today in record—in fact, disaster—proportions, and the President has declared a state of emergency . . ."

We left it on, but none of us was listening any longer; we had disaster enough here. Looking at the couch where Lindy had been sitting just over two weeks ago while I was trying to reach Henry about Celia, I remembered how we'd talked of her mother, of the plans that would need to be made . . . and I remembered her sitting there again while Temple read out that surprising will. . . . The yellow silk looked very aggressively empty. Underneath my tiredness and shock, I could feel something stirring. I realized later that it was anger. I felt tears starting and got up and left the room.

"Goddammit," I muttered to myself, stalking down the hallway, "I'm just constantly crying these days. I hate all this goddam crying; it makes me sick. Sick!"

I went into the kitchen to get some tea; there was only the big silver coffee pot out in the library, and I'd had so much coffee that morning I was beginning to feel like a rattle.

Cook was at the sink, weeping and washing spinach leaves.

"Oh, Grita," she wept, "*qué lugar malo, malo, loco! Yo me se debimos* to stay in *Tejas,* oh *sí,* I know this, *pero la Señora Silia,* she no listen, she no listen, *veas tu: qué paso! Veas!*"

Although Cook spoke reasonably good English when she wanted to, she didn't often want to. Not exclusively, anyway. With me and Celia and the family she spoke a seemingly haphazard combination, about sixty-forty, of Spanish and English. Celia, and our mother before her, had tried to discourage this practice, but to no avail; Cook was a stubborn woman. I'd known her all my life, and if there was anyone from my family I trusted, it was Cook. Which doesn't mean that she wasn't often exasperating.

"*Mi niña*, she hurts no one, no one! *Estos locos con bombas!* Maybe they kill us *todos*, all, *esta familia*, no? We go the *Tejas, sí? À Tejas?* You and Mark, I go, too? *El* doctor, no, he tells me *en la semana proxima* he gets *un apartamento* downtown, *màs acerca* for his work, better for him, maybe. *Pero nosotros, vamanos à Tejas, verdad? Lejos de estos* heepies *y* yeepies *y tambien*," she concluded, "*estos carros que matan mi pobre Señora Silia!*"

"I don't know," I answered slowly, thinking about how it would be for Cook to return to Texas after all those years. "Maybe you should go back, Cook. I know you have family there. I didn't know Henry was getting an apartment—are you sure?"

"*Sí, sí, seguro.* He tell me last week. *Un apartamento* in the city for his work. He say I stay here, Ling So *y las criadas, tambien*, for Mr. Mark. But I think better we all go to *Tejas.*"

"I can't speak for Mark—but I will, anyway," I smiled. "I don't think he would go to Texas. He's never even liked it on visits. And I know I don't want to go back. Even if Henry does get an apartment, though, this house will be kept open. It was set up like that in Celia's will." She looked blank. "*En el testamento de la Señora.* It says the house has to be kept open, no matter who's living here. And you've been with the family so long—but you should think it over very carefully, just what's— what's best for you. If you decide you want to go, I'll help you arrange it, if you want me to."

"*Sí, Grita, gracias, pero*—you think, too; maybe you change your mind. Before you killed, too! *La Señora* left me lotta money, for *ranchito, el retiro*, to retire. Or I come work for you and Mark, in *Tejas.*"

Unlike Cook, I couldn't think of Texas as a refuge from crazy tragedies; it had had its share in the past few years and then some. Kennedy and Oswald and Jack Ruby, the tower sniper, and a man from Dallas who'd carved up eight or ten nurses with a butcher knife came instantly to mind.

The tears were rolling down Cook's face, I noticed, and then I realized they were rolling down mine, too. We clung to each other and wept, there in the kitchen where it felt better to be—

and Cook better to be with—than out in the library with Henry and Mark.

"I guess I go with the lunch now, Grita," Cook finally said, tugging her apron straight and pushing back a string of gray hair that had come loose from the tight bun she always had it in. "*Hay algo quieres*, to eat?"

I felt exhausted. I remembered I had come in to get tea, and I said I'd make it myself. But since I didn't know where anything was, Cook set it all up: teapot, cup, tray, sliced lemon, boiling water, as I was still protesting that I'd do it and that she should go on with the lunch.

I returned reluctantly with the tray to the library, where Henry and Mark were sitting at opposite ends of the room, glum and silent. Henry was holding a cup of coffee in his lap just as when I'd left; it must have been stone cold by then. He appeared to have forgotten all about it. Mark had his usual glass of scotch.

"I suppose there will be some sort of group memorial service," Henry remarked as I entered the room, apparently talking to me. He seemed to be ignoring Mark. I had the sudden thought, "He wished it had been Mark. Instead of Lindy. And Mark knows it. Oh, the poor kid!"

"I remember when a friend of mine at New Haven was killed in a crash," he continued; "that's what they did. A group service. I suppose I could get in touch with Maura Holmes. Or perhaps Charlie's office would be best. What do you think?"

"I would think the office," I answered, surprised at being asked. "Although on the other hand, maybe Mrs. Holmes would like hearing from you, I don't know . . . were you good friends?"

"Not really. Just socially. I suppose his office would have any information there is. On what we can plan for."

"I'd think so," I agreed.

Mark was staring out the window. Yesterday's sun hadn't lasted, and the world out there was a universal gray again, whether from clouds or fog I couldn't tell. I tried to focus my mind on the practical details that would need attending to. I didn't like seeing this naked hate between Mark and his father. Adopted father. The silence was uncomfortable, but "Would you like anything to read?—à la Miss Prothero and the fire fighters—clearly wouldn't do.

"Would you like me to write up something for the newspapers, what you want said about Lindy?" I tried instead.

"No," Henry answered shortly, "I want to do that myself this afternoon. It will give me something to do. Tomorrow I'm going back to work. I am needed there," he added with a cold glance at Mark, "or so they say."

"I'm sure you are," I agreed uncomfortably, then wished I had kept my mouth shut and not said anything. And then, not liking the silence, I added, "Is there anything else that you'd like me to do?"

"Yes, actually, there is, Maggie," Henry said quickly. "Lindy said you were going to, uh, finish going through Celia's things—send them off to the Goodwill or whatever. Would you mind—could you also see what you can do with Lindy's . . ." His voice trailed off, unwilling to go on. It was the only time I ever saw him show any strong feeling until the time, much later, when he broke down completely.

"Yes," I said, "I'll be glad to." I wished I hadn't asked.

"Perhaps some of her friends would like something. I don't know, is that sort of thing done? Cook can tell you who would be appropriate to call, I think, if you decide you want to do that. As you wish, of course. Do what seems best to you; I'll leave all that in your hands."

"Fine," I said, nodding my agreement and thinking that Henry seemed to be in rather a hurry to clear out his wife's and daughter's things. Then I decided it was probably the scientist in him. Tidy.

"Oh—I wanted to ask you—Lindy mentioned to me at the airport that Dunbar Oates had come by to see her. She had the feeling he wanted something, but it wasn't clear what. He came to see me, too. Did he come to see you?"

"No," he said, "why?" But he appeared to be hardly listening.

"I don't know, I just wondered. I noticed him talking very earnestly to Temple at Celia's wa—at the gathering here after Celia's funeral." And to Henry as well, I remembered. "You haven't talked to him, then?"

"No, and I don't want to," Henry said in a way that closed the subject. "By the way—Celia had a lot of things in the guest cottage; you'll need the keys."

He took a small ring with two new-looking keys out of his

jacket pocket and handed them over. He'd obviously been planning all along to have me do the clearing up.

"Two? Are there two locks?"

"It's just a duplicate," he said. "I had a number of them made when we had a new lock put on—quite a good one; there'd been some burglaries in the neighborhood. Just return them to Cook when you've finished. I have some files of papers stored down there—old office records—just leave them to one side, will you?"

As usual, I felt relieved when I left that ornate, unhappy house.

ELEVEN

THE NEWS MEDIA WERE WELL REPRESENTED AT THE MEMOrial service held Wednesday morning for Lindy, the congressman, and the other ninety-two victims of the crash. Not only the local papers and television, but all three networks and several of the big city newspapers were there as well: still photographers, video and sound men, equipment, cables, microphones—all the bustle and hustle of a big news event. Some of the reporters were local stringers, but some of the heavies from New York had also come out, a couple of whom I knew from my documentary-film days there. One of the cameramen, Paul Folsom, I'd known very well indeed, and I waved at him through the confusion. A few of the faces, including one woman's, were familiar from the national evening newscast.

The congressman's widow—and ex-Hollywood actress who had been moderately well known and was still moderately beautiful—and her two young daughters were all photogenic and good copy. They were filmed arriving, with microphones stuck right into the widow's face; one or two mikes even rushed down to the face of the older daughter but failed to catch her question, then rushed back up to the mother's lips to get the answer at least, should there be any. I'd done sound work myself, and I remembered very well that ruthless feeling of total concentration on "getting it," whatever "it" turned out to be. Like a marine landing on the beach, I used to think; the big moment everything else was for, and all the softer feelings gone entirely. Eventually trained right out of you, if you stuck around long enough. Which I hadn't, luckily, although why I left that world I've never been quite sure. Certainly it wasn't to protect my finer feelings.

A good deal of footage, to my surprise, was being devoted to Henry, Mark, Cook, and myself. It was the first experience I'd had on that side of the cameras, and I didn't like it. There is something very annoying about having a bunch of flashbulbs go off in your face, particularly with all those microphones waving around it, too—unless you're a movie star or a politician; presumably then the benefits outweigh the disadvantages. And if you're a movie star or a politician, you're probably also an extrovert and thrive on that sort of thing. The bulbs flashed—not a few right in my introvert face—and I was feeling extremely irritated.

Of all the passengers other than the congressman, Lindy's death was receiving the biggest coverage, partly because it had come only two weeks after her mother's—and also by violence. But mainly, I think, it was because her huge personal fortune (and that from oil) fit in so well with the "people's enemy" aspect of the California Coalition tape.

"DOUBLE TRAGEDY STALKS PROMINENT FAMILY" and "HOLIDAY HORRORS HIT LOCAL HOME" were some of the tackier local headlines, but even *The New York Times* had picked up the story not only as addendum to the Holmes assassination—as it was being called on both coasts—but also as a double family tragedy.

Walking in through the microphones and flashbulbs with Mark, I could see that he was hating it all even more than I was. He looked ready to kill somebody—anybody—at any minute, barely managing to hold himself together under whatever the iron control was that had kept him away from a drink for the last twenty-four hours. The day before, I'd been afraid he was going to shake himself into convulsions. He'd rejected my suggestion of having the doctor come over, so I'd plied him with orange juice—which he threw up—and honey and water—which finally he didn't—all day long. It hadn't seemed a very good time to try for the talk I'd promised myself and Lindy that I'd have with him; I'd just concentrated on getting him sober.

He looked better today, I thought. At least, he didn't look like he'd already been dead for several days the way he had the day before. He also looked absolutely furious—probably a good thing, given the usually withdrawn nature of his hostility. It seemed a small miracle that he didn't bash in the heads of some of the more aggressive photographers with their own cameras.

Glancing back at Henry, who was following behind with Cook, I saw that he was expressionless as usual but still had that sickening gray tinge to his face. I imagined that he resented the kind of copy being made out of the deaths as much as anyone. Cook was weeping unashamedly.

The actual service was closed to the media, and it was a relief to pass through the door of the chapel into the relative quiet and dark of the interior. We entered just behind the congressman's widow, who had one small daughter held tightly in each hand. She had on a short black veil, and inevitably I thought of Jackie Kennedy. And irreverently or irrelevantly, a song from an old Joan Baez album started up in my head:

> She walks
> these hills
> in a long
> bla-ack
> veil
> visits
> my grave

Only for these dead there wouldn't be any graves. Such remains as there were had been cremated together and were to be put in a special mausoleum at the same Colma cemetery where Celia was buried. What was the rest of it?

> But I spoke not a word
> though it meant
> my-ay life
> for I'd been
> in the arms
> of my be-est

> *fri-end's*
> *wife*
>
> *she walks*
> *these hills . . .*

The pastel-house-covered hills of San Francisco, in this case, not the bare and windy Dakota badlands . . .

I dragged my thoughts back to the chapel. Another "nice" minister was walking up to a kind of podium. There was a large crowd, with quite a different feeling to it than there had been at the service for Celia. I tried to pinpoint it. The feeling here was—what? Restlessness? Resentment? Anger? With a sort of unfinished quality . . . excitement, in fact. Which, I suppose, had to do with the lunacy of killing a whole planeload of ordinary people to get one rather ordinary congressman. No big villain, from what I knew of him; just a common minor one, only one or two million dollars richer than when he first entered public service . . .

> *Farther along*
> *we'll*
> *know all about*
> *it . . .*

The organ ground out the old black spiritual now:

> *. . . farther along*
> *we'll*
> *understand why . . .*

Someone, I thought, actually chose something appropriate for once, probably by mistake. . . .

> *. . . we'll understand it*
> *all*
> *bye and bye . . .*

But would we, I wondered, ever learn much more about the California Coalition and the blowing up of the plane than was known now? As far as I could tell from the media reports, the police and FBI weren't making much progress in identifying the group that sent the tape, much less in getting their hands on it. They were pretty sure now that the bomb had been constructed from a new explosive developed at Grabbon International, one of the giant space industries that gave "silicone valley," down the peninsula, its name. Two days before the memorial service, on Monday, one of Grabbon's employees had been found shot to death with what turned out to be his own gun. Judging by the condition of the body, he had been killed about the time the plane was sabotaged. He'd worked in the section of Grabbon that had developed the new explosive. The FBI weren't committing themselves, but the news media assumed the connection as a matter of course.

> Cut down like the grass in the
> morning
> yet so shall they
> rise
> and be with us
> in spirit . . .

This, or something very like it, plus the minister's solemn voice which had suddenly grown louder in what I hoped might be a concluding peroration, brought me back to the service. I looked around. Sitting a few rows down on my left was the old man I'd seen at the airport when I'd gone back to find my book. I'd been right, then, in my idea that he'd been seeing someone off. If it was the little old lady I'd imagined, the companion of a lifetime, was he glad or sad, I wondered, to be left behind? I wouldn't have been glad, but I have the idea that most very old people cling quite tenaciously to life, no matter what the circumstances. Once they've made it that far. Perhaps he was one of those; perhaps the getting from here to there with that cane and back again was the only thing of real importance to him. I wondered who he was, who he'd been.

A couple of rows beyond the old man, I saw the slick blond head of Dunbar Oates. I wondered who he was, too. Underneath the smooth exterior. He was from Dallas, I remembered, and had done some work there for some of Celia's fellow millionaires, who'd then introduced him to her. She'd been very taken with him from the beginning . . . he was rather like her first husband in a way. . . .

The minister wasn't finishing up, as I'd hoped—what I'd heard had been merely a middle peak in a continuing range. My thoughts drifted away again—from the chapel, from the old man, from Dunbar—back to the murdered Grabbon chemist. Who had he been? The Tuesday morning paper had a good many facts, and the Wednesday paper even more, but they weren't adding up to much.

His name was Ronald Lesley Cremmens. He had been thirty-three years old. Born in a small town in southern California, he had gotten a master's degree at the Polytechnic College at San Luis Obispo and then gone to work for Grabbon, where he'd been for ten years. For the past five of those years he'd lived in Mountain View, in one of the giant, impersonal beehive apartment buildings built to house the workers of the huge Peninsula electronics empires. He'd remained a stranger to his neighbors, as is the way there. As is the way now in most of the places where we live, but more so in that place.

His ex-wife, interviewed on TV, said she hadn't seen or heard from him in several years and that she knew nothing about his current life, friends, or enemies.

"Though I can't imagine Ronnie having an enemy, really; there wasn't much one way or the other about him to dislike," she said with decided venom, "if you see what I mean." She paused to think, or to do what passed for thinking in her heavily curled, beehived, dirty-looking head. "The scientist type. If you see what I mean."

Remarried and living in Long Beach, she'd already been found and interviewed in time for the Monday evening news. A slew of scraggly children surrounded her; one little girl's dress was not only dirty but had a big tear in it. The ex-Mrs. Cremmens herself had on what looked like a brand-new outfit, however, a beige pantsuit patterned with red roses and green leaves made out of one of the synthetic fabrics developed by those scientists she seemed to think she had no use for. Looking at that pantsuit, it occurred to me that she might be more right than she knew.

"Oh, no," she continued, giving the smallest boy an absent-minded pat on the head, "these aren't *Ronnie's* children. He couldn't *have* children—"

Her lipsticked mouth opened for more—the appalling woman

was apparently quite prepared to continue with details of this ancient grievance—but the interview had ended there.

> *. . . that we may lay hold on eternal*
> *life, for tomorrow we die . . .*

The minister's voice again, and this time he was ending. People were collecting their things; he left the podium and it was over.

"For tomorrow we will die too." Waiting for the crowd behind us to leave, I was reminded of a church I'd seen in Italy. Down in the south it was; I hadn't thought of it in years. I'd thought it funny and wonderful at the time, decorated all around the outside with a lacy pattern of dancing skeletons, with Latin inscribed in the gray stone across the door:

> *Be miserable with me*
> *Be miserable with me*
> *For tomorrow*
> *You will be dead too*

Amusing at the time, but enough was enough.

The aisles were clearing. The four of us walked back out through the bulb-and-microphone gauntlet, Henry and I going first this time, followed by Mark and Cook. We separated at the curb. There was to be no wake for Lindy, like the one after Celia's funeral; and if there had been, I don't think I would have gone. I'd had enough. We've all had, and to spare.

I waved again to Paul Folsom, who was still behind his camera, and left. The scene was too chaotic to stop and talk, and I was tired all the way down to my bones. Quite unlike the bones that had made such a charming design around the top of the seventeenth-century Italian church; those bones had been sprightly and gay, dancing. Not mine. I willed them to drag the rest of me along home.

TWELVE

LATER THAT AFTERNOON MY CAMERAMAN FRIEND FROM NEW York telephoned, and I agreed to meet him at his hotel for a drink. I'd had time for a nap, and a hot bath, too, so that when I got up to the Mark Hopkins I was feeling a lot better than I had after the service, though I was still awfully tired. Whatever had gone out of me was more than a little sleep and hot water could restore.

"I'd forgotten what remarkable eyes you have, Maggie," Paul said, after we'd gotten settled in the crowded hotel bar. It was on the top floor of the hotel and had tables along three of its four glass walls. We had a table at one end which looked out over the city, the bay, and both bridges, a spectacular view that was spoiled somewhat by a hideous white-and-mustard-colored skyscraper rising squatly in the middle of everything.

"What'll you have?"

"A Coke, please."

"Just a Coke?"

"Just a Coke."

"You're not drinking? Why not?"

"That's right, I'm not drinking, I turned out to be an alcoholic."

"Good Lord, Maggie, how could you? You never drank any more than the rest of us!"

"Maybe, although I'm not sure about that—anyway, it's all right. Being an alcoholic, I mean. I go to AA; that's been a help."

"Oh." Paul looked pained and uncomfortable, the way people tend to do at the mention of AA, and I was sorry I'd brought it up. We both retreated for a few minutes to our drinks, his the perpetual double martini.

"So Dave Elliott went and got himself killed. How long were

you together, about four years? Married about two?'' he asked finally, raising his eyes from his drink and giving me a searching look as if to discover once and for all just what that meant to me.

"Yes to both."

"Had it remained a good relationship?"

Well, Paul was never one to beat around the bush. A good thing in this case, perhaps; it would have been awkward if we'd both skirted around the subject of David all evening. At one time I'd thought I would probably marry Paul. We'd had one of those emotional on-again, off-again New York City relationships going for a couple of years when, during one of the off periods, I'd met David. And that had been that.

"In many ways, yes, it was still a good relationship. And in some others, it wasn't. We were hoping to work those out, eventually. Then David got killed, and that's when the drinking, combined with a lot of pills, got completely out of control. When I say I turned out to be an alcoholic—it's been a big relief, really. To find out what was the matter and be able to stop it. For a long time I knew I drank too much, but I thought when I got my problems sorted out, got my life in better shape, then I'd do something about the drinking. Turns out it only works the other way around. Meanwhile, I saw a lot of shrinks . . . of course, that had started in New York. . . .''

"Dear old Dr. Pudman, oh, yes. I remember him, all right,'' Paul said with a tinge of residual bitterness—he'd always looked upon my Freudian analyst as a sort of adversary.

"Putnam,'' I corrected automatically and smiled at the old joke. "Well, since him I've tried all kinds. He was one of the better ones—at least he had a sense of humor. Now I'm seeing a Jungian. I like Jung's psychology a lot better than Freud's—but none of it was really any help in living my life until I realized I was an alcoholic and stopped drinking. But that's enough about that. What about you? I heard from someone you'd married? To someone—what was it? Not in film, anyway?''

"Yeah—a dynamite lady; you'd like her. Designer—textiles. Very good at it, too; makes heaps of money.'' He looked through the glass wall to the lovely scene beyond, but I thought that what he was seeing was the image of his wife, or his marriage.

"We get along pretty well. Lead our own lives to some extent—an open relationship. No children, which makes that easier. Actually, I'm getting to the point where I wouldn't mind having a couple of kids; senility, perhaps. But Daisy doesn't want to; she's afraid she'd get stuck out in some charming house in Connecticut. Can't say I blame her.''

''No. People do seem to move out once they have children. No matter how much they swore they wouldn't. What about work?''

''I went with the network; of course, you saw that today if you didn't know. About three years ago. It's meant a lot of money, and I've been to a lot of places, shot stories I wouldn't have got to do otherwise. On nice fat budgets. I miss being on my own in some ways, but I don't miss that constant free-lance hustle, and I sure don't miss the dry spells. I still have a burning desire to make my own film—and I still don't have an idea in my head.''

He smiled, the charming smile that lit up his otherwise rather saturnine face and made the less appealing aspects of his character—chunks of arrogance and narcissism—seem less important. He knew himself pretty well in some ways, knew his own limitations, and to some extent he accepted them—another redeeming feature, and rather rare in the business he was in. And he was a wonderful cameraman. Sometimes I think I'd been in love—not with Paul himself, but with the pictures he took. But he lacked the whatever it is that's needed to formulate a framework to put them around. Not passion. Clarity, perhaps. The idea, I suppose; the concept.

''I was surprised to see you there today,'' he went on. ''I had no idea you had any connection with the plane crash.''

''Yes. Linden Sloan was my niece—my half sister Celia's daughter. That was Celia's husband and son, and Cook, that I came with. Celia was killed herself—well, you must know that, since it's been part of the coverage on Lindy. For a while they even suspected one of the rest of us had murdered her! Celia, I mean. It's all been pretty horrible, Paul. There was an inquest, a finding of accidental death, we seemed to be through the worst of it, and then this plane crash . . . What do you know about this California Coalition?''

''No more than you do, probably, if you read the papers or watch the news. Or not much more. The tape they sent was an ordinary one-and-one-half mil, quarter-inch. Scotch brand, sold by the millions in thousands of stores. On a five-inch reel, not a cassette; that's a little unusual these days. No prints, naturally. And that's all the FBI has, as far as I know. The so-called Coalition's own description of themselves on the tape. Fact is, nobody's ever heard of 'em before, and I don't think all the digging they're doing is turning anything up. Of course that guy who got killed—that Grabbon guy, Cremmens—that's their best hope. The wreckage analysis suggested his type of explosive, and the fact that he was killed when he was makes the connection pretty sure. Jesus! We interviewed his ex-wife down in Long Beach on the way up here—did you see that, by any chance?''

"Did you shoot that? Jesus, as you say. Truly grotesque. What else was there that didn't go on the air?''

"Well, she started to go into the details of how Cremmens couldn't have children—'sterilized' as she called it, though I suppose what she meant was 'sterile'. She'd met him out here; she was a waitress at some place he used to go to a lot when he first came to the area, some dinky sandwich joint. They started going out. They got married. They got divorced. A normal couple.'' He grinned.

"As Bob Dylan would say. Well. I guess . . . I guess they're sure there really is such a group as the California Coalition? Doesn't it seem a little strange that nobody's ever heard of them before?''

"In a way. I suppose it could be some other group that just made up a name to mislead the cops. Although that wouldn't make any sense, since the whole point of something like this is the publicity. If something doesn't turn up on them soon, I guess they'll start looking into that possibility. But as far as I know, right now they believe there is such a group, and their main worry is that they *will* hear something more—in the form of another bomb. Or, rather, 'explosive device.' That's one thing that hasn't been mentioned; they asked us to hold it, so don't repeat it, please. There's some indication enough of that stuff is missing to make up several of the things.''

"Good lord, I never thought of that. How horrible!''

"Probably the first thing they did think of—and look for—once the Grabbon connection came into it. Want another, uh, Coke?''

"Why not?''

He got the waiter's attention—no small feat, the bar being

quite crowded—and held up two fingers for two more of the same.

"OK," he said after the drinks came, "now. The New York question. What have you been doing out here in crazy California? Any film work?"

"Well, in the beginning. When David and I first came out, we both worked some. Not together on anything. He did some things for KQED; pseudo-documentary, nothing special. He was working on a thing of his own when he got killed. It's still in my kitchen pantry, unfinished."

"Ever think of finishing it yourself?"

"That's not the worst," I sighed. "I've got an unfinished film of my own in that pantry. I hate going in there to get out a can of soup. I really ought to move the stuff somewhere else. The cans of film, or the cans of soup."

"Think you'll get back to it?"

"I don't know. I haven't thrown it out, anyway. It bothered me a lot for a long time, but now it's more . . . inert. Either I'll get back to it or I won't."

"I hope you do. I liked that film of yours about the little black girl—what was it, west Eightieth Street?"

"Eighty-eighth. I did, too. This one's a lot bigger and more complicated, though."

"What's it about?"

I sighed. "Well, that's part of the problem, I think. Self-destructive Southern women, you could say. Based on myself, naturally, although I didn't realize that so much in the beginning."

"You been working at all for money?"

"No. For a long time after David got killed I just stayed home and drank. Along with a generous ration of various pills. And even now that I'm sober, I haven't felt like trying to work. I haven't any idea what sort of work to look for, for one thing."

"Not film?"

"I don't think so. The farther I get from it, the more I feel I don't want it anymore. I did some stuff out here, commercials mostly, some yukky 'educational' stuff. It's pretty hard to keep body and soul together in the film business, in San Francisco. If I were really hot for film still—and one of the things that tells me I'm not is that I'm not willing to do this—I'd move to L.A., or back to New York. Besides," I added reflectively, seeing it clearly for the first time myself, "I'm not feeling tough enough for that world. Maybe I never was. I can easily imagine never going back to film—though I'd like it if I could finish my own movie someday—but I haven't the least idea where *to* go. I'm kind of waiting. For it to come to me."

"Sounds very California. But like you said, either it will or it won't. What have you been living on, if you don't mind my asking? Or even if you do, of course," he said, smiling the appealing smile and taking a big slug of gin.

"I don't mind. David and I had a cabin on a gold-mine claim, up in the Trinity mountains. I sold it. I've been living—just barely, so the money would last—on that. Now Celia's left me a hundred thousand dollars! It doesn't seem real—but it is. So now I can continue to take my time about figuring out what to do with myself. Speaking of time, what time is it?"

Paul looked at his watch and said: "Shit. It's after eight—I've got to get back to work. We're shooting an interview with an FBI honcho who's flying in tonight. . . ."

He signaled the waiter and pushed his chair back all in one motion. "How about if I call you when I'm finished? You could invite me over to your place—how about it?" Again the charming smile. "For old times' sake?"

"No, thanks."

"Why not?"

"How about—because we can't get back what we had? And aren't in a place to find anything new?" I resolutely didn't mention the dynamite wife in New York. "And," I added, holding out my hand and smiling, "I have really loved having this time with you, Paul."

"OK. Same here. If I get out again, I'll give you a call."

"All right. And I'll call you if I come East this spring. I'm sort of thinking of it."

"Friends, then?"

"Friends."

THIRTEEN

Talking to Paul made me feel better than I had in a very long while—almost like my old self, or some promised new one. The next day I woke up feeling horrible again, though, and soon figured out that I had the flu back again. Like most relapses it was worse than the original illness, and I ended up spending another week at home, most of it in bed.

While I'm always happy when I first realize I'm sick, give in, and go to bed, this only lasts a day or so. Then I get the idea that I should be getting over whatever it is, and this is a miserable time saturated first with the suspicion, then the certainty, that I'm going to feel bad forever, after all. Hopes of dying from my illness creep in then, because what would be the point in living the rest of life feeling so awful?

To distract myself I read mysteries, including the true-life one of Ronald Cremmens. I had morning and evening newspapers delivered and watched the television news religiously as well. Both newspapers and TV showed pictures of the body as it was found, a thinly huddled bundle of old clothes it looked at first, the red-and-green-checked trousers especially pathetic. As though he had dressed up for a special occasion. The body had been stuffed loosely into an old drainage culvert in a particularly deserted area of the salt marsh that extends along the eastern edge of East Palo Alto, a poor, black residential area segregated from affluent white neighbors by the freeway.

"A sort of local lovers' lane in summer," said a local commentator, as a camera panned in rather wobbly fashion around the area, "but mostly barren and deserted at this time of year—as Cremmens' killers were no doubt aware." And as we could perfectly well see for ourselves. "Too Cold for Love but a Good Spot for Murder," a newspaper article capped it. At least the news people were having a good time, I thought, propped grumpily in my bed and alternating between throat lozenges and cigarettes.

The owner of a run-down grocery on the road leading into the marsh was interviewed on TV and said he'd seen some sort of a small, new-looking car—gray, or maybe blue or green— drive into the area around the time Cremmens was killed. He thought there'd been two or three people in it. He'd noticed because it was unusual for that sort of car to be going in there in winter.

Cremmens had a three-year-old Toyota which fit the description; it was found parked on a back street in San Jose. Police speculated Cremmens had gone with one or two persons in his own car to the area, been shot with his own gun, and that then the murderer or murderers, after stuffing his body into the culvert, had driven the car off and parked it. It had been wiped clean of prints inside and out.

Which perhaps meant, I speculated, that the killers had been in the car, as trusted friends, often enough before the murder drive to make the thorough cleaning necessary. I could see them, Cremmens and his killers, who in my fantasy were a young man and woman, both in silver wire-rim eyeglasses—shades of Kerensky and a lot of bad movies. I could see the three of them, stopping at one of the endless quick-food places that litter the Peninsula, eating the cardboard tacos and burritos—enough to make anyone dream of the overthrow of the capitalist system, that food—while they talked, safe in the car, of bombs and "ruthless campaigns." It was hard to stay with this fantasy for long, though. Cremmens fit into the picture so badly. I downed another tetracycline and read on.

All of his known relationships of any and every sort were being checked out, of course, but they were pitifully sparse for a man who'd been in the general area for fifteen years, worked at the same job for ten, and lived in the same place for five. It was as if he were some alien creature dropped from the moon or some far star. His fellow workers knew almost nothing of his life outside Grabbon; as one of them with an upper-class British accent put it, "I always assumed he hadn't any."

Another colleague said he'd had the impression Cremmens had had a girl friend for a while, but all he remembered was that Cremmens, asking him to recommend a good restaurant, had said something about knowing her a long time ago. The man thought Cremmens had been more relaxed for a while after that, but lately he'd been very edgy.

"Meek and quiet as he was, you couldn't help noticing it—and no wonder, ripping off our secret explosive like that. Who would have ever thought? Cremmens! Of all people!"

For several days Cremmens' death and life were the lead story in all the media, but gradually, as the information collected seemed to lead nowhere, the story shrank, and by the end of the week in bed it was covered as just a two-paragraph follow-up in which nothing particular was said. The "FBI officials are still working on" sort of thing. And there seemed to be no further leads on the plane crash or the California Coalition.

On Tuesday morning, finding I could smoke my before-breakfast cigarette with relative ease and therefore must be nearly well, I telephoned Cook and told her I'd be up later to start on the job of packing up Celia's and Lindy's things for the Goodwill.

"Could you get some boxes brought down from the attic, do you think, Cook? Are there quite a few up there? I'll need a lot of them, I'd guess."

"*Sí*, Grita, I have the boxes put in the room of the *Señora*; Ling So will do it. There are lotta boxes there, all you need, *pienso*. *Entonces, si necessitas más, el los traja. Pero, hay* plenty to begin, *seguro.*"

"Have some put in the guest cottage, too, will you? I think I'll do that first."

The new key Henry had given me fit smoothly into the lock, and the door swung open without a sound. The cottage consisted of an anteroom and then one huge room used sometimes for guests and sometimes for Celia's sewing. Not that she sewed herself, but she'd had a "sewing lady" much like our mother's, and, typically, she'd had the best equipment and a wealth of fabric, trim, and patterns for every conceivable sort of sewing project. Lindy had gotten interested in sewing for a while, I remembered, and had used the place fairly often. Possibly as much to get away from the Celia-dominated house, as to sew.

I don't sew myself—I hate it—so that, although some of the material was very lovely, I knew I didn't want to have it around, nagging at me to do something with it. I went through the place fairly quickly and dumped all the sewing things into the three huge cartons standing in the middle of the room. A mouse scurried out of one of the drawers as I emptied it and quickly disappeared.

As an afterthought, I dragged the big sewing machine to the pile—obviously neither Henry nor Mark would use it, and Cook didn't sew, either. I made a note to check with Ling So to see if his family would want it, gave another look around to be sure that only the supplies for the occasional guest—linens, soap, and so forth—were left in the huge built-in cupboards, and left, locking the door behind me.

I walked back up the driveway. Just as I reached for the handle of the side door to the house, it opened. I jumped about a foot and felt my heart suddenly pounding—almost loudly enough for Mary P. Lewis, coming out the door, to hear it, too.

"Oh!" she gasped. "Maggie! I didn't expect—how you startled me!" She put a chocolate-colored kidskin-gloved hand to her breast, and the violence of my own heartbeat subsided.

"Me, too. What are you doing here?"

"Just taking care of some things Celia wanted done for the Crippled Children's," she answered vaguely, then walked around me and hurried off. Which wasn't like Mary P.; if anything, she was usually overly polite and chatty. She and Celia had been best friends all the years Celia had lived in San Francisco, and I thought Celia's death must have upset her more than I'd realized from the social facade I'd seen at the funeral and at the wake.

When I walked into Celia's room, the first thing I did was just stand there and look around. Now that I was there, where to start? As Cook had promised, there were a "lotta boxes" stacked neatly in the center of the room. I wondered why on earth I'd ever told Henry I'd do the job for him—he could have hired somebody, for God's sake, I thought irritably. The real trouble, though, was that I'd promised Lindy, and how could I go back on that? I sure did want to, though.

I tried to cheer myself up with the thought that at least Lindy had already made a start by putting aside the things—like the fur coats and the jewelry—that had to be counted as part of the estate. Which, with the two deaths following one another so closely, was in something of a snarl itself. Lindy had started making a will at Temple's insistence when he was out for Celia's funeral. She'd wanted two-thirds of her inheritance to go to her father and, surprisingly, one-third to go to me. But as she'd penciled in a few changes and sent it back to the lawyers unsigned, it would all go to Henry. He would not be deprived, after all, of the free use of Celia's millions or that he'd always enjoyed.

Thinking about the disposal of Celia's property, however, was getting me no closer to packing up that part for which I'd agreed to be responsible. I threw my cigarette into the fireplace and walked reluctantly over to the big mahogany dresser. It was from Texas and had belonged to a great grandmother; I remembered it from our mother's house. Neat stacks of handkerchiefs monogrammed in white and yellow and pale blue, too small and dainty to be of much use; a whole drawer stacked full of silk scarves; another full of brassieres; one for underpants; then slips. I eyed the slips covetously, narrow-strapped Italian hand-made silks and satins, but knew they wouldn't fit and dumped them into a big cardboard box with the rest.

Celia was shorter and a good deal wider than I am, so I didn't have to think much about whether I wanted most of her clothes for myself. I did set aside an old tweed coat I'd always liked, made from material I remembered Celia bringing back from Scotland before she was first married. I also kept some heavy Irish sweaters and a soft, warm bathrobe.

Cook was also a basically different shape from Celia, being abut the same height but scrawny, short-legged, and long-waisted where Celia was long-legged, short-waisted, and plump. At Lindy's urging she'd gone through and taken what she wanted or thought she could use, but it wasn't much: a plain, black-wool overcoat; a couple of hats; and, surprisingly, a new-looking yellow goosedown ski jacket. A side of Cook I'd never seen? Or bothered to notice? She'd put her things off to one side so I'd be aware of what she was taking.

Luckily, Celia had not been a saver. The rich have no need to save the worn-out washing machines, rusty car parts, the buttons and string and scraps of everything that has gone through their lives, as the poor do. They can simply go out and buy new. I squirmed at the thought of what it would be like for the person who would someday go through my house to dispose of my things. The magpie habits I'd had all my life had certainly not come from want of the material kind, but there are, of course, other sorts.

I walked over to the bigger of the two closets and opened the door. While Celia hadn't been a saver, she'd had plenty of everything—enough for a dozen people or more. It took me the rest of that day and most of the next, between memories, philosophizing, and cigarette breaks, to pack away the things from the big closet and the huge bureaus. This left only her shoe closet—she'd had a special closet just for her shoes—and her desk. I decided to leave the desk for the very last and tackled the shoes.

Low-heeled leather walking shoes, high-heeled pumps in suedes and satins for dressing up; all colors. Shoes for running, for golf, for tennis; boots for walking, hiking, skiing. And a pair of yellow cowboy boots which looked as if they'd never been worn. They were on the top shelf, and instead of dragging a chair over to get them down, I took an umbrella and poked at them until they fell. One of them upended and something fell out, skidded across the polished wood floor, and came to rest in the corner. To my immense surprise, I saw that it was a gun.

It was very small and black, the lady-gangster type that Lauren Bacall might have in a Humphrey Bogart movie—but Celia? I looked at it blankly, then finally picked it up and examined it. It had a small circle with a W superimposed on an S, or vice versa. I opened the chamber, saw that it was loaded, and closed it up again. The bullets looked quite large for such a small gun.

It didn't seem the sort of thing to send to the Goodwill, and finally I got a dark red scarf out of one of the boxes, wrapped up the gun, and put it in the bottom of my purse. I told myself I'd decide what to do with it later. Then I finished packing away the several score shoes that had taken Celia through her various proper, predictable activities. Where in the world did a gun, a loaded gun, fit into those? As I put the shoes away, I felt carefully down inside each one, especially the boots, but found nothing further.

It took another two days to go through Lindy's things. I'd gotten more efficient with practice, but my niece had been something of a saver, and sometimes it was hard to make the decision to throw something out—a photograph or a piece of driftwood she'd collected somewhere, a handful of pebbles from some local or exotic beach—how could I throw them away? But would the Goodwill take pebbles? And at home I had collected enough to be buried under, myself. Lindy's life had been so short, and the disposal of those intimate, private objects seemed, somehow, to shrink it down even more.

Also, since she and I had been much the same size, I had to stop and think it over with various of her clothes, wondering if I wanted this or that, while keeping as firm a control as possible on the magpie part of myself. I had resolved, at the thought of the stranger who would someday go through my own possessions, to reform, to simplify.

By late Friday afternoon, I'd finally gone through the lot—except for Celia's desk—with no further surprises since that very small gun had dropped out of the cowboy boot. I decided to put the desk off until Monday, partly because I didn't want to get overtired and get a fresh case of the flu, but mostly because I didn't want to be around the house on the weekend. Henry would be home then, and we'd be obliged, probably, to spend some time making conversation. So far, in the four days I'd been packing up the earthly remains of his wife and daughter, I hadn't laid eyes on him. Or anyone but Cook and one of the maids, for that matter. The house was feeling more and more, I thought, like a mausoleum.

FOURTEEN

THE WEEKEND WAS UNEVENTFUL, RESTFUL, RAINY. I GOT caught up on some of the things I'd let slide the most while I was sick, like vacuuming the house and washing Orphan as well as my hair—which I hate doing even more than washing the dog. I also got back to my regular AA meetings. I found my mind wandering, though, away from talk of drunkenness and sobriety to the gun I'd found in Celia's closet, and possible reasons for its being there. Burglars? But why hidden away where you couldn't get at it, then? Had I not known Celia at all? Could all that propriety have been just a facade, with a life beneath it quite something else?

> . . . *bar against all information* . . .

The speaker was ending with a quote from Herbert Spencer that concludes the main AA book:

> . . . *cannot fail to keep a man in everlasting
> ignorance—that principle is contempt
> prior to investigation.*

But I just couldn't imagine Celia involved in any sort of intrigue, no matter how hard I tried. . . . Maybe there'd be something in her desk that would give me a clue. . . .

When I woke up Monday morning I saw out my bedroom window an extraordinarily bright and beautiful day, already warm at nine o'clock. One of those first spring days that sometimes comes along in the middle of January in California—a day much too fine and rare, after the weeks of gray and rain, to spend at Celia's desk.

So I put the dogs in the car and drove through the white city and across the red bridge into Marin county, quite green already from the weeks of rain. Everything—the city, the buildings, the bridges, the hills—was positively gleaming with light and well-being. Muir Beach, when I got there, was almost deserted. I walked far down to the left, near where the rocks start, with Diana jumping and running after sandpipers and seagullls she had no hope of catching, and Orphan trailing sedately. I settled myself on a nice soft dune, closed my eyes, floated awhile.

"A bar against . . ." How did it go? Knowledge? Information . . . will keep you in ignorance . . . something prior to . . . contempt. Prior to investigation. And why, I wondered dreamily and for the fiftieth time, had Celia had a gun? In a boot? Should

I be investigating that? Or maybe I had better instead—the old nagging thought came into my head from somewhere—give some thought to answer the old question: What are you going to do with your life, anyway? Or rather, what to do with the rest of it, having—I figured, if I lived to an average old age, which looked likelier than it had a few months ago—already used up about half of it? What to do with the rest of it? This naturally pushed thoughts of Celia right out of my head for a while.

I didn't discover the answer to the question that day; I haven't, still, although sometimes I find a direction to take for the next bit of the way. The Answer, though—that faithful mirage—seemed to hover in the distance; to be almost graspable. It was one of those times when something new is due, is essential, but what? Something . . . I thought sleepily . . . it would be important not to reject . . . before investigating . . .

On the soft sand, in the warm sun, with the hills all around turning green from the rain, the grazing high up cows solid and reassuring and peaceful, the murmuring sea a calm and flat rich blue more soothing than any drug I'd known, the breeze gentle and soft, with small birds chirping and larger ones squawking, the problem dissolved for a while, and I drifted off to sleep.

A beautiful wine-dark sea came up the edges of green marble walkways. I came into a luminous city, found a high, spiraling golden tower, and began climbing. There were heavy paintings on the walls, of Medicis and Borgias, and they struck an ugly note in that shining tower. . . . I was just getting into a new part when Diana came and shook water all over me. I held the fabulous city in my mind as long as I could, it was so magical and pleasing, but it quickly faded. The dark, heavy portraits stayed longer and I didn't like the feeling they left, so I got up and walked with the dogs to the other end of the beach, where three nudists played Frisbee. Then I headed home. One of those quiet days, I thought, driving back, a gift not forgotten even years later when you're old.

When I'm Sixty-Four? . . .

I hummed, crossing the red bridge, paraphrasing the Beatles, their friendly voices humming along with me in my brain,

Will you still
need me?
Will you still
feed me?

Well, I thought, and where is he, my lover? I'd seen no sign of him in years.

I didn't believe I'd ever be sixty-four, though. The sun shone too brightly; the wind coming in from the northwest had too much energy in it.

Celia's study was on the second floor, a small room at the back of the house looking out over her gardens, the bridges and the bay, and the Marin hills beyond. I stood by the window awhile, procrastinating. The sea was gray again, and the sky. Yesterday's wind had brought rain during the night, and the flowers outside in the garden looked just made—a tall wall of falling blue, pink roses, big yellow acacia trees—a very California mixture of summer and spring, in January.

With a sigh I went over to the desk—an old one that had belonged to Celia's father—and rolled up the top. I was surprised at the cluttered, untidy mass of papers that confronted me. I knew the police would have gone through the desk in their search for clues to secret lovers, blackmailers, blackmailees, dangerous knowledge, or whatever else might conceivably lead to murder. Or for signs of despair or discouragement deep enough to cause suicide. They had presumably found no such clues, judging by the inquest. I wouldn't have thought, though, that they would have left the desk in quite such a mess, like someone in a hurry. Someone other than the police, that would be; they never hurried. Henry didn't seem likely; he was such a methodical sort and, anyway, could take his time, if he wanted something. Mark? Dunbar Oates, the day he supposedly came to see Lindy and let himself out? Whoever it was, I wondered what they'd been looking for. And if it had been found. I tucked the question away with the memory of the gun from the cowboy boot.

Most of the papers seemed pretty straightforward—charity things and obvious kinds of bills—and I threw them into a big cardboard box after a mere glance. I was just about to drop a small desk calendar into the box when I decided to have a look inside, at the week Celia was killed. I found her old skull-and-crossbones sign marked on the square for December 17, the day she was killed. It was a symbol Celia had used since she was a teenager, copied from our mother, to indicate something important—and unpleasant—to be done. In those old days, I remembered, it was apt to be some family obligation, or studying for a big test. I wondered what it had been that day, and I wondered if Simmons had noticed the sign. The design looked more like a circle with an X over it than a skull and crossbones—the symbol had gotten streamlined over the years—so he might have attached no particular significance to it. I looked back through the rest of December and found another of the symbols on the seventh with ''Dentist 10'' beside it, and another on the eleventh, unexplained.

Then I glanced through Celia's latest dreambook; she'd kept one off and on since her marriage to Henry as one of her efforts to be part of his career. The last entry was for November 30:

''I was with a group playing bridge—two men and another woman. One of the men was Dunbar, and the other I'm not sure. Perhaps my father or Mark. I didn't know the woman—she was dark and foreign. I was upset because I was losing, only a little at first, and then it was a huge amount which would bankrupt me. Suddenly I realized it was because the others were cheating, even my partner. . . .''

There were no notes alongside to indicate what, if anything, she'd made of the dream. . . . I put that book to one side, also. In the end, without knowing why, I added her big desk-style checkbook, with stubs dating back almost a year, to the small pile of things I was keeping aside. I thought I might want to look through them more carefully another time, although it didn't seem very likely. I think I also had some vague idea that the police might not want them destroyed, even though the case was, presumably, closed. I found out later that they'd all been carefully photo-copied and put into a file which was still, at that moment, in Simmons' office.

In any case, I rolled those few papers up into a cylinder, tied it with a green ribbon I'd found in one of the drawers, and dumped the lot into an old Nassau straw bag I'd fished out of one of the Goodwill boxes still sitting in Celia's bedroom.

I dragged the big cardboard box over to the fireplace and made a huge blaze with the papers I was throwing out. The fire was violent but short-lived, the ashes large and black, and any vague ideas I'd had of understanding what had been going on in Celia's life before she was killed—the unhappy dream, why she'd had a gun, and so forth—seemed to go out the chimney with the smoke. It was all too vague, would be too much trouble, and was silly, anyway, I told myself. When the fire died out, I had the good feeling of being more or less done with the whole affair.

Except, I remembered suddenly, for the talk I'd promised to have with Mark. I realized guiltily that I hadn't seen him since the memorial service. I had, in fact, managed to forget all about him.

I squared my shoulders and walked resolutely, if reluctantly, down the hall to his room. After I knocked several times and got no answer, I cautiously turned the knob. The door wasn't locked, as I'd half expected. But when I stuck my head in, I saw that the room was not only empty but looked like it had been empty for a while.

I went down to the kitchen to ask Cook where, and especially how, Mark was and to let her know I'd finished.

"No sé, no sé donde esta, Pero," and here she paused and looked at me gloomily, shrugging her shoulders, *"*he get a car, *hace una semana en* Thursday, *muy malo, un* wreck, *y le no veo despues. El señor dice no importa! No importa! Yo,* I am worrying, *sí. Pero,* he is not liking to be here, *en casa. Qué viene ahora, con la casa,* with the house, Grita?*"* She was speaking more Spanish than usual.

"The house has to be kept running, Cook. That was in Celia's will, *el testamento,* you know; we talked about that before. Whether Mark stays here or not. Henry will still be here to look after."

"No, Grita, no, *el señor dices que,* he say he moves, to *apartamento,* close by his working place. I tell you this already, no?"

"Yes, you did. But I forgot or thought he didn't mean it. Has he said any more about it? Is he really going to live there full-time? And not here? Even on the weekends?"

"Sí, sí. This weekend, *en Sabado,* he goes with big suitcases, *cuatro. Solamente* Ling So *y las criadas estan aquí conmigo.* I feel it. *Muy sola, muy triste."*

"Of course you feel it! All I know is, though, the house is to be kept running whether anyone's here or not, for the next four years or so. The money for that is specially set aside. Mark had an apartment in North Beach somewhere for a while. I wonder—do you have a telephone number for that place?''

"Sí, sí," she said, brightening, and hurried off, returning with a small black-and-white-checked ledger.

"Cuatro-cinco-siete-ocho-tres-dos-una," she read out slowly, then handed me the book, pointing to the place with a knobby index finger to be sure I'd get it right.

"Pero no sé si Mark has this place *ahora.* . . .''

"Well, I'll try it and see if I can track him down. At least try and find out if he intends to be back here at all, so you'll know what to plan. . . .''

Dialing the number from the muddy-yellow kitchen telephone (a color the phone company calls gold for some reason), I had no great hopes of getting an answer, and was surprised when it was picked up after five or six rings. But it wasn't Mark.

"Is Mark there?"

"No." A male voice, whiny.

"Do you expect him?"

"No." And impatient.

"Is this the right number? For Mark Sloan; does he live there?"

"He did; he doesn't now." And contemptuous of the caller's ignorance.

"Oh. This is Margaret Elliot." I thought that to identify myself as a relative might be unwise, but on the other hand I needed something, and that was all I had. "Mark's aunt," I ventured.

Silence.

"Do you have another number for him? Or address?"

"No," he said again, not elaborating. The wretched slob.

"Well, do you know where he went? It's rather important. Perhaps I should come over there and ask you about all this in person. Is it that you don't like giving out information over the telephone?"

"Oh, no," he said quickly, "don't come here! I mean, it's just that I don't know where he's gone exactly. I mean, there isn't any forwarding address. He said if there was any mail, just to hold it. He went off somewhere in his car. Camping."

The idea of me on his doorstep had loosened him up, all right.

"He said he probably wouldn't be back for a long time. He said he wanted to get away for a while. He was going to just drive around the country."

"The country, like Mendocino, or the country, like America?" I asked vexedly.

"America, I think," he answered sullenly.

"All right. Thank you. If you should hear from him—a postcard or anything with an address on it—would you let me know?" I added, inspired, "Of course, I would want to pay you for your trouble." Or not so inspired, on second thought. He'd probably just make something up.

"Sure," he said, sounding happier.

I repeated my name, address, and phone number; thanked him and hung up.

"Apparently he's gone traveling in that new car of his, Cook. Sounds like you shouldn't plan on his being back anytime soon. Don't worry, he'll turn up again eventually."

I told myself to take my own advice. What did it matter, after all, whether I had an address for Mark or not? In the country he was lost in, nobody could find him, anyway, I thought, except himself. Or God, whatever that is.

I felt sorry for Cook, though, left almost alone in that huge, fast-emptying house after working for the family for so many years. All four gone now: two dead, one moved out, one missing.

I could see the house in my rear-view mirror as I drove off down the driveway, huge, gray, silent. Waiting. For what? To see what would happen next?

PART TWO

FIFTEEN

It WAS OVER TWO YEARS BEFORE I SAW THAT HOUSE, OR COOK or Mark or Henry, again. I was busy feeling my way into new ways of living, without alcohol and without pills, and those people weren't in my mind very much. And I'd never liked the house, or Henry, either, for that matter. So that it was only Mark and Cook who might have kept me in touch with what remained of Celia's family. I heard occasionally from Temple that Mark was alive—no one knew whether ''alive and well'' would fit the case, but I had a feeling not. He kept Temple informed of his changing address by postcards so that Temple would know where to send his allowance. Several came from Detroit, I remember; then a bunch from Omaha.

To look at myself from a concrete, material view, not a whole lot happened during the two years or so that passed before I became involved with Celia's family again, other than the fact that I quit smoking and gained a lot of weight that first year, and spent most of the second getting rid of it.

I fell in love a few times. Always briefly. The only one of my affairs that endured in those days was the one with clay, small c. And for a while I thought I'd found the answer: what to do with my life. It didn't turn out that way, but it was a nice feeling while it lasted. I spent long days at the studio; I would have taken my sleeping bag and the dogs and lived there if I could have. I made a lot of ugly objects, and one or two quite beautiful ones. I spent the year following Celia's and Lindy's deaths, the year I was getting fat, learning to use the potter's wheel. As I concentrated on centering ever-larger chunks of earth, some of the wobbles in myself gradually smoothed out as well. The next year, the dieting year, I dropped the wheel and moved over to hand building and sculpture, where I could be more asymmetric, more eccentric—more myself.

97

There were other things, too—running, for instance, and meditation—that had their part in creating a feeling that developed, unexpectedly and late in life, of being more or less glad to be alive. Usually, anyway. And beneath all this, the bottom line, were lots of AA meetings. Old patterns of thinking were slowly being replaced with ideas about living in the present, instead of the past or future. About doing whatever was in front of me and leaving the results up to whatever is in charge of that. About something called acceptance and something called surrender.

With all this, a lot of the old was dropped off; it had to be, to make room. And so I rarely thought of Mark or Cook or Henry or the big house in Pacific Heights where nobody but the servants lived, kept open in name only to satisfy the requirements of Celia's will. Occasionally in the beginning I remembered Cook and telephoned her, but that gradually dropped off, too. As it happened, I didn't have to feel guilty about it, either. About three months after Mark went on his travels and Henry moved into an apartment, Cook telephoned to tell me, hesitatingly, that she had gotten married.

"Why, that's wonderful, Cook!" I said somewhat falsely, because what I was thinking was, uh oh, probably some rat who found out she's got some money now; I just hope he doesn't break her heart. Cook was suddenly looking to my imagination very much like the heroine of my favorite Fellini movie, a poor, thin prostitute robbed of her heart and her hard-earned savings by a cynical fortune hunter: "Kill me, kill me, just kill me!" she sobs as he grabs the purse from her down in the deserted ravine. "Go ahead and kill me, why don't you?"

"Who have you married?" I asked, fearing to hear the worst.

"Ling So, you no listen; Ling So, Grita. We live now *en apartamento sobre la* garage, he is good man, *verdad?*"

"Oh, that *is* wonderful, Cook!" I said again, really meaning it.

Ling So, the Chinese gardener/chauffeur/bartender at Celia's, was about ten years younger than Cook and, from what I'd seen and heard of him, a patient, kind, authentic sort who didn't seem likely to be after her money, although that may have been an added inducement. I meant to stop by and see them but never got around to it. I did send a silver bowl and a clay one that I'd made as wedding presents. And was glad I didn't need to feel responsible for Cook anymore. She had not been totally deserted and left to a pitiful, lonely old age, after all.

I must admit I again immediately thought of fortune hunting when I received the note from Henry one afternoon about two years after Lindy's death.

"My dear Maggie," it began.

Since when had I been his dear Maggie?

"I am writing because you are one of the people I want to know that I have decided to remarry. Of course, when the tragedies I know we both remember so clearly and unforgettably struck"—awkward, I thought, as well as pompous—"and to all intents and purposes destroyed my home and family (Mark, unfortunately, has had to go and find his own way; I tried to help, but he has had to find his own way), I expected to live the remainder of my life interested primarily in my work, sustaining perhaps a moderate interest in my tennis game, and to live, of course, alone."

It was hard to believe anyone could actually put such stuff down in black and white. And mail it.

"However," the communication continued, "I have been fortunate in coming to know Beatrice over the past year or so," and was it, I wondered, the past year, or the "or so"? It could make quite a different picture, depending . . . In any case, my thoughts were similar to the ones I'd had in response to Cook's announcement, only even more suspicious, for I thought immediately: Now I wonder, is it some little fortune hunter he's met since Celia died? Or rather some little tart that had her eye—and not just her eye—on him well before that? Who perhaps explains that picture of Celia's marriage having gone a bit rocky? I read on; these questions wouldn't be answered, of course, but there might be clues:

". . . since she came to work at my clinic about a year ago. She is an occupational therapist, and, in fact, it was in working together that we first came to know each other and, ultimately, decided to marry.

"We will have a simple civil ceremony at City Hall on February twenty-eighth, and we are asking a few friends to join us that evening in celebrating. . . ."

The letter was typed, with the initials HS:b at the bottom, but there was a handwritten postscript: "I saw Mark a few days ago, and we had a long talk about a number of things, including my forthcoming marriage, which he does not seem to mind. I expect he will be at our little reception, so you will probably see him then, along with meeting Bee. I hope you are able to come." The initials, HS, scrawled the finish.

Though I'd never been close to Celia, had disapproved of her, and had in some ways actively disliked her, I found myself feeling resentful. The idea of Henry's remarrying and living happily ever after on Celia's money did not please me at all. Perhaps it was my suspicion that his "bride" was not such a recent acquaintance as he was making out, or perhaps it was just a residual family possessiveness. Whatever it was, I didn't like the feeling I had and hoped that it would go away. It was no business of mine, I told myself, who Henry married or whatever the hell else he did, for that matter.

My bitchy reaction thus counteracted, at least partly and temporarily, I felt quite a stirring of curiosity to see this Beatrice of Henry's. Usually I loathe parties and I fully expected to loathe this one, but I wouldn't have missed it for anything. I wanted to see what she was like, this new wife. And what Henry was like, as her husband. I remembered the saying about condemnation before investigation but quickly suppressed it with the thought that I would go to the party and see.

I was not so eager, on the other hand, to see what the years had done for—or more likely to—my nephew Mark.

SIXTEEN

"**B**EE, DARLING," HENRY SAID TO THE WOMAN STANDING beside him, taking her arm and turning her in my direction, "I'd like you to meet Maggie, Maggie Elliott. Who was so helpful to me, when, uh—"

"Of *course*," the woman said, turning, smiling, and sticking out the hand of the arm Henry wasn't holding. "I've heard *so* much about you, and I've been looking forward to meeting you, Maggie. I'm sorry it couldn't have been sooner, but we've been *so* busy."

She sounded, I thought sourly, rather as if I'd been trying for a long time to see her and she was explaining why she'd kept putting me off.

"Getting married and setting up a new household," she continued, "on top of all our obligations at work! It's been quite a lot more complicated than I'd expected. But of course," she went on, smiling over at Henry and then back at me again, "everything always is."

For all her smiling face and rather gushy greeting, I didn't feel any real warmth from her. I'd actually felt more from Henry. But why should she feel friendly, for God's sake? On the other hand, why should she pretend to?

I responded to her seemingly false enthusiasm with some equally false commonplaces about being "delighted to meet her, too, and to see Henry looking so happy," etcetera. Yuk. The amount of criticism I can churn out for other people when my own behavior is so absolutely sickening just amazes me sometimes.

"We'll have to have lunch one day so I can really get to know you," she continued. "It's always so hard to really talk at parties."

Was she implying there was so little of me to know that it could be done over a lunch? There I went again. The woman certainly did irritate me. But after all, who or what she was, was really no concern of mine, I told myself again. And what did it matter whether we liked each other or not?

She moved on to the next guests just coming in behind me, a couple who were apparently old friends and called her "Tricia." Poor Mark, I thought, and looked around the room but didn't see him.

"—Joffrey is in town, I understand . . ." a tall, bony woman with a long horse face was saying, over by the bar.

"I don't believe I . . ." responded a round-faced, dumpling figured woman next to her. "Joffrey?"

"The *ballet*, it's a *ballet* company." The brown eyes of the horse-faced woman swept the other with contempt. "At the opera house. The big building on Van Ness."

"Oh, Yes. Of course, the opera," muttered the dumpling

woman. Her round blue eyes fell before the contempt shooting from the other like knives and settled on the very pointed toes of her own shiny black shoes, a style about twenty-five years out of fashion.

The horse-faced woman moved away as I approached the bar and ordered a soda and ice. I sipped it slowly and watched Henry's new wife, this Beatrice, greeting her guests.

I started with the hair. An ordinary sort of ash brown, fairly long and frizzed, whether naturally or artifically I couldn't tell. Which meant that if it was a permanent, it was a good one. And therefore expensive. But, of course, she worked and earned money. What a picky bitch I've turned into, I thought, over this marriage.

I continued my inventory. A thin, simply cut ice-blue silk dress with a narrow brown trim. The colors matched her eyes, which I saw again as she turned to Henry: one blue eye and one brown, the colors alike enough in tone for the difference not to be startling. They gave her face a kind of interest it might not otherwise have had. She appeared to be about thirty-five—younger than Henry, but at least not an infant, as might have been expected as part of his late-middle-age break-out. . . .

Medium height, but she looked taller beside Henry, who was only medium himself. Celia had been as tall as he was. Flat shoes, which Celia hadn't stooped to. I wondered if they were for the comfort of her feet or of Henry's ego.

Medium slender; generally a medium-looking person, in fact, except for the different-colored eyes. A big diamond ring on the appropriate finger, not one I'd seen before; new, then . . .

"Stop it, for heaven's sake," I told myself.

I must have said it out loud because a man getting a drink asked, "Stop it? Stop what?"

"Oh, I didn't mean you; sorry, nothing."

"Well, and what do you think of her? Weren't you, aren't you, Celia's sister?"

"Uh, yes," I said abstractedly and pulled my attention away from Beatrice to a gray-haired man in a conservative dark gray suit and dull gray eyes behind gray, plastic-rimmed glasses. He had on a red tie, to match the broken blood vessels on his pale cheeks. I vaguely remembered him from what I always thought of as Celia's wake but couldn't recall anything in particular about him.

"I remember you from when we were all here," I said, "after Celia's funeral, but I'm afraid—"

"Harvey Stewart," he interjected promptly. "My wife Angela and Celia were pretty good friends. We're divorced now, actually. But old Henry and I have kept in touch; I'm his stockbroker, ha ha! Can I get you another? What'll it be?" He held out his hand for my glass, which was hardly half empty.

"No, thanks. Why don't you get yourself one, though?" I hoped he would go away.

"Don't go 'way then, sweetie." Possibly he intended to sound playful, but he had about thirty too many pounds and years on him to carry it off. Certainly I got the idea he was looking for somebody to play with now the wife was gone, but it wasn't going to be me.

I looked around the room for Mark but didn't see him. I was just about to go over and talk to Mary P. Lewis when the blood-vesselly man came back, took my arm, and said unnecessarily, "I'm back, dear. Let's you and me just pop out somewhere more private and listen to some music. What do you like?"

"Never mind, no, thanks." I removed my arm from his grasp and told myself it was silly to get annoyed. Part of his problem was that he'd had too much to drink. But only a small part, the other side of my head added. A sleek blond head across the room caught my eye, leaning over an expensive-looking woman. The head turned, and sure enough, it was Dunbar Oates. I wondered what he was doing there; he'd been Celia's friend, not Henry's. I noticed then that the wall behind him was blank and remembered Celia's Renoir had always been there before—the Renoir of a woman in a bright garden. The woman who looked rather like Celia had, years ago. . . . Dunbar had found it for her. Getting rid of a Renoir, I thought, was going pretty far in making the place comfortable for the new bride. Or perhaps Henry had got rid of it long before, for his own comfort. . . .

The blood-vesselly man nudged my arm: "Have you met Mrs. Halff?" he asked, turning to the dumpling woman who hadn't known about the ballet. "Mrs. Frieda Halff? She's a great friend of Henry's bride and sometimes looks after her little son."

"How do you do," I said, automatically offering my hand. "Beatrice's son? I didn't know she had children. Or is it just the one? How old?"

"Nineteen months and four days," she replied as proudly as if the child were hers.

She was one of those heavy-set women, built that way to begin with and a little overweight besides, middle-aged or more, with pale eyes and the kind of pale eyelashes, eyebrows, and hair that make the person seem something of a blank. She had a slight accent—German to judge by her name—but only very slight.

"Quite young, then," I offered.

"His father," she continued in a disapproving tone, "was killed before he was born. In an accident. So dear Beatrice had the complete burden. I was sometimes able to help; the child is like a grandchild to me. It is nice to see things turning out so nice for her now." She looked around the room at the expensive-looking people.

"She has always worked, then? Full-time? It must have been difficult."

"Oh, yes. To support herself and the child. She is also in school to obtain another degree. Also, the work is not just to earn money. It is—what is the word?—vacation. A vacation. To help the sick."

"Then it must"—I felt a little helpless in the face of the woman's heavy, simplistic devotion—"be especially important to her, having someone she can count on to take care of the child when she is working. At her, uh, vocation."

"Oh, yes."

"Will you still be looking after him now that she has married?" I was genuinely curious. Mrs. Halff didn't strike me as a type I'd like to have around as a regular part of a newly married household.

"Sometimes, of course. He will come to me. I am like the grandmother. Beatrice has no family. But she has hired, now, a girl to live in here." Her mouth tightened. "For pay, a regular job. With me it was only to help out. Not for money. I live alone."

I didn't know what to say to that, so I didn't say anything. After an uncomfortable pause, she continued; "Now dear Bee is able to pay someone. Of course. This is as it should be." She looked around the room again, almost disapprovingly this time. "I understand this perfectly."

"Of course you do," I said, to be saying something. But I

couldn't think of anything to follow it, and neither, apparently, could she.

So we stood there and looked at each other in a silence of growing discomfort and then looked away. I shifted my drink to my other hand and my weight to my other foot. Beatrice had one devoted follower, I thought, in addition to Henry. And maybe deserved them, for all I knew.

Mrs. Frieda Halff said: "It is a nice party."

"Yes, it is," I agreed.

The voice in my head continued: Nobody suits you today. Not this pathetic German person with her pointy-shoed devotion, not poor old Harvey with his broken blood vessels and his . . . *Stop* it, I told myself. And did, for a minute or two.

Harvey had gone off to get himself yet another drink while I'd been listening to Frieda Halff sing Beatrice's praises, with her under-melody of resentment at being shunted aside now that Beatrice could afford to pay someone. I saw him on his way back to us and quickly excused myself.

Mrs. Frieda Halff. "I live alone." I wondered what had happened to Mr. Halff. She had a widowy feeling to her. Maybe she poisoned him. *Stop* it. I looked around the room for someone to talk to. Mary P. Lewis was no longer in sight, and I still saw no sign of Mark. Dunbar Oates was over in front of the fire now, talking to another rich-looking, middle-aged woman.

I slipped out through a side door into the back hall which led to the kitchen. I was thinking that now that I'd seen Beatrice, I'd also seen enough of her and that I would just say hello to Cook and to Ling So, if he was around. By then, a decent amount of time would have passed and I could leave.

I'd expected it to be Ling So serving the drinks and had been surprised to see a man behind the bar I hadn't seen before. Now, entering the kitchen, I noticed there were a couple of women making hors d'oeuvres with a big, Irish-looking woman obviously in charge. No Cook.

"Can I get you something, miss?" asked the big woman, looking up at the sound of the door swinging open. It had always been creaky.

"No, thank you. I was looking for someone who works here—"

"Oh, you must mean that Mexican woman."

"Yes. Guadalupe Riveras. Mrs. So, or Ling, now. Isn't she here?"

"No, miss, they—she and her husband, that is—retired when the house was reopened. Seems like it's going to be a lot more work now, what with a child in the house and all, and Mrs. Sloan working, too, you see. The Mexican woman wasn't feeling up to it, or so I'm told."

I was surprised Henry hadn't mentioned this to me, but then we had talked only briefly when I came in, so he hadn't really had an opportunity to. Knowing Henry, he probably didn't even realize I'd be interested. But he'd have their address; I'd have to remember to get it.

"Where did they go, do you know?"

"Out to the country somewhere. They bought a little retirement home, I believe. Dr. Sloan will know, miss."

She looked at me with great curiosity, but obviously didn't want to come right out and *ask* who I was.

"It's just that she worked a long time for my family; I suppose it was at least thirty years."

"Oh, you must be related to Dr. Sloan's first wife, then?"

"Yes, she was my sister. My name is Margaret, Margaret Elliott," I said, sticking out my hand. "And you?"

"Frances Broome," she replied, putting forth her own cool, limp fingers and almost immediately withdrawing them. "Pleased to meet you."

"Thank you."

Back at the party I found Henry momentarily alone, getting drinks at the bar.

"I'm afraid I have to go now, Henry," I began.

"Don't do that," he said. "I've hardly had a chance to talk to you. I haven't even seen you for—what is it—must be almost two years. What are you doing these days? Are you working?"

Henry had always been big on the Protestant ethic.

"No. Not working. I've been going to school, though." Something he could have approved of, only probably wouldn't, I thought, since it was art courses. "Art courses."

"There's really quite a lot you can do with art these days. You should have a talk with Beatrice." He sent a proud glance toward the little group that surrounded her over by the windows. "She uses art in her work, you know."

"An occupational therapist, you said in your note. That's interesting. . . ."

"Actually, she's still working on the master's degree at State. I want her to transfer to Berkeley; that sort of prestige never hurts, you know. She's a wonderful therapist, truly wonderful. Very dedicated."

"So I hear. I was introduced to a Mrs. Frieda Halff when I first came in. She said there's a little boy. . . ."

"Didn't I mention that?" He smiled but looked displeased for some reason. "Alexander. We call him Sandy. Bee's done a fine job with him on her own. But it should be easier for her now. Strange how things repeat themselves. . . ."

"Yes," I agreed, thinking of Mark and Lindy and how he had legally adopted them as small children. "Are you going to adopt him? The little boy?"

"Of course. I have a lawyer drawing up the papers now. It isn't so complicated, actually; the father of this child is . . . dead." He took a swig of his drink, then another. "What are these courses you're taking? And where?"

"City College, nothing fancy. But I got very involved with ceramics. And sculpture. That's what I'm mainly doing now."

"That's Beatrice's specialty, ceramics. When she has the time. I've had a kiln put in here, in the cottage. Made it over into a studio for her as a wedding present. To her specifications."

"Gas?" I asked enviously. "A gas kiln?"

"Yes—what's it called? Oxidation? Reduction? She tells me, but I forget. It cost a small fortune, anyway; it's very big. She works so hard at the clinic. I want her to have every opportunity to do her own creative work, too."

"Is she still going to be working full-time?"

"We haven't quite decided. Or she hasn't. You women"—the smile on his lips did not travel to his eyes—"are so independent these days. I'd like her to go to half-time, or even quit the job altogether and finish the degree, or even relax a little. And taking care of a young child can be a full-time job, too, of course. If you want it to be." He paused; probably we both were thinking of Celia. "Which she doesn't. Very keen therapist, very keen. But," he concluded, taking a final swig of scotch, "she's reluctant to leave the clinic also because people there count on her so much."

"Wonderful," I said glumly. "Oh, I meant to ask you. I went

back to the kitchen to say hello to Cook—and was told they've retired?''

"Yes. Yes. Seemed a bit much for her. I put some money in with what Celia left her, and they retired. Cook wanted it that way; she felt that working for a family again would be too much, especially with a young child. Bit beyond that now. And best really to start fresh, we thought. Fine woman we have; used to be with the Seeligsons, do you remember them? Had the big yellow house up on Broderick? They moved into an apartment—children gone, house too big—so I was able to get Mrs. Broome.''

"She seemed quite pleasant. Where did Cook and Ling So—they're still together?''

"Oh, yes. Seems to be a very happy marriage.''

"I'm glad to hear it. Where did they retire to, exactly? Mrs. Broome just said the country.''

"Up around Napa somewhere; they got hold of a small farm. Some kind of vegetables, I think. I have the address somewhere. I'll send it along if you like.''

"I would, thanks. And I really do need to be going.''

His face brightened.

"But I didn't see Mark. How is he?''

"Mark,'' said Beatrice, coming up from behind her husband and taking his arm, "is doing just wonderfully, isn't he, darling? I'd really expected a walking disaster, but he seems to be pulling himself together marvelously. I quite like him.''

"I'm glad to hear it,'' I said, not feeling particularly glad at the "I quite like him'' bit, though; whyever not? "Is he not drinking, then?''

"No, he's drinking, but moderately. He's got control of it. Henry says it's the best he's been in a very long time.'' She smiled at him.

"I think you're going to be just the influence he needs, darling.'' He smiled back with a sappy expression on his face.

"Well, next time you see him, tell him hello, will you? And that I'd love to hear from him if he wants to call me. Where's he living now?''

"Well, of course, this is his home as long as he wants it,'' Beatrice replied, although I'd addressed the question to Henry. "But he also has an apartment somewhere—was it the Mission,

Henry? Or Bernal Heights? Around there, anyway; I just haven't had time . . ."

"Of course not, with all the wonderful work you do, *and* being a mother, *and* a new wife and running this huge house," I said with only a slight edge to my voice. "It's been lovely meeting you, Beatrice. I have to be leaving now. It was a nice party."

She wasn't stupid; she'd heard something in my voice, and she looked at me for a moment—questioningly, assessingly, coldly, and so fleetingly I couldn't be sure I'd seen that cold assessment. Then she smiled her narrow smile once more.

"We'll *definitely* have to get together for lunch. I'll call you, Maggie."

"All right, fine; I hope you will. Thank you again for the lovely party."

One thing that hadn't changed in the two years, I noticed as I left, was the feeling of relief when I walked out the door of that house.

SEVENTEEN

A FEW NIGHTS LATER I HAPPENED TO GO TO ANOTHER PARTY in that neighborhood—given by a friend from my film-making days who'd hit the big time and was living it up accordingly. I found myself a little depressed, though, whether with envy or at the rather dreary form that the success seemed to be taking, I couldn't tell. Anyway, I left early. It was about ten-thirty, cold and crisp and clear outside. It had been very dark when I'd gone in, but now there was a big full moon hanging over the bay, and it was quite light out.

Light enough to see, walking down the sidewalk coming toward me as I headed uphill to where I'd parked my car, a familiar, tall figure, a battered-looking face: the policeman—no, ex-policeman, I remembered—who'd been there at Celia's accident and who I'd last seen when he testified in court at her inquest.

"Are *you* coming to this party?" I asked him without a word of preamble, feeling very surprised.

"I wasn't planning on it," he answered easily. "Whose party is it? Should I be?"

Up close I saw he was older than I'd thought, maybe fifty. He did not smile and looked at me as if seriously questioning whether to go to the party or not.

"I'm sorry," I said, feeling like a fool. "You're"—the name emerged surprisingly full and immediate from depths of memory—"Richard Patrick O'Reagan."

"I am," he agreed, as if calmly acknowledging the truth of an accusation, like "you're dishonest," or "you're a snob . . .''

"And you're the little sister, right? Eleanor?"

"Margaret. Margaret Elliott. It's, uh, lovely to see you again." I smiled mechanically. "Is that any better?" He looked back at me with no expression. I sighed.

"It doesn't matter," he said.

"I suppose not. Well, are you? Going in there?"

"I almost never go to parties, I don't like 'em. However, if you think I should . . ." He paused, eyebrows lifted, as if waiting for my decision: yes or no. When I didn't say anything, he asked again: "Whose party is it? That ought to help me decide."

"I'm sorry. I was just so surprised to see you out here. It's a pretty boring party, actually. Film people, and that's all they seem to talk about. So and so's film and so and so's . . . everyone in there really irritated me for some reason. I haven't felt this cranky in a year." I felt a sudden strong desire for a cigarette.

"I don't think I want to go to the party, in that case," he said gravely. "Cigarette?" He pushed the red and white box toward me.

"My brand, even. Ex-brand. Are you psychic, or what? No, thanks." The hideous craving would pass; it always did.

"I don't know about psychic"—he paused to cup his hand around the match, lighting his Marlboro—"but I'm cold, standing around out here. I was on my way to get a mud pie. Would you care to join me?"

"Yes, I would," I answered immediately, mentally abandoning the diet I was on at the time. "On Union Street, you mean? Cafe Cantata?"

"Funny running into you like this—just now particularly and in this neighborhood," I said, after we were settled at a small table with coffee and mud pies ordered.

"Why now, and why in this neighborhood?"

"Because of connecting you with Celia's accident. Her house—her husband's, now—is just around the corner. I was there only a few nights ago for the first time in a couple of years, for a wedding reception. After not even thinking about any of them for a long time. A *long* time."

"Wedding reception? The son?"

"Nope—Henry. Celia's husband. He just got married again, and they had a big reception at the house."

He looked thoughtful and took a slow sip of coffee, then asked: "What's she like?"

"The bride?"

"The bride."

"A paragon of all the virtues. I loathed her."

"Naturally," he smiled. It was a lopsided smile that warmed his otherwise rather cold gray eyes astonishingly. He was about to say something, but the waiter brought our mud pies. Then we just ate for a while. A mud pie is a dish of very rich chocolate in a shell of super pastry with layers here and there of ice cream and some delicious sauce. It's peerless. Neither of us said another word until we'd finished. Unfortunately, they aren't very large, mud pies.

O'Reagan is a tall, big man who, while you would never call him fat, is certainly solid. He held up two fingers to the waiter for a repeat, looking a question at me. I made no objection. It had been a long time between mud pies. He drank some of his coffee, which had Irish whiskey in it, and I drank some of mine, which didn't. Which was another thing I liked about him.

Another thing? I wondered over that one briefly. He hadn't asked me "Why not?" when I'd said no to a drink. Just nodded and given the order.

"I'm curious," he said now. "Tell me about this paragon of all the virtues. Name?"

"Beatrice, of all the pretentious things," I answered. "I suspect she read the *Divine Comedy* in high school and then renamed herself. She acts like she thinks she's just divine, anyway. She's a wonderful therapist, according to Henry, and a quote beautiful little mother unquote according to this German she's had looking after the kid—''

"Kid?"

"Son. Around a year and a half. Father not around. 'Dead,' according to Henry."

"You put that in quotes? Dead?"

"Yes, now that you mention it."

"Why?"

"Let me see." I thought back to Henry standing there by the bar, sipping his watery, pale scotch and talking.

"He paused, sort of, when he said it—that he is adopting the child, I mean, as he did with Mark and Lindy, who were from Celia's first marriage. He said something like, it isn't complicated the way it was with them, because the father of this child is . . . dead. He said it like that."

"You didn't believe him?"

"I don't know. I have no real reason not to."

"What's your fantasy about it, then?"

"Umm. That she slept around so much, Beatrice, that she doesn't have any idea herself who the father is. But that Henry's so proper and conventional, in spite of hanging around with Buddhists and such lately, that the 'dead' is just face saving. Hers or his, I don't know. That's not very clear, maybe, but that's my fantasy." I started in on my second mud pie but stopped long enough to ask, "What's yours? Do you have one?"

"I can always get one. Let's see." He chewed ruminatively on the last bites of his second mud pie. "How about, that the kid is really Sloan's? They don't want anybody to know that, naturally, since Sloan was still married to your sister at the time the kid was conceived. He's now about a year and a half, you said, right? This would give him—well, never mind that. Anyway, he can't acknowledge the kid as his. How's that?"

"Fine. Except that Henry's—he couldn't, can't have any children."

"Damn."

We sipped on our coffee for a while in companionable silence, thinking it over.

"More coffee? Or a drink?" he finally asked.

"Coffee, but make it Sanka. What time is it?"

He looked at his watch, a plain, silver-colored one that had seen better days, but not much better. "Eleven-thirty."

"That's not too bad. But Sanka anyhow."

The waiter came over and took the order and then took away the dirty dishes. Cafe Cantata wasn't crowded. One of the reasons I'd always liked it was that even when it was full, you could sit there and talk as long as you wanted.

"Tell me more about the paragon."

"OK." I closed my eyes, visualizing her. "Five feet four or five, medium height. Medium weight but with rather large, pointy breasts. For her size. Medium-brown hair, frizzy; a permanent, I think. One blue eye and one brown. Hazel. Medium nose, thin lips, round face. Mid-thirties, I'd think. No scars visible. How'm I doing?"

"Sounding like you just graduated from police school," he smiled. "More?"

"All right. A wonderful therapist, mother, and hard worker with a vocation for helping the sick. An artist, on top of all that, in clay. Which is my medium, and I particularly resent it accordingly. Henry's had a huge gas kiln built for her, which I envy. That's it, I suppose; envy. Do you think? This awful sniping reaction I have to her?"

He looked down into his cup for a minute as if the answer might be found there in the muddy mixture of coffee and cream and Jameson's, then looked across the table at me, his face expressionless, the gray eyes, without the smile, rather cold.

"Could be. Are you?"

"I don't know," I sighed. "I know I don't like feeling this way, though."

"If you were envious," he prodded quietly, "what would you be envious about?"

"I guess the way she does *everything*. And to perfection, if you believe her admirers. Work. Art. Motherhood. Now, Marriage. All with capital letters, in case you can't hear them."

"I can hear them."

"Having it all under control—and having it all. Maybe. Or maybe it's just her manner, I don't know. She sure unnerved me. But, as I kept telling myself at the party, why should we like each other? Do you know Jung's work at all?"

"Who?"

"Carl Jung?"

"Oh. A little. What're your thinking of? The shadow?"

"You do know. God! That whole idea used to infuriate me—that if you don't like someone it's probably just those qualities that you don't like in yourself; you're seeing those qualities in them, instead of in yourself. But"—I sighed deeply—"I find it's true all too often. In this case, indicating a simpering-bitch, little-Miss-Perfect shadow side to me. I hope that's not true, but I'm afraid it might be. Sickening."

O'Reagan didn't say anything, which is one of the things I like most about him. He's not the type to say, "Oh, no, *you* could never be like that"—when in fact you perfectly well could be.

"Sorry to go rambling on and on about her. But it's been a help talking about it. I was feeling so hideous when I left there the other night I really needed to do something with it. Thanks for listening." I felt like smiling for the first time all evening, and did.

"That's all right," he smiled back; "it's been interesting. And you did tell me a good deal about the paragon, you know, whatever your shadow is or isn't. I do get a sense of a kind of 'little Miss Perfect,' as you said—which is not particularly attractive, after all. Right?"

"Yes. Right."

"I think"—he turned and looked toward the adjoining room and the waiters—"I have room for one more mud pie. They've gotten so little, with all this inflation. Would you like one?"

"I'd like one, all right, but I'm not going to have it. Thanks. Since I quit smoking—which I only did because I couldn't breathe any more; I loved to smoke, especially Marlboros—" I wistfully eyed his pack on the table between us—"I have to watch out for getting fat. Fatter."

"Yeah, I noticed you put on some weight since I saw you. What's it been? Couple of years? What have you been doing besides gaining weight?"

"Working on losing it again." What had I been doing? Going to AA meetings. "And taking some art classes," I finally answered.

"Oh, yeah? Where? I like to draw. Paint, sometimes."

"City College. Did you ever go there? Are you a native?"

"Yes, I was born here," he smiled, "and no, I never took any courses at City. I did some work at State, a long time ago.

Their art department has a good reputation. City's. Are you painting.''

"Not much. I took one painting course when I first went there. Then I started on clay, which is what I like best. Sculpture, mostly, at this point."

"That's right; you said clay when you were telling me about the paragon. What sort of stuff do you do?"

"Ugly stuff, sometimes."

He nodded like he knew what I was talking about. I was finding him easier to talk to than I had anyone in a long time. Especially any man. Maybe because he was a good deal older, I thought, and the sexual question wasn't particularly pressing. Though I doubt his age had much to do with that because he's a very sexy man in his battered way, O'Reagan, and I imagine women will be chasing after him in hordes till he drops over dead. But I had a sense at that time that a relationship between us, if there was going to be one, would not be primarily sexual.

I pulled back from thoughts of the man to his actual presence. "Where was I?"

"Making ugly objects some of the time."

"Right. What my sculpture teacher calls monsters. The freedom to blow it. Anyway, to answer your question, lately what I've been doing is combining clay heads—sort of abstract, or maybe you'd say primitive—also hands and feet and arms and legs, it varies some, with driftwood bodies. And then I add other stuff—needles, feathers, whatever they seem to need from whatever I have lying around. I like them. And it feels like a good direction. One I can keep going in. For a while, at least."

"They sound interesting. I'd like to see them," he said simply, sounding like he meant that, no innuendos of anything else and no false politeness, either.

"I've only done a few; I just started working these out about six months ago. I'd be glad for you to see them, if you really would like to."

"I would," he repeated. "Do you work? For money, I mean?"

"No," I replied uncomfortably, as I always did to that question, feeling guilty. "I'm still trying to figure out what I want to do when I grow up, I'm afraid. Or at least figure it out over again. I've tried out a few answers to that question, but they didn't hold. Celia left me some money, and that was probably the main thing that made the police—do you know Simmons?''

"Yes."

"I always believed I was his favorite suspect, or favorite after Henry, when he was so hot for the idea that Celia'd been murdered, because of that money. A hundred thousand dollars. Which I thought was absurd, at the time." I felt rather guilty about the money, too, which was probably why I blurted out the amount like that.

"Absurd that she'd been murdered, or absurd to suspect you just because of a little money like that?" he asked, smiling.

"Both, but mainly absurd that she'd been murdered."

"You thought it was absurd at the time," he repeated; "and now?"

"Oh—still absurd. Of course. Only at the party—or when I got the note from Henry inviting me—I did wonder just how long they've known each other."

"You said she's some sort of therapist. They know each other from work?"

"Yes, occupational—'using' art, as Henry put it so charmingly. But according to him, they only got to know each other a year ago. When she came to work there, at his clinic."

"If they work in the same field, they could have known each other before easily enough. Why don't you believe him?"

"I don't know. I've just been feeling suspicious. Nasty and suspicious. And telling myself it's none of my business, even if they were having an affair while Celia was alive. And continuing with the suspicions."

"Of?"

"I don't know."

"That your sister's death wasn't an accident? It's the first thing the police would have checked, you know; they would have tried pretty hard to dig up another woman in Sloan's life. And if he'd had one, of course, it wouldn't necessarily have meant, uh, murder. It could have meant just an average marriage."

"I wonder if Simmons did find out anything, though?"

"I'd guess not. If he had, he would've held onto the murder angle a lot longer than he did. I still know some people in the department here. I could find out."

"Could you? Would you? I think I'd like that. Just out of curiosity—admitting that it's none of my business, I'd still like to know. What would they do, look up the case? Would Simmons know?''

''That I was asking? Or someone?''

''Yes.''

''Wouldn't have to. You'd rather he didn't, I take it.''

''I'm leery of getting him interested again. I don't want to put ideas in his head.''

I stirred my cold coffee, feeling restless, wanting something to do with my hands. ''What were you doing up here tonight, anyway? Do you live in Pacific Heights?'' He didn't seem the type.

''Do you mean where do I live? Or do you mean what's my interest in all this?''

''Both,'' I admitted.

''OK. I live in Bernal Heights. Where I have a printing business. Small one. From which I was delivering an order we just finished up this evening; the client was in a hurry for it. And as the client is also an old friend, we had dinner.''

''Oh.'' I wondered if the old friend was a man or a woman and waited to see if he would answer the other question.

After a while, he did: ''The second part is harder to answer because I'm not entirely sure myself. I *am* interested. Curiosity? Boredom? Missing the good old days as a police detective? I don't know. Before I ran into you tonight, I hadn't thought about the case for a while. But I was there, you know. And frankly, I never believed in the accident explanation. It never felt right, and it's been on my mind, off and on.''

''*You* think Celia was murdered?'' I asked in astonishment. A suspicious Simmons was one thing; this man, somehow, quite another.

''Well—yes. I always thought it was most likely murder.''

I sat in stunned silence for what seemed a long time. O'Reagan, on the other hand, looked perfectly composed, relaxed, even happy. ''What do you—could anything be done?'' I finally asked, not clear myself about what I meant.

''It wouldn't hurt to find out a few things, maybe. I'm curious. Are you? What do people call you, anyway? Margaret? Margot? You don't look Irish enough for Peggy. In spite of those amazing green eyes of yours.''

''I'm not. Margaret or Maggie, usually,'' I answered his question, ignoring the part about my eyes. ''Celia's cook—she used

to work for our mother—calls me *'la grita,'* it means 'the cry.'
I was usually so angry, growing up. And in school it was Mag-
pie. I do tend to collect things, although I'm trying to reform.
And yes—I'm curious, too. What about you? Richard? Patrick?
O'Reagan?''

"Depends on who it is." The lopsided smile briefly lit the
gray eyes as he thought of some private situation. "Most of my
friends call me Pat, or O'Reagan. Take your pick."

"Thanks. I think of you as O'Reagan; I'll stick to that. Maybe
Pat will emerge. You said," I continued slowly, "you could ask
somebody in the police whether they found any signs of an extra
woman in Henry's life. And if so, was it Beatrice? Will you do
that? And let me know what you find out?"

"I'll let you know."

"When, do you think? I don't mean," I added quickly, "that
there's any rush. I'm leaving town tomorrow for a couple of
weeks—so if you find anything out, don't try and get in touch
with me until around the fifteenth."

"OK. Where you going?"

"New York. Somebody offered me the use of an empty apartment, so I decided to go. I used to live in New York; I haven't
been back in a long time. Too long."

"They got snow there now?"

"Not right now, apparently. I'm hoping they'll get some while
I'm there. I always used to like it when it first snowed in New
York. It gets messy later, but just in the beginning it's beautiful.
You ever spend any time there?"

"A little. Enough." He did not continue. I've since learned
that when he abruptly stops going into detail over parts of his
past, it usually means they have to do with the time when he
was married.

I looked at my watch. "Do you realize it's almost one
o'clock?"

"Time to go," he agreed and signaled to the waiter, who
now looked a little droopy. But still perfectly pleasant.

"Will you call me, then, and tell me what you find out? Or
come over for coffee, and I'll show you my sculptures."

"I'd like that. It should be interesting, either way. I wonder . . ."

"You wonder what?" I asked when he didn't continue.

"Nothing. I'll tell you when I see you," he answered contradictorily.

I dug around in my purse for a pencil, then tore a deposit slip out of my checkbook. I didn't use many deposit slips in a month and they make fine calling cards, printed as they are with name, address, and telephone number.

"You might see also what, if anything, they dug up on a man named Dunbar Oates."

"Who's he?"

"He was Celia's decorator, a sort of protégé. Came to see me just after she was killed. Lindy, too. Seemed a little fishy, that's all."

We walked out into the San Francisco Union Street night. It was after one o'clock and Cafés were closing, city lights were dimming, and stars brightening. The perfect wide circle of the moon was high up now, far away and small.

EIGHTEEN

THERE MAY BE MUSEUMS IN THIS WORLD MORE PERFECT THAN New York's Frick, but I don't know them. Some of the best of my New York hours have been spent there, and that quick trip back East was no exception.

Mainly it's the size, I think, the smallness, and the fact that it was lived in, a house—the art a part of the everyday life of Mr. Millionaire Frick—long before it was made into a museum. Just stepping into the central marble courtyard with the large shallow pool in the center is soothing, coming as you do from late-twentieth-century New York City streets into an earlier, calmer, slower world. The rooms themselves are small, by museum standards; there's still some furniture around, and then, of course, there are the paintings.

Henry Clay Frick made a lot of money in Pittsburgh with coke and steel and the labor policies of a monster. He spent a fat portion of that money in Europe, buying up, with the guidance of hired experts, a truly fabulous pastiche of the most glorious paintings produced by Western civilization. Starting, as the painting itself did by and large, with the very earliest of the early Italian Renaissance.

I'd spent a lot of time in the Frick in the years I lived in New York. On Seventieth just off Fifth Avenue, it's an easy place to just drop in on, spend whatever time you have, a lot or a little, and then continue on with the rest of your day. The paintings there are old friends of mine, and I was glad to see them again.

In spite of my joy in having some time to spend with them again, though, I didn't seem to be able to leave my questions about Henry and his new wife back in California where they decently belonged.

The huge Ingres portrait I've always loved so much, the Comtesse D'Haussonville in ice-blue satin, her back reflected in the giant mirror of her dressing table, looks out at the spectator with—what? Disdain? Complacency? Or simply a rock-solid sense of who she is, a person of absolute bourgeois consequence in the Paris of the 1850s? An incredible presence, an enigma. And as I looked at her once again—the expression, the costume, the portrait—what came to mind was Beatrice.

I moved on. But Rembrandt's portrait of himself in middle age, gazing back at me so real and true, now looked like Henry. Was that the story, I wondered? A middle-aged man, a little afraid about what his life was adding up to at that vulnerable time, obsessively attracted by that cold blue satin younger woman, so sure of herself, so sure of herself that she was quite irresistible to this tired, self-doubting man who would so soon be old? His last chance? His last chance . . .

Rembrandt's self-portrait in his old age, though, the golden, glorious one that says: "I have arrived, I have entered my kingdom, I have become myself and I know who that is," reminded me only of itself, thank God. Of them all, I think that I would have been saddest to lose that one to what I was beginning to think of as my "California obsession."

The Polish Rider, slim, fleeting, mysterious, which had once reminded me of David now made me think of Mark. Where did he come from? Was something terrible not far behind? Where was he going; did he know? Would he get there?

Then the fat Borgia child, richly dressed for the portrait by

Bronzino in green velvet and gold, holding the dead bird—the little bird he'd just squeezed the life out of. I thought of Beatrice's son. Sandy, Alexander; I imagined him to be just like that—spoiled, arrogant. . . .

Walking to the next room, the small one at the back, I found the remembered "Temptation of Christ"; the early, early Renaissance now, primitive and sophisticated at once. Christ, standing high above the stylized medieval buildings which represent the kingdoms of the earth. The black and batlike devil, hovering, offering, tempting. But if my thoughts strayed once more to Henry, to Beatrice, and even to Dunbar Oates, which was the kingdom, and which the devil?

I gave it up for the day. I decided what I needed was people, not paintings, not fantasies. I told myself that when I came back another day the ridiculous obsession would be gone; another day or so of New York would dissolve my West Coast fantasy of mystery and evil. Of murder? Of the murder of my sister?

And so out through the pastel-and-golden, luscious playful room of panels painted by Boucher, every rosy, rounded, smiling face, every charming arm and ripely feminine seductive curve and graceful draping of pink and blue and gold a reminder now of Celia.

I went to some AA meetings, and I looked up a few old friends. Both were good and tough, with that fine New York hard edge that I miss on the West Coast, where people are sometimes so mellow as to be a little waffley. I forced myself to look up people I'd lost contact with so long ago they seemed to belong to another lifetime. Which, in a way, they did. Some had become strangers; some had not. There were films to see, a few good, a few bad, but most of them interesting, if only because I knew the person who'd made the film.

I also looked up a couple of old college roommates. One of them, Muffy Tucker, had been a reporter for *Time* for a number of years by then. We had lunch at the Russian Tea Room, and I asked her if she'd ever heard anything more about the California Coalition. No arrests had been made, and they'd gradually just disappeared from the news.

"Not much," she replied. "Nothing, in fact. All the information anyone ever had came from that tape of theirs, when you get right down to it. Why?"

"I just wondered. And thought you'd be in a position to know."

"I'll check the files, if you like. It was your niece who was killed on the plane? I was thinking of snagging an interview with you at the time. Didn't sit right so I left you alone, meant to write. Never did."

"Thanks," I smiled. "And yes—see what you can dig up on them, will you?"

Later that day I went out to see a friend from the West Coast who was living with her rich parents in Connecticut. They could afford to pay for the trips to Silver Hill Sanitarium when the breakdowns came, as they continued to. Artist, schizophrenic, magic, sometimes wrecked, she was well that time, and we had a satisfying visit. I stayed over, and she took me to the train the next morning. The train was late, as it usually is.

"A snowflake is not a subway train." she commented, looking up at a sky so gray and heavy and low it seemed about to crash down on us, the southbound platform, the whole town of Stamford. A train came through then, going away from New York, and on impulse I said good-bye and ran down the stairs, through the concrete tunnel beneath the tracks, and up the other side. I got on the train that took me north, to New Haven.

I walked around the Yale campus for an hour or so, thinking of Lindy. It started to snow, big, soft, slow flakes, coming down out of the sunless skies as if they had all the time in the world. Lindy, who had not had much time. Who would have been graduating at the end of the semester that was beginning now, if she'd had more.

I thought, too, about weekends years ago when I came up from Vassar, remembered a boy from Oyster Bay I'd been crazy about—quite literally—I hadn't thought of him in years. October and November, scotch-and-soda and football. April and May, gin-and-tonic and picnics in the outdoor Connecticut springtime.

And protest. Revolution? Students who went South to free the blacks, then marched against the war in Vietnam to free the rest of us from the corporate tyrants who ran, who run, the country . . . the world . . .

Funny how the rhetoric had changed, though, I thought, considering the California Coalition tape. Partly the tone had gotten shriller with failure, but it was more than that, I mused; the whole feeling was different. What was it? A kind of rot? I remembered the immense innocence and purity—and guilt and naiveté—of those sixties revolutionaries:

> *Those were the days, my friend,*
> *we thought they'd never end, . . .*

How had it gone?

> *We'd live the life we choose,*
> *we'd fight and never lose . . .©*

Who had sung that? I couldn't remember, only the sound, a sort of Lotte Lenya/Mack the Knife sound . . .

And the more I thought about it the more the tone of the Coalition tape sounded all wrong. I couldn't put my finger on why, exactly; the words were right . . . more or less. . . . I was suddenly cold—the snow was coming down in earnest—and I half ran, half walked back to the station. A southbound train was standing in its concrete stall, rumbling and hissing. I jumped up onto the worn metal steps just as it began pulling slowly out of the station.

"Remember the California Coalition, Paul?"

We were having dinner late that evening on Bleecker Street at the Bocce restaurant. It was a favorite of mine and not changed much except for the prices. The old Italian men, who looked like the same old men, still threw the metal disk to the end of the narrow clay court that ran along one side of the restaurant, accompanied by the same Italian cries of excitement and dismay. The wooden balls rolled, and the customers ate and talked and watched. We were three: Paul Folsom, his wife Daisy, and myself.

"The California Coalition? I certainly do. Question?"

"Have you ever heard anything more about them? At all? There's never been anything in the papers, but you as a privileged insider . . ."

"Knower of secrets, digger out, digger outer of hidden—hidden what? Murk? Muck. I once had desires to be a famous murk racker, it's true, but I've become just a hack technician instead. . . ." He smiled a cheerless smile and knocked back the rest of his fourth after-dinner brandy. Actually, it was a poet he'd wanted to be, I remembered. . . .

"Speaking of which, why don't you just chuck it?" his wife said, in a tone of voice that also said she'd said it too many times before. Too many times for him, and too many for her. And to which there wasn't, apparently, any useful answer.

He gave a useless one. "Scared, darling, you know that; you've told me so often enough. Daisy, darling Daisy." He smiled at her with a lot of hostility. "However, Magpie dear," turning to me, the hostility receding but still ready to leap out with the least encouragement, "to answer your question. The answer is, the answer is. What was the question? Oh, I remember. The answer is, no. I have never heard another peep about the nefarious California Coalition. And far's I know, nobody else has, either."

"Strange, huh?"

"As you say. Strange, huh."

I walked back home up Fifth Avenue and then east along Twelfth Street. The big March snowflakes that had come to New Haven that afternoon, and had just begun drifting down from the nighttime New York City sky when we went in to dinner, had now covered the streets, the doorsteps, and the bare branches of the trees with white and quiet. It was very peaceful. A man walking toward me in a black overcoat and hat was carrying a baby leopard in his arms, tawny yellow against the dark coat, the huge paws a baby animal has yet to grow up to dangling over the man's arms. We smiled at each other, because of the new snow and the leopard.

And went on our separate ways. For him, a jungle perhaps, a silk room high above Manhattan. For me, back to the borrowed apartment for one last night, and in the morning back to San Francisco. To have, I remembered, something of my curiosity satisfied about Henry and his Beatrice. Perhaps.

NINETEEN

"**N**ICE PLACE YOU HAVE HERE," O'REAGAN SAID JUST AS most people did, looking around my front room.

"Thanks, I feel lucky to have it. With all that"—my arm swept toward the windows and the view out over the bay—"it's also very low rent. Get *down*, Diana!"

"It's all right, I like dogs. How old is she?"

"Around six years, not six months like she's acting. I'm glad you don't mind being jumped on. She sheds, too. Luckily those clothes don't look like they'd pick much up."

He had on heavy brown twill trousers, hard surfaced, and a plaid wool shirt of browns and dark red that reminded me of the tweed coat I'd kept from Celia's things. I wondered what he'd found out.

"Would you like something to drink? Coffee, or wine?"

"Coffee, thanks."

"Follow me back to the kitchen, then."

The kitchen also looked out over the bay, and O'Reagan said: "I feel like I'm on a ship up here."

It was Sunday, about two o'clock in the afternoon of a warm and smoggy day.

"Have you spent time at sea? On ships?" That would fit with something about him, I thought; maybe the battered quality. Although that had a city feeling to it somehow. . . .

"A little. Not a lot." He sat down at the kitchen table, in the chair that had the best view, and looked out.

I poured the boiling water into the Melita, put a plate of sweet rolls I'd made that morning on the table between us, and asked: "Did you find anything out? Any signs of a past affair between Henry and this Beatrice?"

"Yes and no. Nothing definite. This is good coffee."

"Malvina's. Italian roast. What did you find out?"

"It looks like a good possibility that he was playing around with someone. And for several months, at least, before your sister was killed."

"Good! I mean—that's good news somehow. Perversely. Who did you talk to? What did they say?" I felt I was being a little pushy and added, "I'm sorry I sound so impatient. Just start at the beginning, and I'll try and not interrupt any more." I put a little more cancer-causing saccharin into my coffee, stirred it, and then forgot to drink it in my interest in O'Reagan's news.

"That's all right. There's not a lot. A friend of mine is pretty high up with the city now; DA's office. Bob Patton—we were in a training thing together years ago. We get together for a drink from time to time, anyway; I just made it sooner. We talk old times and the police force mostly, cops and robbers. Good sweet rolls. You make 'em?"

"Yes. Thanks. You talk cops and robbers."

"Yeah. I started talking about being a witness to your sister's death, how I didn't actually see anything wrong but never felt right about it, either. Got him talking about what he remembered of the case."

He took a long slug of coffee and downed another sweet roll. They were rather small. He had another. I waited.

"It was two years ago, of course, so he was pretty hazy at first. And not a particularly important case, in his world. But a few martinis cleared his head up pretty good. After he got into it, I asked if Simmons had ever found anything against the husband, as we called him—we were at the Buena Vista and not talking names—'that accident with the cable car,' and so forth. Though it was a week night, and nobody much was around.

"He said as far as he remembered, Simmons had been hot on the trail of some hanky-panky of the husband's, particularly after they found out the wife had changed the will and more or less cut him out—although, in another way, that gave him less motive. Anyway, Simmons was all ready to charge in and arrest him at one point. He's always been one to go off half-cocked, and he did have definite information that Sloan was away from home a lot, in the evenings and on weekends, during the year before Mrs. Sloan was killed. And that was a new pattern; up until then he'd kept pretty regular hours and otherwise been at home.''

"Claimed he was working late, I bet. Henry was never very imaginative.''

"Right. And most important, Patton said there'd been something from the son that indicated another woman, though he couldn't remember what. But then the kid clammed up, apparently, and Simmons couldn't get any more out of him. So he dug around his damndest but didn't come up with anything else, and he had to let it go. Sloan stuck to his story that he was doing research; he said the clinic was a quiet place to work.''

"He had a quiet place to work at home. Not the library—they all used that as a kind of sitting room—but a study.''

"Patton said Simmons didn't buy it. And the feel it has to me is that Sloan was lying. But that's not to prove why, what he was really doing, or who, if anyone, he was really with.''

"How did Simmons find out he was gone so much, anyway?''

"From one of the servants, the cook, I think, mainly. Patton said he got a sense from the transcripts that she didn't like Sloan all that much.''

"I don't know. She worked for them—well, she worked for Celia, really, since she was married the first time, and for our mother before that. I've known her all my life; it's certainly possible she disliked Henry, although I wasn't aware of it.''

"If we decide to go any further with this, that could be a big help. You could probably get a hell of a lot more out of her than the police did. If there's more to get. Does she like you?''

"Adores me. I think. Or used to. I'll have to get her address from Henry, though. She married the gardener, a Chinese guy, about three months after Lindy was killed. He and she were keeping the house open according to the dictates of Celia's will, but none of the family was living there. At the reception Henry said they've retired, somewhere up in Napa. He's supposed to send me the address, but if he doesn't I can ask again. It would be perfectly natural for me to want to keep in touch with her. If,'' I echoed, "we should decide to go any further.''

"Good. Patton says the other servants were less definite about his being gone so much, except the butler, chauffeur, the Chinese guy he thought had corroborated the cook's story. Sloan's car being out most evenings that year, and so forth. And Simmons couldn't get any more, couldn't prove he wasn't—that Sloan wasn't—at the clinic working, like he said. Just an ordinary hard-working, noble American doctor, sacrificing his family for his patients.'' O'Reagan made a sour-faced grimace—as if he'd just had something unpleasant shoved under his nose.

"I always thought Henry was a little on the lazy side. He *talked* a lot about working, but they were always going off on trips. And Simmons found no other traces of an extra woman in his life? Other than—maybe—something Mark said and then took back?''

"Right. Which doesn't mean there wasn't one. Just that they were extremely careful if there was. Think you could get anything out of the son? Your nephew?''

"I could try. If I can find him. He left town, and no one heard from him for a couple of years—except for Celia's lawyers, who send his money from the trust fund. But apparently he's back; Henry and Beatrice have seen him and say he's in good shape— he drinks.''

"He's how old?''

"Umm. Twenty-two, it must be.''

"Think he would have made something up like that about his father?''

"I don't know. They weren't getting along at all, from what I saw at the time. But no—I don't think he'd make something like that up. Whether he'd unclam for me at this point—I don't know. Why would they be so careful, do you think? If they were seeing each other, Henry and Beatrice.''

"I don't know, but it must have been more than ordinary care to stand up under that kind of police investigation. That's the dope, anyway, as far as the police got with it. What do you think?''

"That it certainly sounds like Henry was involved with some-one. But if it was Beatrice, she would have been about three months pregnant when Celia was killed, and Henry couldn't get her pregnant—so it seems stretching things to think that they were involved with each other then.''

"Couldn't have been someone else . . .''

"That Henry was seeing? Or that got Beatrice pregnant, you mean, while she was also seeing Henry?''

"Either."

"I wonder if Celia really hadn't told Henry she'd changed her will? Seems to me she would have—that the whole point of changing it was to force him back into being a society shrink."

"What makes you think so?"

I thought back to that day in my apartment when Celia had been speaking the reasonable, accepting words about Henry's changed work. I tried to pinpoint where the feeling had come from that wasn't really the way she felt about it at all. Just deduction, or had there been something else?

"It was a feeling I got, let's see, that what she was saying was what she thought she ought to feel, what a person like her idea of herself would feel—but that the reality was . . . entirely different. And the trouble was, she didn't exactly know this herself. Our mother was like that; Celia was very like her in tending to buy her own bullshit façades . . . more than most people do, I mean.

"She did actually say, too, after she'd finished the supportive-wife bit, that she'd be sorry to see him drop the private practice he'd built up. She used the word sorry, but she sounded angry. And the teaching, she didn't want him to drop that either; it was fairly prestigious, I guess. . . ."

"Partly a feeling and partly what she said, then?" He picked up the Marlboro packet from the table and absentmindedly flicked up some cigarettes and pointed them at me.

"No, thanks. Yes to your question, partly feeling and partly what she said—based on my general knowledge of her. But if Henry was out of the big money, anyway, why would he kill her? Why not divorce?"

"Maybe he didn't know the full extent of the changes in the will. Or maybe—how much did he get, anyway?"

"I don't remember exactly—and it got superseded so soon by Lindy's death. But it was around thirty thousand a year—I think it was for five years—and the house eventually. I can't even imagine how much that place is worth, with the inflation we've had. Three quarters of a million? A million?"

"Plenty, anyway, to make a motive for murder."

"Then he was to get some thousands, I forget how many, for life, after the five years."

"If she'd found out he had another woman and was going to divorce him and cut him out altogether . . ."

"He might have decided to kill her," I finished the sentence for him.

"If we went any further . . ." He paused and blew a perfect smoke ring. We both watched in silence until it spread itself thin enough to disappear.

"If we went any further," I repeated slowly. "That keeps coming up, doesn't it? OK. I say yes. Just because I don't like him? And hate the idea of their living happily ever after on Celia's money—if he killed her for it? And on Lindy's money, as it turned out."

"As it turned out. As it turned out; it certainly made all the difference."

"You mean maybe he arranged—" I felt a little sick and didn't want to put the next part into words. Even though it had been in the back of my mind since New Haven, in a way, to put it into words would make it more real, and I didn't feel ready for that. Then I went ahead, anyway: "You think maybe he murdered her, too? Lindy? That's harder for me to believe."

"Why?"

"Because I always thought he was genuinely fond of Lindy. He and Mark never got along, from the beginning. Not just since Celia was killed, but it got so bad by then I thought Henry really hated Mark. If he was going to murder one of the children for the money, I think it would have been Mark.

"Come to think of it," I added, "Mark was pretty sick a few days before Lindy was killed."

"Sick, how?"

"Supposedly attempted suicide. Something about taking a bottle of sleeping pills along with a bottle of brandy . . ."

"When was this?"

"About a week before the plane crash. He said he didn't remember taking the pills; we all thought he'd done it in a blackout. Or that's what I thought. From alcohol. Lindy said Henry was furious with him—for being so stupid, I think she quoted him, when they were all so upset about Celia."

"Interesting."

"Yes. I can imagine Henry trying to murder Mark—maybe he was angry because it was an attempted murder that failed."

"That would be annoying," O'Reagan agreed. "Then after that, maybe he had an opportunity with Lindy that he didn't have again with Mark."

"I thought Henry looked truly upset, though, by Lindy's death, O'Reagan. I'd be surprised if I was wrong about that. But I could be." I smiled across the table at him. "I am occasionally wrong."

He smiled back; his real smile, the charming one he doesn't use so often. Usually it's that grimace, expressive enough but hardly warming.

"He's a doctor," he said. "He could have taken something to make himself look sick easily enough. Or he could have been upset about something else—remorse or fear of getting caught. He may have been genuinely fond of her—and even fonder of money."

"And he might have been afraid that his dear Beatrice wouldn't have him without the money," I added, thinking of the aging, insecure-looking Rembrandt in the Frick museum. "Worried enough to kill Lindy and only feel sick about it afterwards. Horrible, but I guess possible."

O'Reagan said abruptly, "We should think of all the possibilities, you know. Not just of Henry—or Henry with Beatrice helping, perhaps—just because we don't like them."

"And would a girl friend help in something like that? A girl friend pregnant by somebody else? Even, as you say—if she isn't very likable . . ."

"Yes, well, there are other possibilities, too, you know."

"Like what?" I asked with a feeling I didn't want to hear the answer.

"Well—there's Mark. He inherited right away, after all. Did his mother keep him on a tight string for money?"

"She was threatening to," I answered reluctantly. "She was so worried about his drinking . . ."

"She might've told him—go to AA or no more money?"

"Many an alcoholic would seriously consider murder before AA," I agreed, smiling at the thought. "But he nearly died himself with those sleeping pills, so surely—"

"Could've been attempted suicide," O'Reagan countered promptly. "Killed his mother—terrible remorse—tried to kill himself. Failed, sobered up, didn't try again."

"I suppose it *could* be—but I like Mark!" I protested. "Although that would leave the plane crash an accident—as far as Lindy was concerned, I mean. I can't see where Henry *or* Mark would have any connection with that man who made the bomb. Cremmens, his name was."

"You never can tell. Mark's a bar drinker, right? You can meet anyone in a bar. Someone who'd be quite willing to help— for a big slice of a big inheritance. Although as you say, if it was Mark—" he held up a big hand to still further protest. "Calm down; we're only trying on theories. If it was Mark, I agree that the plane crash then had nothing to do with Lindy; the kid would have plenty from his mother. . . ."

"In an Agatha Christie I was reading lately," I said, "there was something about a 'little Lilly somebody, poor child of the slums.' An aunt took her in—she was twelve—and when the unfortunate woman refused her permission to go to the movies, the poor child of the slums grabbed the meat cleaver and cleaved that aunt through the head. Seriously, though, Henry does seem a lot more likely—he's so cold! But then the plane crash would have been his doing, and aimed at Lindy."

"Cremmens could have been a patient of his, something like that."

"What about Dunbar Oates, by the way? Did your friend know anything about him?"

"Oh. No. He's going to check the records for me and let me know if there is anything. What did you mean, anyway, he was 'acting fishy'? "

I told him how Dunbar had been when he came to see me and what Lindy had told me of his visit to her. He was a much more desirable suspect than Mark, and I made his behavior sound as peculiar as I could with any honesty at all.

"All right," O'Reagan said, "if we go any further with this we'll have to check him out pretty thoroughly, too."

Neither of us said any more for a while. O'Reagan smoked in the silence, and I started squirming around in my chair.

"I'd like some exercise. I'm tired of sitting so long," I finally said, getting up. "Would you like to come with me while I take the dogs out? My head needs some fresh air after all this— whatever it is. Air, anyway," I added, looking out the window at the smog-smudged sky across the water, with Oakland, Berkeley, and their hills barely showing through it.

O'Reagan nodded agreement and got up and stretched. My kitchen ceiling is a high one, but his outstretched hands weren't all that far from touching it. He smiled down at me, and I felt—I wasn't sure what I felt. I collected the dogs hurriedly, and we walked slowly up to Vermont Park, just over the top of Potrero Hill on the other side, and sat down on the side of the hill. The March green grass was already two feet high. The sunny white city was spread out beneath us. A wind from the ocean had blown away most of the smog on that side of the hill, and the sky was a radiant blue except over on the western edges, where fog, thick and white as cotton, was rolling in through Twin Peaks, creeping into the valleys in big puffy chunks. I had one of those moments I get every so often in San Francisco; an acute realization of how much I love the city and of how glad I am that I live here.

In unspoken agreement we dropped the subjects of Henry, Beatrice, Mark, Lindy, murder. Diana dug in the soft spring earth for gophers and fantasies. Orphan watched.

"You live alone in that huge place?" O'Reagan finally asked.

"Yes."

I thought about that for a minute and decided to continue. "I lived there in the beginning with my husband. He was killed several years ago in a motorcycle accident. Then I drank a lot for a while and took pills and felt very, very sorry for myself. Then I went somewhere and dried out, and then I went to AA; that's about two years ago. A few months before Celia was killed, in fact."

He was silent, looking out over the far hills. Then he said, "I drink on binges from time to time—but it's never been bad enough to interfere with anything I cared about. You've lived there alone, then, all this time?"

"Most if it. I tried having a roommate for a while but didn't like it. It's been worth it to me to pay the whole rent and have the place to myself—even before Celia's hundred thousand. There's a man I've been involved with off and on the past couple of years. I thought of living there with him at one time—but it didn't work out. We're not seeing each other right now." I paused, then asked, "What about you?"

"I have a house in Bernal Heights. Live there alone. I was married, too, a long time ago"—he made that grimace like there was a bad smell around—"but not in the house I live in now. That ended long before."

Neither of us said anything for a while, looking down at the white, cluttered city and both thinking, presumably, of our broken marriages. And other relationships.

"Ended by divorce, you mean?"

"Yes, divorce."

More silence, a surprisingly comfortable one.

"Loners," I sighed. "Sometimes I don't like it so much. At least, I think I like spending time by myself all *too* much. I'm afraid maybe I couldn't live with anyone again. Too set in my ways, rigid, selfish. But I'd like to, if that possibility comes up. You wouldn't?"

"I don't think so."

"The longer I live by myself, the more I understand that feeling. It scares me."

Back at my kitchen table, covered with the remains of a big takeout pizza and with my sculptures, duly admired, we got back to the subject of murder.

The walk had given me a chance to let the idea of Lindy's death—as part of the pattern of Celia's—rest quietly in my mind, gathering reality. In place of the old idea that it was part of a political assassination.

"O'Reagan?"

"Yeah?"

"I have a question."

"Ask it."

"All right. I do want to go on with this. Especially now the question's come up about Lindy. But what about you? I'm very grateful to you for getting the information the police had and for helping think about . . . the possible meanings. But—I don't know quite how to put this—you sound like you want to go on with it, too—why? Do you? What's in it for you?"

"I don't know that I can answer that, Maggie. I'll try."

He took a Marlboro out of the pack and lit it, inhaling deeply. "I've been asking myself the same question ever since I ran into you that night in Pacific Heights and we spent three hours talking about what I find myself calling 'the cable car case.' Facetiously, I told myself; but I don't feel facetious, I feel . . . serious. Maybe because I was there, I don't know. And I've wondered if my continuing interest means I made a mistake leaving the police force. I've thought about it a lot.''

He didn't say anything more for a while. The room was starting to get dark, so I got up and turned on the ceiling light, put our dirty dishes in the sink, and stuck the empty pizza carton in the garbage.

I sat down again. My sculptures stood around, silent and expectant; the Princess, the Fool, and the Cosmic Laborer all seemed to be waiting to hear what would be decided.

I suddenly had one of those almost unbearable urges for a cigarette and took three deep breaths. The feeling went back to wherever it came from.

Finally, O'Reagan said slowly, ''I've had to come to the conclusion that I'm pretty bored with my printing business. I also concluded that the reasons I left off being a cop were good ones. I wouldn't want to go back to that, taken as a whole. But there are parts of it I miss.''

''A kind of knight errantry?'' I guessed.

''Perhaps,'' he agreed. ''In a brave new world that's thrown away its soul and gone completely material. And that material poison plastic, more often than not. Or some other shoddy rip-off.''

His voice had roughened, and he looked for a moment very bitter. Then he looked embarrassed and smiled, a tight smile.

''Sorry. I don't usually get carried away like that. Anyway, for reasons I'm not sure of, yes, I'm interested in going on with this.''

''A deal then?''

''A deal.''

''What exactly is it we've agreed to do? Satisfy ourselves, at least, as to the truth about Celia's death? And Lindy's?''

''That's about the size of it.'' he agreed.

''How do we go about it? You're the one with the experience—did you ever think of being a private detective?''

''I've thought about it. Most cops have. All those movies and books, you can't help yourself. Humphrey Bogart, Dashiell

Hammett, they're inescapable. Lew Archer. But there're a lot of hassles involved, and a certain money investment. Plus the question of where the clients are going to come from. I'd have to be a lot surer I wanted to try it than I am now.''

"And our cable car case might help you become surer? One way or the other?''

"Might. We could work it out together. . . .''

"I'm happy with that. Do you see me more as your client, or more as your partner?''

"Oh, partner, by all means. There are a lot of things you can do on this better than I can. You know the people. If you can put some time into it?''

"I can. I'll be the junior partner, though, this being my first—case? Case. Also, I'm something of a coward, I should warn you.''

"That's all right,'' he smiled; "so am I.''

I raised my cup. "To detection, then.''

"To detection,'' he agreed, clinking it with his own to seal the bargain.

We settled down to working out a plan of action.

TWENTY

ONCE A MONTH I WAS IN CHARGE OF THE WEEKLY AA meeting in the D-Tox at City Hospital. When I got off the elevator to set up the meeting the Tuesday after seeing O'Reagan, the first person I ran into was my nephew Mark. He was sitting in one of the big chairs in the small central lobby across from the elevators.

He'd looked pretty bad at the memorial service for Lindy, which was the last time I'd seen him, but he looked a lot worse now: black eyes, two of them. A heavy, dirty cast all the way up his left leg. A tired-looking plastic—or I suppose nylon—shirt with an ugly orange and green design of what some optimist had hoped might pass for palm trees and fish. Droopy old man's checkered trousers he probably got in one of the pawn places on Sixth Street, with one leg cut off to make room for the cast. Very thin. Pasty-white skin.

Good, I thought, the worse the better, as long as it doesn't actually kill him. Maybe this'll be the place he hits bottom.

"Mark?"

He looked around very slowly, like an old man. He saw me and the sight didn't seem to cheer him up at all.

"Hello, Aunt." He stopped and seemed to be trying to think but finding it difficult.

"How'd you know I was here?" he finally asked but as if he was not very interested in the answer, as if that maybe wasn't even what he really wanted to know but the real question eluded him, and that was the best he could manage on such short notice. Then his expression brightened, and he asked, "You got a cigarette?"

"No, I don't. Sorry. And I didn't know you were here. I set up the AA meeting every second Tuesday of the month, and this is a second Tuesday. How long have you been here?"

Not long, by the looks of him.

"Three days," he said after stopping to think again. "I think."

A transvestite type walked past, male but with the clothes and manner of a flamboyant woman. He was cheerful, sprightly, and in much better shape than Mark, though he needed a shave.

"Marie!" Mark called. "Got a smoke?"

Marie stopped and dug around in the flowing but dirty white lace blouse he was wearing, pulled out some menthols and offered them. His fingers were covered with cheap costume rings, coarse black hairs poking out between the bits of colored glass and twisted imitation silver and gold. He had a friendly smile.

Mark took two; Marie didn't seem to mind.

"I've got to get the stuff out for the meeting, Mark—if this is your first week I guess you'll be there." I looked in my purse for some money. "Here's some money for cigarettes; there's a machine downstairs."

"Thanks." He took the money and pocketed it in a flash, skid-row style.

"I'll talk to you later."

"All right," he agreed blankly, lit one of Marie's cigarettes with hands shaking so badly it took three matches, and went back to staring at the dingy green wall.

City de-Tox, which is free, is an end-of-the-line kind of place, a place to go after you've run through the classier cures. The guys there come from the streets, skid row, mostly, and mostly they go back to skid row, too. A lot of them are young, in their twenties. A very small proportion are women. They come to the AA meeting the first week they're there because it's required. They stay another three weeks and get some of their health back; they go faithfully to their daily therapy groups—then they go back out, most of them, to get drunk and live among the garbage cans, doorways, and dirt again. A few get sober, eventually. One in thirty-six, the statistics say, stay sober. The rest of them die. Eventually.

The speaker I had that night was good for that group, a thirty-year-old black guy from Oakland who street-talked his way through fifteen years of assaults, armed robberies, disasters with women, alcohol, other drugs, and trips to San Quentin with simple believability. He'd been there. Also, he had that extra whatever-it-is—energy, sex appeal, vitality—that makes people listen.

Not a story Mark would identify with in its events, but he could probably relate to the anger, all right; the hatred of any and all authority. If his head had cleared up enough in three days to hear anything at all, I amended. I wondered where he'd been and what he'd been doing the past two years. He had a skid-row look to him, wherever he had been.

"What it was like, what happened, and what it's like now." The rough outline for every AA pitch. The speaker covered it all, and there were even some questions and discussion when he finished. After the meeting was over and I'd pushed what AA meeting directories I could on the unwilling residents, I took Mark off to the linen room with me, which is the room where the meeting supplies are stored and also the only place on the ward where there is any privacy.

"I'm having lunch with your father's new wife tomorrow, Beatrice. You knew he remarried? Henry said you'd be at the reception. I looked for you."

"Yeah," he mumbled, "I met her."

We were sitting at a big round table half covered with stacks of coarse white sheets. Mark was chain-smoking, lighting one from another as if he were in a race to see how much smoke he could get down his throat in the shortest possible time. It reminded me of the way I used to smoke, especially when I was drying out. At a place not unlike this one, I thought, though fancier. I remembered thinking over and over, "Thank heavens I can still smoke! Thank heavens I don't have to give that up! Thank heavens I can still smoke!"

It was the only bright spot I could remember from that time.

"What'd you think of her? Beatrice?"

"She's all right." He lit still another cigarette, slowly, because his hands were shaking. "Gave me some stuff to read on how to drink, in fact; behaviorist stuff, you know. But"—he was still putting the words and thoughts together with difficulty—"it doesn't seem to have worked, does it?" He smiled, a raggedy one but genuine.

"I wouldn't say so offhand," I agreed, smiling back. "From just a quick superficial look at you. I hope you'll give AA a try now. Because that's what helped me. But I'm not going to nag you about it."

"*Good,*" he said with heavy emphasis, then smiled again but with a degree of hostility this time.

"All right, let me finish, please. If you want, I'll take you to meetings or mark the ones in the book I think you'd probably like best—there are about fifteen a day to choose from. If you want to be left alone, I'll leave you alone. If you have any questions about AA, or getting sober, I'll answer them if I can. But it's up to you. And I really do know, from my experience, that AA works. And I don't know of anything else that does. And that's all I'm going to say about it."

"Good," he repeated, but more calmly.

"Here's my phone number"—I tore out a deposit slip and handed it to him—"or if you lose that, you can get it from Henry. I'm not in the book."

"I don't know how long I'll be here."

"It's a twenty-one-day program, isn't it? Or twenty-eight?"

"Twenty-eight. But they said since I have money—theoretically, that is, in fact I don't have any until my allowance next month—anyway, they said they might transfer me to another place."

"How come?"

"Don't know. I think—the counselor said since I have that trust fund, somebody would probably spring some money, so I may not be eligible. For this place. Do you think I should try and go someplace else? Do you think Temple would go for it?"

"Sure, I think he would. You haven't anything to lose by asking him, anyway. About where you should be, that I don't know. I dried out in Marin County, a place called Cameron Hospital—private, profit making—I doubt it's any better than here, but it's pleasanter. Trees. I don't think it matters so much where you go as where you are with your drinking when you go there, and whether or not you're willing to try AA."

I got up and started putting away the AA literature that I'd had out for the meeting.

"Does your father know you're here? When I have lunch with Beatrice tomorrow, do you want me not to mention seeing you, or what?"

"It doesn't matter. Henry's going to know I'm here, anyway," he answered gloomily. He used to call his father Dad, not Henry, I remembered. "The shrink here knows I'm his stepson; we met before at some tennis thing. He'll be sure and tell him, too, he's that type—motherfucker. I don't care, anyway. It doesn't matter."

I could hear it in his voice. I remembered the feeling: It didn't matter, because nothing did. And something about trying to sound tough, in shreds.

"I've been thinking about when your mother was killed, lately. Trying to understand better what was happening in her life just then. You know, we weren't close—in a lot of ways I disliked her—but now I'm finding I want to understand her better. Was something going on between her and your father? Some problem, I mean? That you—"

"All right, Sloan, time for meds; come along now."

A counselor I didn't know was leaning against the door, her carroty-topped head stuck into the room and her large brown eyes fixed on Mark. They switched to me: "Visiting hours were up long ago. I'm afraid you'll have to leave now." She stayed there, waiting.

"My last day for Valium," Mark said. "They call it easing you off gradually. Ha."

We both got up, and the woman in the doorway left.

"About your mother and father . . ."

"Stepfather. I heard him on the telephone once—'oh, my darling,' he said—and he wasn't talking to my mother; it was disgusting!"

"When was this?"

"A couple of weeks before she was killed."

"Did your mother know?"

"I don't know."

"Do you think it was Beatrice he was seeing then?"

"I don't know. I don't know who it was. Now I think of it— no, I don't think it was Beatrice."

"Why not?"

"I don't have any—"

"Come *on*, Mark," the nurse interrupted. She was standing in the doorway again with her arms crossed over an ample chest, and she obviously wasn't going to leave until she took Mark with her.

"All right, I'm going," I said. "Call me if you want to, Mark. I'll probably be back in a day or so. Call me if there's anything you need."

TWENTY-ONE

"**I** WAS SURPRISED, BEATRICE," I SAID TO HER THE NEXT day, after the waiter had taken our order and gone off, "to get your note inviting me to lunch. I know you said you wanted to get together—but people so rarely do what they say. People including me, of course. I always mean well but then don't get around to whatever it is I was meaning well about."

The part about being surprised was true, but the implied admiration wasn't. It was part of the tactics I'd decided on to try to find out more about her. And if she hadn't initiated the luncheon, I would have. My self-labeled ineptness was the other half of my plan. It didn't feel like much, sitting there right across the table from her sharp, two-colored eyes, but it was all I had. I had no idea what I was looking for—that she was likely to tell me, at least—but I figured flattery was always a good place to start.

"I have so little time," she purred, "that I *know* I have to plan ahead and arrange things if I'm going to get to them at all. Since you don't work"—she paused briefly—"you probably think you have all the time in the world and can do whatever you want to, anytime. . . ."

" 'Floating in the illusory amplitude of his youth,' " I muttered.

"What?"

"Nothing, just something a man named Walker Evans said about a friend of his," I said hastily. Obscure quotes about James Agee wouldn't go with my tactics of flattery and humility; I'd have to watch my step.

"My mother was like that," she said. "She never got anything done, either."

I bristled inwardly but smiled sweetly, rolling my eyes around as if in agreement.

142

"Rotten bitch," I thought, "It's one thing for *me* to say I don't get around to things—and quite another for her to agree!"

I didn't like being equated with her mother, either. Beatrice said her age was thirty (she looked older), which if true made her five years younger than I was. But she had a condescending way of talking down as though she were the elder and certainly the wiser of the two of us. I wondered sourly if she had any friends, or only worshipers like Frieda Halff and Henry. Did she pull these numbers on her patients, or clients, or whatever she called them? Not so good for the improvement of their mental health. I considered whether they could possibly like her. They were, of course, supposed to be crazy. Speculation like that wouldn't get me any farther, I reminded myself as the waiter served our lunch; I had better get busy and start asking her some questions.

"Is she still living? Your mother?"

My main—in fact only—plan, was to get as much random information as I could and hope some of it would suggest a follow-up.

"No," she answered; "she died. Many years ago."

"While you were still a child? I always think that's so sad."

"Well, actually it was after I left. Which was pretty young. I had my way to make in the world, and I knew I'd better get on with it if I wanted to get anywhere. Quite different from Henry's first wife. Your sister. Her accident must have been a terrible sorrow to you."

So that's it, I thought; she wants to fish around in the Celia waters, see what's there. . . . I finished chewing a large mouthful of spinach canneloni—I am excessively fond of spinach canneloni—and swallowed it hastily.

"Not so much," I answered truthfully. "Celia and I weren't close at all, you see. In fact, I never saw that much of her, even when we were children. She was ten years older and went away to school from the ninth grade on. We didn't have much in common—she was very rich and I wasn't, for one thing."

"Oh, *that* needn't make any difference, surely?" she protested, smiling coyly. "I'm biased, of course, but I'm not just thinking of me and Henry."

"I think it's different, or can be, for a man and a woman—especially when it's the man who has the money. I always thought it must be a strain on Henry's relationship with Celia, the fact that she was the one with the money. She was a little on the bossy side, you know.''

I didn't want to give the impression that I'd sensed anything actually wrong with their marriage, though, so I quickly added, ''Although they seemed to be very comfortably married in spite of that. Not a great passion, perhaps, especially on his part. It was always Celia who was simply wild about him. But he had a lot of loyalty, I could tell that, and for that kind of marriage it was a good enough one, I think. I guess you must have a certain amount of curiosity about it? I would, in your place. What does Henry say?''

''Not much. And I am curious; I hate to admit it, but I am,'' she said with relish, not seeming to hate it in the least. ''You're really a very understanding sort of person.''

I couldn't think of anything to say to that, so I smirked modestly and concentrated on my cannelloni. Beatrice had chosen a small, expensive Italian restaurant near the clinic where she and Henry worked. The food was excellent, but we were almost the only people there. Which was perhaps why she'd chosen it.

''Since I saw so little of them, I don't really know much about their marriage, so I'm afraid I don't have much to add. I just had the idea that it was fairly average, comfortable, decent; nothing spectacular. Were you married before?''

''Oh, very briefly, a long time ago. Just a kid thing; it didn't last.''

''And you didn't have any children then?''

''No, luckily. Since I was barely able to take care of myself. But the time I had Alexander I was ready for a child—though that relationship didn't last, either.''

''Few do anymore, it seems,'' I sighed. ''Did you go back to your maiden name, then? After your first marriage?''

She looked at me a little oddly, so I tried smiling and added, ''I'm always so interested in what women do about that; left over from the women's movement, I guess. Did you go back to your own name?''

''I did, as a matter of fact. The marriage was so fleeting it seems completely unreal to me now.''

And may well be, I thought. ''That has the advantage, anyway, that when you remarry it's your own name you're marrying with and not some—by that time—perfect stranger's. Don't you agree?''

"Oh, I do, Maggie, I certainly do."

She frowned earnestly, pulled some hair back from her fore-head, and tucked it behind her right ear. She had large diamond studs in her ears, a rather insensitive choice, I thought, for work-ing with the impoverished mentally ill. I'd seen her clientele when I picked her up for lunch, sitting like stones on straight-back chairs around the edges of the big front room, odds and ends of humans in odds and ends of old clothes, shabby, hope-less, many of them looking frightened as well. For people who sit around so much, it seemed too bad they couldn't have some comfortable chairs.

"You said your mother died after you left home? Where was home, anyway?"

"Well, all over the place." She smiled.

"All over the place like where?" I smiled back.

"Not California—the southwest—New Mexico and Arizona a lot, plus some Oklahoma and a little Arkansas. My father was a welder; we moved around a lot. Dead-end jobs."

"Northern Arizona or southern? Northern Arizona is *so* beau-tiful. I don't know the southern part."

"Southern, Phoenix, partly. We were never in one place very long."

"Were you born in Phoenix?" I was starting to feel quite tired. Having to drag every little fact from her was as much work as pulling teeth. Or seemed so.

"Why, yes."

"And then your family was there off and on, you said? Is that the place you think of as being from? Did you go to high school there?"

"Part of the time. I don't think of anyplace as home, really. As being from there, I mean. San Francisco, of course, is home to me now. . . ."

"Did you mind? Moving so often?"

"Mind? No, I liked it. Always moving on. Seeing new places. Though some of them don't seem very exciting when I look back on them now. But I always had a sense of—conquest, about coming in to a new place. A brand-new territory . . ." Her eyes lit with a memory, and I was reminded of my cat creeping across the roof of my neighbor's shed, stalking.

"You should have been named Alexandra instead of Be-atrice."

"You know," she said, still smiling dreamily, "I never thought of that. My son's name is Alexander . . . maybe that's why. I want the world for him, I guess; that's true."

"You didn't name him after his father, then. Or your father? What was his name?"

"My father's name," she repeated slowly, still preoccupied with some thought or memory of her own. "Henry, oddly enough. James Henry," she added, no longer absentminded. "He was killed. In Vietnam."

"He was in the army?"

"No. One of those civilian jobs, the kind men took because they couldn't get anything else. That was a terrible war."

It was, but somehow the way she'd conveniently shoved her father off to die in it struck a false note. Anyway, I had her father's name now, or would have when put together with the maiden name from her marriage certificate. Better check that, though. . . .

"Were your mother and father still together then?"

"Until my mother died. This sure is a lot of questions!" She smiled to indicate she didn't really mind. "I haven't thought about all this in a long time."

"Well, I'm interested," I said, quite truthfully, although, of course, she wouldn't like my motives much if she knew what they were.

"Your father went off to Vietnam after you left home, then. You left young, you said. What happened then? I always admire people so much who have made their own way, without help from their families, I mean, like Celia had. I did, too, through college."

"It was difficult at first." Her lips tightened into a harsh line, remembering. "I worked a lot of crummy jobs, grocery stores, that sort of thing. Hard work, low pay."

"In Phoenix?"

"Pretty soon I moved to L.A. That was my first time in California. The jobs got a little better, and the money was better there. I managed to save a little, got my G.E.D. at night school. Eventually I took some courses at a junior college. Finally I took some loans out and went back full-time."

"Impressive perseverance," I said. "What was your school?"

"Pomona, just a community college, but it was a start. Then I finished up at State. That's when I came to San Francisco. It was there I got involved in art courses and ended up going for the O.T. degree. Technically counseling, but I'm doing graduate work there now for the actual O.T.''

"I'd like to see your work in ceramics. Henry told me that's your medium when you find the time—which must be hard with everything else you do," I gushed admiringly.

"I haven't had the time to put into it I need. But did Henry tell you that he had the cottage made into a studio as a wedding present? It's a kind of office, too, where I can go and get away when I need to study. All mine—no one else is allowed in there! At least—he has some things stored there but doesn't come in without permission. It has absolutely everything I need for clay, too; it's wonderful! A really big kiln. I'm hoping I'll be able to get back into the ceramics on a regular basis. And now that Sandy's older.''

"You have someone, a live-in person, to look after him, don't you? I met that nice German woman at your reception; Mrs. Halff, I think it was? She said she'd looked after him a lot but wouldn't be anymore?''

"That's right. We've hired a marvelous Swedish woman. Frieda is really a little old to be looking after an almost two-year-old. And she has her own home. She was a wonderful help, though, when I first went back to work; she lived near me, and I just dropped him off every morning. I'm glad those days are over, though.''

"Understandably. Did you live around here, near the clinic?''

"Daly City. I never liked it, but the price was right.''

"It sounds like you've worked hard and deserve an easier life for a change. I guess you're going to have it, too.'' I smiled. There was certainly a lot of smiling going on at this lunch.

"Henry seems so happy," I continued. "How long have you known each other?''

"Only about a year—and we only started dating about six months ago, so the whole thing's been rather sudden. But we decided there was no real reason to delay, once we decided to marry. And, of course, I'm pleased he's so crazy about Sandy. He's adopting him, you know.''

"Yes, he told me at the party. What happened to Sandy's father? First father.''

"Killed before he was born. Sandy never knew him.''

"Tragic," I said. "How?''

"How?"

"How was he killed, I mean?" I wondered if I was to be fed a lie and settled my face into an attitude of believing attention.

"Car wreck. South of San Jose, that awful 'Blood Alley' section north of Morgan Hill. You know it?"

"I know it. Scares me to death whenever I'm down that way. Were you living together at the time?"

"No, we had split up."

I wanted to ask the name of the father of her child but couldn't think of any roundabout way to do it, so I just took a deep breath and asked outright, "What was—how long were you and he together? What was his name?"

"What was his name?" She looked at me blankly and then answered only: "We weren't together very long. We never actually lived together. He wanted to get married, but I didn't. By the time I realized I was pregnant, I'd also realized the relationship was—just wasn't what I wanted. So I ended it."

"Then he got killed? What was his name? My husband was killed in a highway accident." Did I dare say on Blood Alley? No. Better not. "I seem to remember reading about an accident down there a couple of years ago," I added, instead, "that reminded me of my husband's. What was his name?"

"Thompson," she said shortly, picked up her fork, and looked at her watch.

We concentrated on our lunches in silence. Mine was nearly gone, anyway. When she finished, I said: "More coffee? Do you have time?"

"I guess. I have a lot of work, but then I always have a lot of work. I don't have any interviews or groups for another hour, but I do have some paperwork I need to get at," she anwsered, looking at her watch again, a rather large, round gold circle with sapphires embedded here and there around the rim. "One more cup."

She signaled to the waiter by lifting her cup in the air and waving it. He came over and poured fresh coffee into both our cups and went away again.

I tried to think what else I should ask her about, since time was running out, but she beat me to it.

"You did feel, then, that Henry and Celia were happily married, didn't you?"

"Well, comfortably, anyway. Yes. No serious disagreements that I know of or anything of that sort."

"Henry's said so little. And I've always felt that second marriages are more successful when the first was a good one—that's why I'm curious. I've waited a long time, and it's very important to me to have a good marriage. I hope you haven't minded my asking you about Henry and Celia, that I haven't made you uncomfortable in any way?"

"No," I replied and wondered what she thought about all the questions—outrageous, some of them—that I'd been asking her. I hoped she'd put it down to simple family curiosity on my part, and perhaps a kind of greedy insensitivity.

She turned the check over, glanced at it casually, and covered it with a twenty and a ten.

I thought I had better set up a future meeting. I hadn't found out very much from this one.

"Henry said I should talk with you about your work—in terms of what I'm doing myself. I don't know if he mentioned it, but I've been taking a lot of art courses the past couple of years, which has been pleasant—but isn't getting me anywhere as far as getting back to work in the real world." (She should like that phrase, I thought; Henry certainly would.) "He suggested I might like the kind of work you do, and I'd like to find out more about it. If you've time, another day? I know how busy you are."

"Why, certainly. Call me and we'll arrange a definite time—at the house would be best; you can come for dinner."

"Thanks, I'd like that," I said untruthfully. When I saw her again I didn't want Henry present. And I didn't want ever to have another dinner in that house if I could help it. "I'll call you. And you can show me your wonderful new studio."

Driving home, thinking over what I had and hadn't found out, I realized I was going to have to get braver about questioning people; pumping them, that was the term. Or forget the detection business.

TWENTY-TWO

THE LUNCH WITH BEATRICE HAD BEEN ON WEDNESDAY. I telephoned Henry at work later that afternoon and told him how much I'd enjoyed visiting with his new wife and asked him for Cook's address. Which I hoped sounded like an unimportant afterthought.

Cook answered the phone on the second ring and gave me some complicated-sounding directions. I put in a call to Mark, but he was in a group session and couldn't come to the phone. Then I went out to dinner with an ex-boyfriend and tried to forget the whole business for a while.

The next day, Thursday, I drove across the red bridge at about one o'clock and headed north on Highway 101. To go and pump what information I could out of Cook.

The city feeling, which just a few years ago stopped on the other side of San Raphael, spreads very far north now, beyond Santa Rosa. I turned off just below Novato, heading east, north, and east again on what is still a lovely zigzag through the fat, round hills of Sonoma County. Big spiraling oak trees, old white dairy farms, peaceful cows of black or brown and white eating the emerald-green grass—these haven't changed much in the past hundred years or so. It would have been hard to believe, out there in the beautiful rural emptiness, that the benefits of civilization were creeping up so close but for the sky. For the skies are grim and smoggy over all the million acres of Sonoma now: Sonoma, the Indians called it, the Valley of the Moon. Its hills and trees, farmhouses and cows waited quietly for the coming transformation: the developers and tract houses and big, blank shopping centers that would make the area as hideous as any of the hundred thousand others that blight the state. They waited quietly, but not peacefully. They could tell something bad was approaching by the way the sky had changed.

I drove through the old stone town of Sonoma, out again through peaceful country lanes, past small rural holdings offering ducks and rabbits and eggs "4 sale." A left turn down a long stretch lined on both sides by tall old eucalyptus trees planted by Spanish settlers as a windbreak. Left again at the next crossroads and right at the first mailbox: yellow, with Hoong newly painted in large black letters. Cook's *ranchito*, California style; Sonoma County style, anyway—a chicken farm.

Up until World War Two there were a lot of Japanese farmers in Sonoma County. People say you could always tell which farms were Japanese because they were the cleanest, shining with fresh paint and order. After Pearl Harbor these first- and second- and third-generation American citizens were rounded up and put in concentration camps. Their farms were bought up for a few cents on the dollar by their Anglo neighbors. I wasn't aware of any Chinese heritage in chicken farming here, though. I hoped Ling So knew something about it because I was pretty sure Cook didn't.

The late lunch Cook had waiting was, predictably, chicken, fried in her special batter that I've loved all my life and never been able to duplicate.

"Maybe you should just open a restaurant," I suggested between mouthfuls.

"Too much work, Mrs. Elliott," Ling So smiled slightly. "Also, we want mainly quiet here. A restaurant," he added seriously, "would be very noisy!"

"That's true." My chair faced the wall with the windows, and out of them I could see a sweep of tall trees, an empty road, a lot of healthy-looking weeds, a couple of goats, and some hills in the far distance. "It's beautiful here, very peaceful and quiet. . . ."

"But still much work to be done. Excuse me, please, I must go now and attend to some." He smiled a prim little smile and left us.

Cook wouldn't let me help her clear the table, so I waited in the living room until she was done, slowly sipping a cup of very good coffee that she said was Mexican and thinking about what I wanted to ask her. The room was full—rather too full—of new looking furniture, lamps, a figured carpet in somber tones of brown and green. I wondered how to start and decided that abruptly was as good a way as any. Considering that Cook had known me all my life and could always tell when I was—as she called it—"down to something." And also considering the skimpy returns I'd got for all my devious pumping—at least I hoped it was devious—of Beatrice.

"I want you to tell me everything you know about the marriage between Celia and Henry, Cook." I began when she had finished clearing up and had sat down at the other end of the new green couch. "Will you do that for me? I'm not just prying, I need to know. I can't tell you why right now, but it won't go any further than me."

I figured O'Reagan didn't exactly count, and anyway, strict truthfulness didn't have any place in the detection business. In any case there were no officials involved, of whom Cook had a jaundiced view in general and a hostile one in particular when it came to those who'd investigated Celia's death. Not that I blamed her for that; so did I.

"What are you down to, Grita? Good, or no good?"

"Good, of course. Please—just trust me?"

I could see her thinking it over, sitting there in her new front room looking at me speculatively with the flat black eyes, and finally making up her mind. She seemed nervous.

"You want to know if there was trouble between them, *sí*?"

"Sí," I answered with relief. "Exactly."

For the first time since I'd known her, Cook was talking mostly English. I wondered if it was her marriage that had caused the change.

"OK. I talk to you first of about one year before the Señora is killed, maybe one year and one half."

She paused and lit a cigarette, puffed awhile in silence, looking out her front window at Sonoma County but seeing scenes in Pacific Heights now three years dead and done with.

"Always Señor Sloan, he works in the week, *verdad*? Then he is home always for the night, and the weekend. Unless they go someplace, *los dos*. And there are many parties in the house; many people come, very fine dinners, always since we come from *Tejas*. And they get along pretty good, Silia and Señor Sloan, no fights, not that I am knowing about. A few fights, of no importance I think, *comprendes*?

"*Entonces, hasta sobre un año antes—* before she is killed, about one year." She smiled apologetically and threw up her hands in a gesture of impatience. "Ling So wish me to speak English now, but I forget sometimes."

"You're doing beautifully. I never heard you talk so much English in my life."

"Thank you. *Entonces*, so, later I hear them making many arguments; it is no longer like before."

"When did this start?"

"About one year before the Señora is killed, or a little more, maybe."

"What were they about, the arguments?"

"This I do not know. I do not listen, you understand. *Pero*, it is changed in the house. We have no so many parties, and the Señora say Señor Sloan has much work; he is all a sudden very busy and many times no *en casa*, not at home. Also, I see sometimes the Señora is crying. And the Señor comes late, many times not for dinner, sometimes no breakfast also. The Señora says he works, but I think, pah! And then no more fights. *En facto hay*, there is, how do you call it *la courtesia*— but the Señora, I know her *los treinta años*, thirty years, she is unhappy. I know."

"What did you think was going on?"

"I will tell you." She said it slowly, reluctantly. "I think there is a woman somewhere." She widened her eyes suddenly and tightened her lips. A look, I knew all too well from my childhood, of extreme disapproval and anger.

"Did you—was there ever anything else? To make you think that? A woman telephoning?"

"I do not answer the phone in that house; I am the cook, *verdad*? I run the house in order, and I do my job good, too, *pero* the Señora is no more happy. She go to parties *sola*, alone."

"You must have just happened to overhear once or twice, Cook, what they were arguing about. How could you help it, being around them so much?"

"Well. Once or twice maybe, I do think the Señora asks him about the woman—"

"What woman?"

"Some woman, who this is I don't hear. Señor Sloan say no, he say no woman, but one, two times, the Señora, she is accusing him."

She paused, and then asked abruptly, "Why you want to know

all this, Grita? You think something is wrong, maybe, with how she is killed? *Como la policia*?"

I wasn't ready to admit to this, but I didn't deny it, either. "I'm wondering about this new marriage of his, for one thing."

"Ah!" she exclaimed, her eyes widening and nostrils dilating in outrage. "This is why I no stay, Grita. When the Señor tell me he marries and they come to live in the house, I tell him no, I do not stay there."

"Why?"

"*Porque*—because, it is in my mind this woman is bad woman—is the one he has been knowing before, maybe."

"You didn't tell him that? Did you?" Cook was sometimes so outspoken it was not unlikely.

"No, no, I say only I no stay. I say I talk it over with Ling So, and it is much work, we are old."

"Was he disappointed?"

"*Como?*"

"I mean, Henry—do you think Dr. Sloan wanted you to stay, or do you think he was glad to have you go?"

"I think he is glad we go, Grita. Because he say right away, no argument, he give us money for retirement. *Màs que* the Señora. *Me siento*, to leave Mark, *pero* he is no in the house, *nunca*, never. *Entonces*, we leave."

She spread her hands wide, the fingers curled at the ends as if the gesture contained the actual body of the story she now considered finished.

"Did you ever hear any talk of divorce?"

She hesitated, then finally answered, as if grudgingly: "*Sí.*"

"You did! When?"

"It is some days, I forget, before the Señora is killed. Three, four days, maybe. She and the Señor are at breakfast; I hear this word, several times."

"Who said it?"

"The Señora, she says it. Like she is surprised, I think. I think she does not wish it."

"You thought at the time that they were talking about divorce for themselves? To end their marriage?"

"*Sí,*" she sighed and looked ready to cry.

"And you thought it was Dr. Sloan who was suggesting divorce, and that Celia wasn't, didn't want it?"

"*Sí,*" She sighed again.

"Did you tell the police that?"

She compressed her lips together into a straight, hard line. "Pah! The fat man? No!"

"Why not?"

"It is not his business, I think."

I would have loved to have seen Simmons' face if he could have heard that!

"OK, now, that day Celia was killed, the day or so before. Can you remember anything else the least little bit unusual? Anything that seemed odd to you, strange, anything you wondered about? Any telephone calls, anything about the mail that morning? Or the day or so before?"

"The letters, *sí*," she murmured, almost to herself, "the day before she is killed; she has her mail in the library always, but on this day she is late having lunch and has the letters with her, with the lunch. And she does not eat her food; *en facto*, she is— how do you say—she is looking sick. Later I remember this, and I think maybe this is how it happens, with the cable car, that she is sick."

"What happened with the letters?"

"Nothing happens. She does not eat the lunch, and she say she is going to the bank and do I want anything? From the store. I say no—only the ducks, from Petrini's, you understand—then she goes."

"The bank, that's interesting. She didn't say anything more?"

"I remember no more, Grita."

"Is there anything else you remember of that time?"

"No, Grita. *Nada màs.*"

"OK. You've been a huge help. Thank you for telling me all this. Will you do me one more favor and talk to Ling So, find out if he knows anything about any trouble between Henry and Celia? I've got to get back to the city, and probably you could ask him better than I could, anyway. Ask him if he knows of any trouble between Henry and Celia. Talk of divorce, arguments, odd times he wasn't home, anything that might indicate another woman in Henry's life."

She hesitated, then finally nodded.

"You're an angel. I'll call you. Tomorrow?"

"*Sí, mañana.* Tomorrow." She smiled tightly.

Outside, Ling So was working in what looked as if it would be a vegetable garden someday. I waved good-bye to him and again to Cook, standing in the door of the neat white farmhouse. A big red sun was sliding down behind one of the round green hills as I turned my car around and headed back to the city, thinking about what Cook had said and wondering how best to approach the next person on my list: Mary P. Lewis, Celia's best friend. The direct approach seemed to work best when the person was friendly. What would Mary P. be? Neutral? Friendly? Hostile?

Divorce! So that was why Celia changed her will the year before. Not cutting Henry off entirely while she waited for him to get over the affair with the other woman. But making sure the children would get the bulk of her money if anything happened to her in the meantime?

TWENTY-THREE

MARY P. LEWIS WAS IN HAWAII, IT TURNED OUT, BUT I HAD some unexpected luck on Union Street on Saturday. I'd just come out of the Body Shop when I heard my name: "Ma-ggie Lin-den!"

There were a lot of people on the sidewalks, and it took another yell, even louder and shriller, if possible, "Gree-ta!" before I spotted her.

"Carlotta!" I jaywalked through the slow-moving Union Street traffic, most of the drivers looking for a place to park so they could join the promenade of shoppers.

"Carlotta!" I repeated, after we'd hugged and looked each other over. What had the past few years done? "What're you doing here? I thought you were strictly Paris and Rome these days—gosh, I'm glad to see you!"

"You look *just* the same, Maggie, exactly. Come on, let's go have some coffee and catch up. *'Sta bueno*?"

"*Sí, amiga, como no?*" I replied in her language, and we walked down a few doors to a sidewalk coffee-and-pastry place. "What great luck to run into you today!"

Carlotta had been Celia's roommate in boarding school and

the first year of college. She was from Mexico City and usually stopped off to visit us in Texas on the way to and from school. Then her family had lost all their money, so she'd left school and gone to work for an interior decorator in Mexico while studying design at night at the University. She'd always been especially fond of me, and I of her.

It was a heaven-sent opportunity to collect information about Celia's marriage to Henry, and perhaps her first one as well. Although they'd had less and less in common as the years passed, Carlotta and Celia had kept in touch. Carlotta eventually ended up channeling her boundless energy, good design sense, and ritzy connections into first one and then a series of small and extremely expensive boutiques. She'd combined the traditional handcrafted Mexican peasant designs, bright, coarse, earthy, with her own highly sophisticated flair for high fashion and come up with a unique line of casual clothes. She charged the earth for them—and got it—and had made herself as rich or richer than her Cherry Orchard family had been to begin with. She'd been copied a lot since, of course, but by now her name on the label was a part of the value.

I hadn't seen her for several years, not since I'd lived in New York. But Celia had mentioned her from time to time, and I saw things about her in *Time* occasionally, or *People*, which I read sometimes while waiting in doctors' offices. She was one of the "Best Dressed" usually, and she had a flair for colorful men, as well as clothes, which kept her in the news off and on.

"What great luck running into you today, Carlotta!" I repeated, after the waiter had brought our order. "There're some things I'm trying to find out about Celia. Not," I added, "that I wouldn't be just ecstatic to see you, anyway—you know that! What are you doing in this poky little town?"

"This poky little town has a lotta money flowing through it, my dear one, and I decided to get my hands on some of it. In other words, I'm opening a shop. I set them up, you know; do a big opening, keep it stocked, but then otherwise leave it with a manager. And collect the money." She smiled happily. "But what is all this about Celia? And Lindy! I was in Nepal after some fabric and didn't hear right away. Then I ran into somebody in Paris we'd known in school who told me. I felt—sick. Sick."

"I know. It made me sick, too, especially about Lindy. And

the police thought for a while maybe one of us had murdered Celia. That was sickening enough."

"Oh, yes? How horrible! We'd grown apart in very many ways, but—Celia was always a very good friend to me. I miss her," she added simply. "She had one quality I do not find much, you know? I know you two weren't close. She had loyalty, though. She had loyalty for me, and she had it for you always, also. Did you—but I don't mean to read you a lecture. Only to say I have . . . I have felt her loss, very much. The daughter I didn't know, never much, so that was more generally sad, if you know what I mean. But Celia—a *cable* car; it's crazy!"

I knew what she said was true about Celia's loyalty. It was something that I hadn't given her much credit for, either, I thought, remembering the yearly Christmas presents and her persistence in keeping in some sort of touch with me despite my rebuffs. Arrogance . . .

"In a way, Carlotta," I said slowly, "in a way I'm just starting to get to know Celia now. Or trying to. Did you know Henry very well?"

"No—I was at their wedding—which, since she'd been married before, was very quiet, you remember—and I sometimes stayed with them here in San Francisco, but not for very long, ever; a day or so, that's all. And we saw each other in Mexico several times, although usually they stayed in a hotel, which Henry preferred. So, although I've known him these twenty years, I have never really *known* him. Only that Celia was crazy about him always. Why is it that you are asking?"

I took a deep breath. "Well—" I took another deep breath. Was I going to say that I was trying to find out if Henry had murdered Celia? And possibly her daughter as well (along with a random load of airplane passengers)? I didn't feel ready for that yet, even with Carlotta. Not in so many words. I couldn't. I took another deep breath; I'd just have to waffle around as best I could.

"Well," I repeated. "I can't really say why in so many words, Carlotta. It's just—I've developed a peculiar curiosity about their marriage. When I see where that leads, maybe there'll be more to say; I don't know. Sounds crazy, huh? Probably is. Will you tell me what you know about it and just leave the why aside? For now?"

"All right, *chica*. As you wish. For *now*," she added sternly.

"You have made me most curious, though. What is it you want to know, exactly? I will warn you, I don't think I know much about it."

I decided to start with the most recent past first and work backwards to the part which she should know more about than anyone else. Except Henry, of course, and I could hardly ask him.

"Well, in general, what did you think of their marriage? And in particular, did you happen to see them in the last year or so before Celia died? And if so, did you get any sense of . . . trouble between them?"

"OK, let me think. In general I thought the marriage was pretty good—but also boring. That's what I mostly thought, although sometimes"—she made a grimace, turned the still lovely mouth down at one corner and shrugged her shoulders—"sometimes I admit I envied her that boring situation. Myself, I have married *several* times, you know? Occasionally I think my life could stand to be a little more boring, you know? But mostly not really! Anyway. Celia was in love with Henry from the time she met him until—the end, as far as I know. I'm not so sure about Henry."

"What do you mean?" I asked quickly.

"Oh, nothing special, nothing . . ." She gave me a look that seemed half amusement, half disbelief. "Nothing . . . sinister, if that's what you're getting at. Only he seemed always rather . . . cold, you know. It was so easy to imagine him with his patients, the expensive leather couch, nodding his head and never saying anything—very Freudian!" She made an expression of distaste. "The Yankee phlegmatic thing, or the German. It would be hard to imagine Henry wildly in love, for instance."

"Well, you should see him now—he's just remarried."

"So? And is truly in love? Poor Celia! Although," she continued thoughtfully, "that stiff-board quality of his was part of his appeal for her, I think. The father kind of thing. She was a little scatterbrained, you know, and in that stiffness of his was a lot of the—the stability she wanted, you know? Anyway, who has he married?"

"Nobody you'd know. Someone from work. Don't get me started on her; I can't stand her. I'll tell you what I know about her later, if you want, but for now, stay on this—have you got time, or do you need to be somewhere?"

"Actually"—she glanced down at a very small watch surrounded by a lot of not-so-small diamonds and sapphires—"I was just on the way to having my hair done for my big to-do tonight." She felt around her head, more sapphires and diamonds flashing on the slim fingers, along with some rubies. "I can fix it myself, though, and the poor hairdresser will be relieved—he was just going to squeeze me in." The superbly cut and shining fall of dark red-brown showed not the slightest need for attention. "Or I'll wear a cloche. I'm meeting someone for dinner at six, though, so we'll have only an hour. Will that do? Do you want to have dinner with us? Do you want to come to the opening?"

"No, thanks—I hate all that social stuff. I like being asked, though. But back to Celia and Henry. Did you see any signs of trouble between them, say in the last year or so?"

"I didn't see them in that time, unfortunately. I was in Rome most of that year, still married to Guido. . . ." She looked wistful for a moment. Guido was a gorgeous and successful Italian movie star, a good deal younger than Carlotta. She smoothed her hair and continued: "But sometime in there, Celia did write. It took a long time getting to me; it went to Mexico first. I didn't get around to answering, and then I heard she was dead. But she did sound a bit unhappy. Something about that decorator of hers, but I thought it was mostly Henry. Some change in his work she seemed upset about, though she didn't come right out and say so. She would never actually complain about anything he did, not even to me! I had the idea he didn't have much time for her."

"Yes—he changed from his private practice to some clinic and apparently started being away from home a lot."

"Oh? That could be a woman, only knowing Henry, it probably was just work," she said contemptuously. "Although if he *were* to fall in love . . . he might be very foolish. Yes. I knew a man like him once who—but that does *not* apply. What else can I tell you?"

"How about when Celia was first married? Married the first time, I mean. And had Mark, and then Lindy, and then her husband ran off and left her—did you see her much then?"

"Let's see . . . that was when I was back in Mexico. And for the first time working. Very hard, also going to school and very determined, I remember"—she smiled gently, remembering that young Carlotta—"determined to make a big success of something. How I hated being poor! And hated the way my father's—but that's nothing to do with this and is finished now. . . .

"Back to your question, the first marriage, let me see. She eloped, so there was no big wedding for me to be maid of honor; I was annoyed about that! I only saw that husband twice, I think, a couple of times when he was playing tennis in Cuernavaca. All the women were crazy over him. Do you remember him at all? He was *very* handsome in those days. Dark, very seductive . . . I saw him around in Europe years later, but he was old then; he'd gained weight and was puffy from too many parties. But when he was with Celia, I didn't see her much then. I was too busy. Except the odd weekend or so in Cuernavaca as I said. I didn't see the children until later . . . it was so horrible about Lindy."

"Yes."

I signaled the waiter and asked for a glass of water; I had a headache and wanted to take an aspirin. Carlotta nodded yes to more espresso. I waited for the waiter to bring our order and go away again.

"Did Celia ever tell you that she and Henry didn't have children because he couldn't have any?" I asked abruptly when he had gone. The hour Carlotta had said she could spend with me was over half gone.

"We—el," she said, considering, "I suppose she did, more or less."

"When was that?"

"After they'd been married a few years, three or four, I think. I'd opened my first shop, and the line was doing quite well. Celia came down one Christmas with the children and spent several weeks in my house in Zihuatanejo. That town is ruined now—excrement! It was so lovely then. . . . She stayed in my house; I came down for several weekends—we had some good visits. She said that was the one disappointment in the marriage, not having more children, Henry's children."

"But it was definitely Henry who couldn't have the children, and not her?"

"Oh, yes; at least, that was the impression I got. I never questioned it. I was surprised in a way, because I knew she'd had a difficult pregnancy with Lindy and had been warned then not to have any more children."

"She was? Specifically told not to? I never knew that. How did you know?"

"She'd written, I think; I didn't see her then, but we kept in touch with letters. She was very depressed. The marriage—the first one—was falling to pieces, and she was so very sick most of the time she was pregnant. Then she had the two baby children on her hands, alone. I remember feeling glad I hadn't married! The husband was gone, running around with other women most of the time. Then he ran off with that Zenia Drummond; I knew her later, too. She's dead now. . . ."

"I never realized she was so unhappy and . . . and badly treated then. No wonder she fell for Henry, after Bobby Taft! But I didn't mean to interrupt; go on. About Mexico. That Christmas."

"There isn't any more. I remember being surprised and saying something about the fact that I'd thought she wasn't supposed to have more children, anyway, and I think she said something like, no, that's all right; they were mistaken, or something like that. That there had never been anything really wrong; it as just her being so upset over the marriage.

"We had a lovely visit—Henry had gone back by then. And you know Celia was always so elaborate! I remember one day she arranged for servants and a huge fancy picnic and burros, of all things. We made the expedition over the mountain to the beach on the other side. It was a beautiful day we had. . . ."

"That's a magical beach, or was—what's it called?"

"Mahagua. Mahagua. That wonderful big tree. God, it was lovely in those days. There's a road there now, not to mention the freeway all around the town. It's *horrible*."

"I'd heard that. It must be ten years since I was there. Ah, well," I smiled, "by the time I hear of a place it's probably on it's way out, anyway." A horn blared, then others joined in; I noticed the street was starting to get that end-of-the-day, not-enough-time-left feeling.

"How's the time?"

"Lord!" She looked at the outlandish watch again. "Almost six! I'll be late again—that makes him so annoyed with me!"

"My car's just around the corner—I'll drop you off. Where?"

"The Huntington; I always stay there. That would be a huge help, Grita." She put a handful of dollar bills on the table. *"Vamanos!"*

The traffic is bad that time of day in that part of town, though we hadn't far to go.

"What was that you said," I asked after we got started, "about Celia's decorator—Dunbar Oates? You said her letter to you said something about him' That she was upset with him?"

"It was something about a picture; let me see." She gazed unseeingly out the front window, thinking back. "A painting— an expensive one—very. Celia thought he cheated her with it, that it was a fake and that he knew all along. . . ."

"Did she know this for certain?"

"She was still checking—but she was sure, if you know what I mean."

"Was it a Renoir, do you know? Supposedly?"

"I think perhaps; I'm not sure. . . . She was very angry, though—Ah! Here we are! *Gracias infinitas,* dear one. Come and visit me in Rome?"

"Lovely—maybe, " I smiled. "Do you still have that letter? Did Celia seem upset about anything else?"

"I don't think so—I'll be home in a few days—I'll send it—I *must* go," she said hurriedly as she opened the door. "Good-bye darling." We smiled, touched cheeks, and she got out.

Carlotta is nothing if not conspicuous, and my old Karmann Ghia, dented and battered, is also rather noticeable, especially on Nob Hill amongst the shining new Mercedes and Cadillacs.

And both the car and Carlotta were noticed, unfortunately, by Henry and Beatrice—all dressed up and walking up the sidewalk toward the Huntington entrance and Carlotta.

I waved but kept going. In the rear-view mirror I saw Carlotta stop and say something, shake hands with Beatrice, then rush in ahead of them.

Oh, well, I thought, perfectly natural for me to see Carlotta, and they can't know what we were talking about, after all.

When I got home the phone was ringing. It was Mary P. Lewis back from Hawaii.

"I was lucky and caught Henry at home this afternoon," she said, "and got your number—I lost the message you'd called that had it on, and you're not in the book. I'm going right back to Maui tomorrow so things are in a jumble, but I thought it might be important?"

As well she might, considering the fact that I hadn't seen or talked to her since meeting her at Celia's house just after Lindy's memorial. As well Henry might, if he thought about it. Combined with Cook and Carlotta.

Most of the questions I wanted to ask Mary P. I could ask only in person. Questions such as had Celia talked to her about any troubles with Henry, the idea he was seeing someone else, the possibility of divorce, etcetera. They had, after all, been best friends.

"Could I stop by and see you for a few minutes before you go off again? It's important."

"No, darling, I'm sorry—I honestly don't have a free minute. I'll be back again in a week, though—how about that?"

There was one question that I could ask on the phone: "All right. But tell me—did Celia say anything to you about her Renoir being a fake? And that she thought Dunbar deliberately cheated her?"

"How on earth did you get on to that, after all this time? She did think so—and she was right, as a matter of fact, about the painting. But not about Dunbar; he was taken in himself, poor lamb. I felt *so* sorry for him; he thought the world of Celia, you know. But after she was killed we had a talk with Henry. He agreed to drop any notion of prosecuting if the people really responsible gave back the money. He did get back most of it, I believe. . . ."

"What happened to the painting?"

"The people in France took it back—protesting their innocence, but who knows? Anyway, it was all settled, finally, to everyone's satisfaction. Why?"

"I just wondered. I'll come see you in a week. Thanks."

TWENTY-FOUR

USUALLY ONLY WENT TO THE CITY HOSPITAL AA MEETING
I was in charge of once a month. But I went the following Tuesday, thinking it would be a good opportunity to see Mark. I'd been calling and missing him all week.

He was sitting again in the foyer across from the elevator. Sitting there with him was the wreck of a beautiful woman. She was older than I'd thought at first glance, I decided, when I got closer.

"How do you do," she said politely in a bored voice, not looking at me. The sentence sounded like it would continue on to something more important, only it didn't. Her eyes, cornflower blue and bloodshot, kept wandering all around the area, down the hall, across the ceiling, and over the scruffy, dark green floor; restless, but she herself sat perfectly still. As if she were waiting for something terrible to happen but didn't know from what direction it might come.

"She just got here today," Mark said in explanation.

A very tall, very thin drunk—the wino kind, the kind you see on skid row—shuffled down the long hallway and came to rest nearby. "Say, haven't I seen you somewhere before?" he asked.

He seemed to be addressing the question to Mark, whose face suddenly turned so white I was reminded of the way he'd looked when I'd told him his mother was dead.

"I don't know what you're talking about; you must be crazy," he mumbled at the old drunk, not looking at him. Then he turned and hobbled off down the hall without looking back.

The wino shrugged his thin shoulders, leered weakly at the beautiful, ravaged woman, and then the watery gaze settled on me. He looked me up and down in an exaggerated way that would have been annoying except that it was so pathetic. The ruins of a great ladies' man, perhaps—but the ruins were in such

165

an advanced state it was hard to tell. He was wearing a beige raincoat—perhaps in its better days the proud possession of some British spy—and it hung open loosely, flapping around the bony, sockless ankles as if upon a scarecrow in some dusty cornfield. His hands were in the pockets, and he stood there swaying in posed nonchalance. I felt some alarm that he might just topple over any minute.

"I'd never forget *your* face, honey, and that's the truth," he whined on. "Haven't I seen you somewhere before? It's them eyes—" He started to sing tunelessly:

> *I fell in love with you*
> *first time I looked into*
> *them there eyes*

but then gave it up and broke back into speech. "I just know I've seen you somewhere," he repeated and stretched his mouth into the form of a smile that might once have had great charm. In fact, I could see the dim remains of a certain spirit lurking behind the sparse and rotting teeth.

"I mean it. You're from Frisco, ain't you? I know I've seen you . . . seen them eyes for sure. . . ." His voice trailed off, but he looked prepared to stay the evening, swaying to and fro there in his raincoat.

"I don't know," I answered. "I don't remember seeing you. Do you ever go to AA? You might have seen me there."

"Naw," he answered, "I tried it. It doesn't work."

"Oh, well," I said, "otherwise I don't think I've seen you."

"Lay lady lay," suddenly contributed the woman with the wandering, bloodshot eyes. "If you're desperate enough . . ." She muttered on, but her voice got so low I couldn't hear the rest.

The old wino, still mumbling ". . . sure I've seen that gal before . . ." turned and tottered off down the hall, back to wherever he'd come from. After he'd gone, Mark rejoined us.

"Sorry," he said, "that guy gives me the creeps for some reason. You here for the meeting?"

"That, and to see you. You're looking better."

"Yeah, well"—he shrugged his shoulders and looked down at his clothes, expensively faded dungarees and a navy blue Shetland sweater—"Henry and Beatrice came by a little while ago and brought me some stuff to wear. I still have a lot of things at the house, I guess.''

"That was nice. It's more than the clothes, though.''

People, mostly men, were coming down the hall from both directions now, heading toward the conference room.

"The meeting will be starting. I need to talk to you afterwards, OK? Are you going to be staying on here?''

"I don't know; they haven't decided.''

"Man," the girl in the chair interjected suddenly. "Man, seen you before—I'm psychic, you know,'' she added conversationally, making the blue eyes huge and pulling her lips back, baring stained yellow teeth. "I'm a witch, a wicked, enor-mous witch, did you know?''

The beautiful but bloodshot eyes were pointed at Mark, although I doubt she saw anything much beyond her own internal process.

"Yeah," he answered, "I can always tell you witches. In fact, I was in love with one of you guys once. But it didn't work out. You better get on to the meeting, Aunt.''

"You're right. I'll see you after—I really do need to talk to you.''

At the end of the meeting I stayed on talking to a guy I knew who'd come from outside, Welfare Jerry—as opposed to Wall Street Jerry, Crazy Jerry, and Jerry of Jerry and Rita. People get these labels in AA because we don't use last names. In this case, the label referred to the fact that he worked for Welfare, not that he was on it. As many are when they first get sober. Only it was called SSI now, sounding like some Nazi secret police group.

"What're you doing at this meeting?'' I asked.

"I might take one of these hospital meetings—so I came along to see what they're like. This looks like it would be a hard one to do,'' he replied.

"It is. They'd be better if they were set up so more people from outside the hospital came. In my opinion. I've got the second Tuesday.''

"What're you doing here tonight then?''

"My nephew's here—drying out—and I wanted to see him.''

There were a bunch of people standing around the elevator when we got out there: the AA secretary and the speaker; the man in charge of the Hospital and Institution meetings and a few people he'd brought; and five or six of the resident alcoholics.

They were two more or less distinct groups, the outsiders and the insiders, and nobody was saying anything. The outsiders didn't look like they were getting ready to leave, though—a couple of them were sitting in the chairs over in the foyer.

One of the counselors, a soft-spoken, good-looking black guy named Jim, was standing in front of the elevator doors.

"What's the matter?" Welfare Jerry asked. "Aren't the elevators working?"

"There are some stairs. . . ." I said.

"No stairs, Maggie," Jim said quickly. "Nobody's supposed to leave; we've had some trouble. I called the police."

"The police!" Welfare Jerry yelped. "What happened?"

"The police!" I echoed. "What happened?"

"One of the patients got hurt. The cop I talked to said, quote, don't talk about it; just keep everybody there till we get there unquote. I'm sorry, but it won't be long. Maybe."

I felt a sudden leap of alarm that it might be Mark, but Jim had headed back to the office so I couldn't ask. Subdued reactions were coming out now in low voices.

"I got a busy day tomorra. . . ."

"What's it got to do with me is what I wanna know. . . ."

"Shouldn't have come to this fucking meeting. . . ."

Nobody seemed to be listening to anyone else.

Finally, the elevator doors opened, and several uniformed policemen hurried out, all bustle. Jim introduced himself, and they all went back into the office, which was a three-desk affair and pretty big.

One of the cops came back out after a few minutes and said for us to wait a little longer and then somebody would be talking to us. He told us to go down to the lounge at the end of the hall and shooed us down there like a bunch of chickens—grumbling chickens. I was glad, though; I'd rather wait sitting down than standing up any day, and the big stuffed chairs in there are pretty comfortable, even if they are hideous. On the wall near the chair I sat down in was a mock college banner made out of red felt, with "The College of Experience" diminishing down from tall to short in white letters across its long, triangular surface.

"I get tired of all this experience, sometimes," I said to Welfare Jerry, nodding to the pennant.

We sat for what seemed a long time but was actually only about twenty minutes. There was a big clock on the wall that jumped a minute at a time, its second hand unmoving on the nine. I could see down the hall from where I sat. After a while some men who looked like plainclothes policemen got off the elevator, and then some others arrived, carrying equipment of various sorts—fingerprints, I supposed, medical stuff and photographers and all the other things I'd read about in murder fiction. Whoever had been hurt must have been hurt to death, I decided, judging by the hardware. I saw no sign of Mark and continued to feel apprehensive.

Finally, one of the plainclothes cops came down the hall and looked around the room, his eyes skipping over the other two women in the room who were new arrivals at the de-tox and looked it, and settled on me.

"You Elliott?"

"Yes."

"You first, then. Come with me."

I got up and followed him down the hall, thinking, why me? and still wondering what it was all about.

What it was all about was the tall thin drunk, the would-be debonair spy-cum-ladies man, that deteriorated hulk, who had for some reason—or possibly no reason, in a place like this— been stabbed to death.

Twice, in the back, with a hospital kitchen knife left sticking out through the ancient trench coat. They thought the first stab had done the job and the second was just to make sure, which the autopsy later confirmed. I wasn't told most of this at the time, though. They wanted to get their questions answered, not answer mine. The reason they had picked on me to start was that Jim the counselor had noticed me and Mark and the witch talking with the murdered man before the AA meeting. And so far nobody had admitted to seeing or talking to him since. I felt a huge relief that it wasn't Mark who was dead.

One of the plainclothes policemen said: "Jim here says the four of you was talking before the AA meeting: that right?"

"Sort of," I said.

"Know him before?"

"No. I don't think so. What happened was, we were sitting there, the three of us—"

"Which three?"

"How about if I just start from the beginning, OK?"

"OK. Shoot."

"I came up here for the meeting a little early to see my nephew, Mark Sloan. When I got off the elevator—"

"He's a patient here? The nephew?"

"Yes."

"OK, then what?"

"Well, then I walked off the elevator, and Mark was sitting across from it, in that little foyer with this wi—with this woman who he said just came in today to dry out."

The policeman looked at some notes he had on the desk. "That would be Mary Lee Colony, according to Jim here."

"I never knew her name. Anyway, Mark and I said hello, I can't remember what exactly . . . I said he looked better; he said his father and stepmother brought some clothes by for him earlier. Then this emaciated skid-row type, the one who got killed, I guess—what was his name, anyway?"

"Gentleman Malone they have him down for; that's the name he gave. Go on."

"He was coming down the hall—"

"Which way was he coming from?"

"From down the hall where the AA meeting was, not this one—"

"The hall going back to his room, right?" the cop interrupted, asking Jim.

"That's right."

"OK, go on now," the cop said, his attention back on me.

"Well, he said something corny, like, 'Haven't I seen you somewhere,' sort of to all of us, and then he seemed to settle on me—"

"And had you seen him before?"

"No. Not that I remember, anyway."

"He said that to everybody," Jim interjected. "He was always saying that. To women, especially. But not exclusively."

"Then what?" the cop asked.

"Well, that's about all. Haven't I seen you somewhere and leering at me and standing there kind of swaying—he looked in pretty bad shape. And I said, just to be silly, I said something about that I go to a lot of AA meetings and maybe he'd seen me there. He said he tried AA and it doesn't work. Then he wandered off down the hall again. The witch started mumbling some crazy stuff. Then he wandered off."

"The witch?"

"The woman we were sitting with—Mary Lou?"

"Mary Lee. She started talking to him?"

"Not to him especially."

"Well, what was it about?"

"Something about men, and then she said she was a witch, and Mark pointed out that I'd be late to the meeting, so I got up and left."

"That's how she's listed on the intake, officer," Jim volunteered.

The cop turned in his chair toward Jim and looked irritated, as if he didn't want information when he hadn't asked for it.

"Yeah?" he queried in a somewhat menacing tone.

"Mary Lee Colony, it says here," Jim insisted, waving a printed form with handwriting on it—purple handwriting. "I got the intake out. I thought you might want to see it. That's what it says here. Occupation: witch." He grinned.

"Wonderful," said the policeman, sounding tired; he turned to me again.

"OK, Mrs. Elliott. Then the drunk, Malone, went off?"

"Yes."

"Which way?"

"Back up the hall the way he'd come."

"Toward his room that would be. You didn't see him again?"

"No."

"Then you went to the meeting and were there until it was over?"

"Yes. No. I left the meeting for a few minutes to go to the ladies' room—there's one just down that same hall, at the end."

"When was this? Beginning of the meeting? End?"

"Beginning. I was only gone a few minutes."

"OK, we can check that with the others. See anybody in the hall, or down at that end? Coming or going?"

I stopped to think. "I wasn't noticing particularly. Most everybody was in the meeting tonight. For a change. Let's see." I put my mind back to leaving the meeting, going down the hall. "There was an orderly or something; he was walking down the hall that that hall butts into."

"Which way?"

"He was walking away from the part to the left, down in the other direction, toward the end with the windows. His back was to me. He was just walking off down that way, and I went on back to the AA meeting. I didn't see anyone else. Except I remember looking way down to the end of this hall and seeing that there were several guys in the lounge, watching TV.''

''Would you know which ones?''

''No.''

''What did he look like, this orderly? Describe him.''

''As I said, I wasn't really paying attention . . . he had black hair . . .'' I put my mind back to the garishly lit corridor and tried to visualize the figure I'd seen. ''He had on a uniform, white, a smock, over some white pants, white shoes. Black hair, fairly long.''

''How long?''

''Almost shoulder-length, about the same as mine.''

''Straight? Curly? Fine? Coarse?''

''Well, coarse. And not superstraight, but not really curly, either.''

''Know who that might be?'' he asked Jim.

''Not offhand. Could be some cleaning or maintenance person, I guess. But mostly, the people who work on de-tox don't wear hospital clothes. They're trying to make it more like what's called a social-setting de-tox, which is a new—''

''Yeah, OK,'' the cop interrupted. ''Now, Mrs. Elliott. How tall was this man? Short? Tall?''

''Medium. About my height, maybe—five seven or a little taller. But that's just a guess; he wasn't especially short and he wasn't especially tall.''

''Thin? Heavy?''

''Well, medium again. On the thin side, maybe. I really wasn't looking, and with that smock thing and baggy pants . . .''

''Think you could identify this individual if you saw him again?''

''No,'' I answered decidedly. ''At the most, I could maybe say that it could—or could not—be him. I think he wore glasses, though.''

''What d'ya mean you *think* he wore glasses? Did he or didn't he?''

''Well, I'm trying to see him in my mind. It's not very clear, but I have the impression—that there were glasses. Its just a vague impression. Dark rims.''

"OK. Anything else about this guy?"

"No."

"Now. When the three of you were talking. Your nephew"
—he glanced at his notes again—"Mark Sloan, and this patient,
Mary Lee Colony. When'd she come in, anyway?" he asked
Jim.

"Today, just this afternoon."

"And Malone?"

"He came in this morning."

"Any idea they knew each other?"

"I have no reason to think so."

"How about you, Mrs. Elliott? Were they talking to each
other?"

"No, not especially. He started out sort of talking to all three
of us, but then he seemed to settle on me, as I said. And she
wasn't talking to anybody, really—it was just gibberish. She'd
have been the same no matter who was there, I think; it was all
internal. I mean, having to do with the inside of her own head."

"Lotta pills involved in her case, officer," Jim interjected.
"She's still way out there. I doubt you'll get any sense out of
her."

"I'll have to have a go at it, anyway. When d'ya think she'll
be back down?"

"Couple, three days, I'd say."

"By that time it probably won't be my job, thank God! I hate
these weirdos—they never make any sense! OK, Mrs. Elliott,
thank you. We'll get this typed up"—he gestured toward a silent
man in the corner who'd been operating a tape machine, which
they'd gotten my permission to use before we started—"and we'll
ask you to come down and sign it tomorrow sometime. Someone
will call you."

"Come down where?"

"Headquarters. Eight-fifty Bryant."

"Can I go now?"

"You can go home, but we may need you again, so don't take
any long trips, huh?"

"All right."

"And don't talk to any of the others on your way out."

"I wanted to talk to my nephew tonight—couldn't I just talk
to him?"

"Not tonight," he said firmly. "Sorry." He didn't sound sorry. "If you think of anything else—about this orderly you saw, or whatever—give us a call, huh?"

"All right. What's your name? I know you told me, but I forgot."

"Hadley. But I don't know who'll be taking this case. I'm here tonight because I was on tonight, but I'm due for a vacation. If you want to call, here's the number." He took a business card out of his jacket pocket and handed it to me. "Just tell them it's regarding the stabbing in the de-tox. They'll know who to connect you with. And thanks for your help."

I almost said, "Thank *you.*" I was pretty tired by then and disappointed not to be able to talk to Mark. I said good-night and went directly home. My report hadn't been exactly accurate, I reflected, but I figured Mark had enough problems without his rather peculiar reaction to Malone being noted. Hopefully he wouldn't say anything about it, either—and it was pretty certain that Mary Lee Colony couldn't.

Even though I was tired, I was wide awake but in that state of mind where thinking is a bad idea because it's bad thinking, unproductive, circular. An hour or so of Agatha Christie and some herb tea, a blend I'd concocted that's almost as good as Tuinal, finally got me off to sleep. To dream of rain, a cold, heavy rain, and fog. I'd loaned my raincoat to someone who hadn't given it back, and I just *had* to have it. I tried and tried to remember who it was, but I couldn't. There was a big pond—the water was a nasty-looking yellow-brown, the way it is after a big rain sometimes. A giant turtle was swimming around in it, and somehow I knew it was a snapping turtle. Then it turned into a snake, a black one, thin and poisonous.

TWENTY-FIVE

I CALLED O'REAGAN THE FIRST THING THE NEXT DAY, BUT HE wasn't at his shop and he wasn't at home, either, so I left a message with the answering service. I'd talked to him after my lunch with Beatrice, but I hadn't told him yet what I'd leaned from Cook and Carlotta. And I wanted to tell him about the stabbing at the de-tox.

While I was finishing my breakfast about ten, having slept late, the phone rang. I hoped it would be O'Reagan, but it wasn't. It was the police. They told me to come by sometime and sign that statement. I agreed to come at the end of the day, after my clay workshop up at Fort Mason.

As I was going out the door, the phone rang again, so I ran back upstairs. It was O'Reagan that time; he offered to meet me at the police station and take me out to dinner.

Fort Mason is a collection of big white buildings on the bay on the north side of town, just east of the Golden Gate Bridge and the Marina. It used to be an army base but recently was made into a National Recreation Area, its buildings used for various things like theater, ecology, and so forth. Building 310 houses a big public art center—although the passage of an anti-property-tax bill had made its future doubtful. It was still going strong then, though, and I usually fired the clay parts of my sculptures there.

I got up to the studio about eleven, early enough to get about half the pieces I was firing—four heads and assorted limbs—into the first kiln load. In the four hours or so I had to wait until they were ready to be pulled out, I threw a half dozen cups and some plates. As I worked, completely engrossed first in making the forms, then in the mandala designs I applied with the colored slips I was experimenting with then, I forgot all about Celia,

175

Gentleman Malone, Mark, O'Reagan, Henry. It was a rest my head badly needed.

Finally, when I peered through the tiny hole in the kiln door, I found the pieces were ready to be pulled; literally red-hot, with the glazed parts slick and shiny as the liquid fire they were. Another potter and I got asbestos gloves and long metal tongs. A beginning student, also asbestos-gloved, held open the kiln door for us while we pulled out the fiery pieces one by one, quickly carrying them outside to the waiting newspaper-filled garbage cans. Two more asbestos-gloved potters opened the lids and then quickly closed them once each piece was safely inside, where the burning newspapers were busy using up all the available oxygen. This turns all the clay that's not glazed a dark black and is the main reason I like to use this particular method, called raku firing, for the clay parts of my sculptures.

We reloaded the kiln and I got the rest of my pieces in. We only had to wait about half an hour this time, as the kiln was already red-hot. We pulled that load, and by then my pieces in the garbage cans had cooled enough to be pulled out with the long tongs and dumped into water-filled buckets, where they cooled down enough to be handled. I scrubbed away the excess carbon and dried them off, well pleased with how they'd turned out. One of them, I saw to my own surprise—mostly black now except for a few small glazed areas in iridescent silvers and greens—looked quite a lot like Beatrice. I packed them up—the one I was starting to call in my own mind "The Fortune Hunter" along with the others—and put them in my car.

I still had an hour or so before I was due at the police station and I didn't feel like starting anything new, so I walked up behind the buildings to the big hill above the bay to watch the sea gulls fishing for their dinners and the pelicans, large and awkward and prehistoric-looking, making their incredible crash-landing dives into the water. Big ships were coming in and going out the Golden Gate, and small white ferryboats were going back and forth to Sausalito and Tiburon, all very slow and stately and peaceful from up there on high.

I thought about Gentleman Malone and wondered who had stabbed him, and why. West Virginia was given as his place of birth on the form. He'd come a long way from West Virginia, all downhill. I wondered if the witch had done it; she hadn't been at the meeting, and she was crazy and spacey enough. But probably not. She was *so* crazy and spacey, she'd most likely have been found wandering around still holding onto the knife, if she had.

Hadley hadn't told me much about what had happened, but he had asked if I'd seen any kitchen knives around the de-tox anywhere—to which I'd replied in the negative—and later he'd said that was what Malone had been stabbed with. An easy weapon to get hold of there, apparently—and impossible to pin down to anyone in particular. A logical choice, too—mostly those guys don't have anything but the clothes on their backs by the time they get to City Hospital.

It was comfortable, sitting there on the hill in the sunshine, looking at the birds and the boats, the blue water and the green hills beyond it, and thinking rather idly about the stabbing the night before. When I thought to look at my watch, it was almost five o'clock—which meant I'd be late.

When I got down to the police station, O'Reagan was already there, sitting in a waiting area. I suddenly felt very much better in that cold stone building for his big, solid presence.

"Sorry," I said. "I'm late for no good reason, but I hope this won't take long. Where do I go?"

He looked up from a tattered *Newsweek* with a welcoming smile and nodded toward the desk. The cop there said to come with him, after I told him what I was there for, and took me down a hallway to a small, windowless room with a couple of straight-back, gray-metal chairs and a small table. After a few minutes, the quiet cop who'd originally recorded my statement brought it in.

"Read it over first, then sign it here in front of me. There has to be a witness."

I skimmed through the pages quickly, hurrying because O'Reagan was waiting. It all seemed all right, so I signed it, and the cop signed below and dated it. We both had to sign several times.

"That place gives me the creeps," I said to O'Reagan after we were seated in one of the huge booths at the Far East Cafe, in Chinatown. The walls of the booths go almost to the ceiling, and you enter through a wall with a curtain for a door, so they are really more like small private rooms. The waiter had gone away with our order, came back with tea, and gone away again.

"Brr. It was very cheering to find you sitting there—a friend amidst the frozen wastes, or something." I smiled across at his tough, friendly face.

"Bryant Street?" He smiled, too, more sardonically. "I don't think it was ever intended to make anyone feel comfortable. How would you design it, then? Remembering its purpose?"

"Umm. Lots of light, I think. I don't know. How are you?"

He started to say something but changed his mind, picked up a cigarette and lit it, instead. "Can't complain," he finally answered. "How about you? You're looking pretty good. Considering everything."

"I've had a nice day with clay and firing some sculptures. Tea?" He nodded, and I filled the two thick, handleless white cups.

"So tell me about this latest murder you've gotten yourself mixed up in," he demanded when I'd finished.

"Mixed up in?"

"Well?"

"Mixed up in. But then I want to tell you what Cook said, and Mark, and an old friend of Celia's I ran into, Carlotta—and Mary P. Lewis on the telephone."

"Sure. On this murder, though, you seem to have been the star witness. How come? Who was this guy, anyway?"

"I don't know. He called himself Gentleman Malone, and he was from West Virginia. Although it was a long time ago, I imagine, that he was from anywhere but skid row. Anyway, I was the star witness, as you put it, because I was talking to Mark and this woman who calls herself a witch"—I smiled, but he didn't smile back—"before the AA meeting. I was planning to have a talk with Mark by himself afterwards. We three were talking, and this guy Malone came over and went through a number about hadn't he seen me before—later the counselor said he said that to everybody. Hadn't he seen me before, where'd I get them eyes—only it wasn't obnoxious because he was just pathetic. Skin and bones, and he had on this old spy raincoat, and he was—"

"Raincoat!"

O'Reagan had been slouched back in his seat idly sipping tea, but at the mention of that raincoat he sat up straight, looked at the cup he was holding suspended in midair, put it down, and leaned forward. His gray eyes, usually lazy and a little sarcastic-looking—as if somewhere he was laughing, at you or at some-thing—now glittered.

"Raincoat!" he repeated. "What did he look like?"

"Tall, six feet at least, very thin. Uh, high cheekbones, skimpy hair, dark with some gray, lank. Dark brown eyes, black they looked, sort of pointed eyebrows, thin eyebrows . . ."

"How old?"

"Oh, skid-row old, maybe only about sixty, but a very old sixty."

"And the raincoat?"

"Really old, too—it looked like he never took it off, and I guess he didn't; he was wearing it inside the hospital. That spy style, trench coat, you know, that goes with British spies and black Jaguars, or the Berlin Wall. Dirty, beige, a couple of those, how do you call them, brown, round leather buttons—that's probably one reason he had it hanging loose; most of the buttons were gone. Those extra strap things on the shoulders and, uh, lower sleeves; that's about it. No belt, but it was the kind that had a belt, once."

He sat there, thinking, and I sat there waiting for him to tell me what it was all about.

"I have to make a trip to the morgue," he said.

"Why?"

"I want to have a look at this guy, that's why. Come on!"

He straightened out his big tall body in sections, like one of those folding lawn chairs.

"But we haven't got our food yet," I objected.

"This'll cover it, come on." He put a ten and a five on the table, weighting them down with the teapot, but fortunately couldn't get out the door because the waiter came through it with the food.

"But I'm starving—I haven't eaten since breakfast. Wait a minute! Waiter, please bring us some dog bags. To go out. Cartons."

"OK, miss, to go," he agreed, after a brief look of annoyance or surprise, and hurried off.

"I'll meet you if you want to go ahead," I told O'Reagan. "What's so important about this guy?"

"Do you remember at the inquest on your sister's death I testified I'd seen a skid-row type who I thought had grabbed her purse and run off with it?"

"No," I said, "I don't remember that. You think Malone might be him?"

"Yeah. That guy wore an old trench coat. And the rest fits, too."

"My God, O'Reagan. If he was there—and if Celia *was* pushed—and he had this habit of saying to almost everybody, 'Say, haven't I seen you somewhere before?' . . ."

"Yeah. He might have picked the wrong person to say that to. Someone who'd been there when your sister was killed—and shouldn't have been."

"And he might have remembered them—or only said he did, because he always said that! Henry and Beatrice, as a matter of fact, had been there just before I came that night—last night. It seems longer. Mark said they brought him some clothes."

I thought of Mark's reaction when the drunk said he'd seen him before and put the thought aside. The waiter came in with the cartons, and we quickly scooped our dinners into them.

"If Malone did see Henry—or someone who wasn't supposed to be there, someone we know, presumably—why didn't *you* see them?"

"I don't know. Come on. No use wasting time on speculation until we know whether it's the same guy or not."

TWENTY-SIX

MY THIRD TRIP TO THE MORGUE WASN'T AS BAD AS THE first one when I went to identify David, or the second when it was Celia.

"I must be getting inured to this," I said to O'Reagan as we left.

"What does 'inured' mean?"

"Look it up. Well? Was it him? Your tramp?"

"It was him all right. Let's go get your car and meet at your place—or mine? We can eat while we talk. Whose place?"

"Mine. The dogs are there, and anyway, I'd rather already be home when we finish."

When I got down there, O'Reagan was sitting on the front steps waiting for me. It wasn't that late, only about eight o'clock, but the houses all around were dark, there was no moon, and the neighborhood looked lonely and dismal. A cold wind was blowing fog in from the northwest.

There was a letter in my mailbox from Muffy Tucker.

"Good," I said as we went upstairs, "here's a letter from my friend who works for *Time*—did I tell you about her?"

"Nope."

"I saw her when I was in New York—asked her to check their files on the California Coalition because their existence was beginning to seem a little dubious to me. . . . I'd been in New Haven that afternoon, thinking about Lindy . . . so I asked Muffy to let me know if there was any new information on them."

I put the letter and the cartons of Chinese food on the kitchen table and went into the bathroom to scrub my hands in case any morgue was on them. Then I poked one of my clean fingers into a carton of what looked like the pineapple chicken and licked it.

"Not hot. I'll heat it up."

"Don't bother for me. Can I use your phone?"

"Sure. The one in the bedroom's closest, or there's one in the living room if you want privacy."

He picked up the phone in the bedroom and dialed a number that he didn't have to look up. I skimmed through Muffy's letter and then put the food in the oven and listened.

"Homicide." A pause, fairly long. "Yes. I'd like to leave a message for whoever's on the de-tox stabbing at City Hospital last night. No, morning's fine. O'Reagan. Eight-two-six-four-six-nine-three."

He drummed his fingers on the marble top of my telephone table. The marble sounds elegant, but actually I'd gotten it out of a dumpster in the days when I used to have a pickup truck; the edges were jagged and the shape a bit arbitrary.

"OK, thanks." He hung up. "I have to let them know about Malone," he explained, unnecessarily, since I'd been listening the whole time. "Should have done it from the morgue. They'll probably be pissed."

"Oh, well. Anyway, the food's hot. Here's a plate. And fork, or do you want chopsticks?"

"Chopsticks, if you've got 'em. You make this?"

"Yes." It was a plate with the full moon, the ocean, and a large white fish. I had the one with a big rising sun.

"Nice."

"Thanks. One of my better ones. So. Where are we in our—what'd you call it—cable car case? I'm sorry poor Gentleman Malone got stabbed—I felt so sad to see him there in the morgue, finally separated from his raincoat. But I must admit it's exciting he turned out to be your wino. That makes it certain, don't you think?"

"That your sister was murdered?"

"Yes. That Celia was murdered." It felt strange to be saying that. "But I also feel—creepy about it. It's a little bit frightening."

"I don't know. I think it was more frightening before because it was so successful. There was nothing you could get your hands on. This could be the first big mistake. Assuming the connection's there, and I feel pretty certain about that. Well, let's get started."

"OK. Want more coffee? How shall we do this? Chronologically, or what?"

"What does your friend say?" He nodded to the letter lying open on the table.

"Oh. She says she found nothing except one little fact someone dug up—that Cremmens had been in the habit—for several months before he was killed, but not *right* before—of taking off Thursday afternoons from work. No one, according to the files, ever found out where he went except that it was thought to be San Francisco, she doesn't say why. The assumption was that he was meeting with Coalition people, but there was no proof of that."

"Interesting. Because if Sloan killed his wife—then the chances are good that he was responsible for the plane crash that resulted in his getting half of the wife's money."

"In which case," I completed the thought, "he'd have to have known Cremmens somehow, presumably. Maybe he could have been seeing him as a patient? He still had some private patients then."

"Could be. I wish I could get into that house and have a good look around. If he knew Cremmens he wouldn't keep any records of it, but there might be something. Do the servants sleep in the house?''

"No, at least they never did in Celia's day. There are some rooms over the garage. But the woman she's got to take care of her little boy must sleep in. Maybe I could think up some reason to be there—looking for something of Celia's, maybe. But the place to look would be the cottage.''

"Cottage?''

"It used to be a guest cottage. Henry's had it made over into a studio and office for Beatrice; it's her private space, or so she said at lunch. She said even the maids don't go in there, so they won't break any of her fragile ceramics-in-the-works. She also said that a lot of old papers of Henry's are stored in there. I have some keys to the place, too, somewhere. From when I was clearing out Celia's things.''

"I could start there, anyway. You have any cream? Milk?''

"Sorry.'' I got a half-gallon carton from the refrigerator and handed it to him. "What did you find out about Beatrice? Anything?''

"I started with their marriage license. She's down on that as maiden name of Brown and place of birth Phoenix. Interesting thing is, though—'' he paused and took a slug of coffee out of one of the uglier cups I'd made that year—"interesting thing is, there isn't any record of a Beatrice Brown born thirty years ago in Phoenix. Or for ten years on either side.''

"She did say she was using her maiden name and that she was born in Phoenix. I wonder why she lied?''

"Offhand, I'd guess there's something in her past she doesn't want anybody to know about. Not necessarily illegal, of course.''

"How'd you find this out, anyway?''

"On the telephone, initially. Then I decided to go out there and check out a few more things. That's where I was when you couldn't reach me.''

"Oh, O'Reagan! That's expensive!''

"No more than paying somebody else to do it—or not much. Anyway, I'm getting restless with the printing business, and there's not a hell of a lot going on there right now. Want to know what else I found? Or didn't find?''

"Of course.''

"Well, fifteen or twenty years ago Phoenix was a good deal

smaller than it is now. Still a city, that's probably why she picked it. But a small city. I went through the yearbooks of the high schools. They're mostly concerned with the senior class, but they go back all the way to the eighth grade, most of them with pictures. There wasn't any young Beatrice Brown gracing those pages, either.''

"She certainly told me she'd been to high school there. You think she never lived there?"

"I think she probably was there sometime. She'd be afraid to pick a place for background she didn't know at all. The question is, when? And what was her name?"

"Well, how are we going to find out?"

"I don't know. I'd like to have a chance to look through her things, too. And if the cottage is her private place, that'd be good for a start."

"Is that it? On Beatrice?"

"One more thing. I've been saving this for last. There was a Beatrice Brown granted a G.E.D. in L.A. ten years ago. And a Beatrice Brown graduated from Pomona Junior College six years ago. Counseling and fine arts."

"I'm glad to hear it. I was beginning to think I'd made her up. Maybe they just lost the birth certificate in Phoenix; doesn't that happen sometimes?"

"Sometimes."

"But if she changed her name, she did it about ten years ago, then? When she went back to school?"

"Looks like it. And that's all I got. Not conclusive of anything in particular, but suggestive in general. What about you?"

I told him what I'd learned from Cook: that Henry had been gone a lot the year or so before Celia was killed; that there'd been a period of arguments; that Celia had been unhappy; that Cook had overheard accusations concerning another woman and had also overheard them talking about divorce a few days before Celia was killed. And that Celia'd received something in the mail that same day that upset her and sent her off to the bank.

"And Mark said the same. I only had a chance to talk to him for a few minutes because the nurse came and dragged him off for medication. But he said he overheard Henry on the telephone and knew from that he was seeing another woman. He said Henry called her 'oh, my darling,' and he—Mark—was completely disgusted. He said he had no idea who the woman was, though."

"We do progress, definitely." He got up and stretched, then paced slowly around the room as I told him about my interview with Carlotta.

"Upset with Dunbar Oates, huh? That fits with your descriptions of his visits to you and Lindy well enough. My friend Patton checked the records, by the way, and found nothing on him. On the question of alibi, Oates was having lunch with a lady-friend at the crucial time. No attempt was made to shake it—no one saw any reason to, particularly. But he keeps coming up, doesn't he? Just a bad penny? Or something more?"

"Don't know," I smiled. "I guess we'll have to try and find out, though. What do you think?"

"I'm afraid so. I'd rather concentrate on Sloan right now, but we better not ignore this Oates guy any longer. You think he was afraid she'd prosecute?"

"He certainly seemed afraid of something. And Carlotta said Celia was very angry. It was an incredibly expensive painting, you know, even for someone like Celia. And 'after all she'd done for him . . .' And Mary P. Lewis, on the telephone, said the painting was definitely fake but that Dunbar was innocent. He went to her for help, apparently. She helped him convince Henry not to prosecute if the money was returned, and I guess most of it was. Even without prosecuting, though, Celia would have totally ruined him just by telling all her rich friends about it. Should I have a talk with him and see what else I can find out?"

"Yeah—good idea."

O'Reagan stopped pacing and sat down and poured himself another cup of coffee. I was feeling restless by then myself and started slowly circling the room as I reported on the rest of my talk with Carlotta. He was especially interested in what she'd said on the question of whether it was Henry or Celia who couldn't have children.

"How did *you* know, by the way, that Sloan was the culprit?"

"That Henry couldn't have children? That he was sterile?"

"Yeah. Did you just assume it, because he and Celia didn't have any?"

"I see what you mean. Well, I think Celia said so. Or maybe it was my mother. I don't think I just assumed it, though."

I thought back to the early years of their marriage. "I always had the impression that they wanted children of their own and couldn't have them. And Celia had the two children, so it obviously wasn't her fault. . . . They moved out here pretty soon after they married, and I didn't see them for quite a while. I think it was my mother. I was home from college one summer. The sewing lady . . . it's coming back to me now. Letty was there to sew, and they were talking about how Celia had never been very strong physically. How she fainted once when Letty was pinning up hems, like she was doing on me just then. Funny, I'd forgotten all about this.'' I started to take a sip of coffee, absently.

"Your sister was never very strong, they said. And?''

"And my mother said something about how it was probably just as well 'Dr. Sloan'—she always called him that with servants, or what she considered servants—that Dr. Sloan couldn't have children. That having Mark and especially Lindy nearly killed Celia as it was. And Letty said something about two children being just the right number, anyway. And my mother agreed, especially if one was a boy and one a girl. I wasn't paying much attention, just standing there very uncomfortably while Letty was pinning my hem; I was very hung over that day. I remember I resented that about two being a good number if one's a boy, which I took to mean that I was the wrong sex. Anyway, then my mother went off on her thing about her own delicate health, and how having Celia and me nearly killed her, and so forth and so on. And I got tireder and more aggravated and finally stomped off.''

"She didn't say how she knew Sloan couldn't have children?''

"No, but she wouldn't have. Especially in front of an unmarried maiden daughter. As she thought. And, of course, I wouldn't have asked, either. Besides which, I was so hung over. I remember just constantly going to parties those summers, drinking as much as I could. Anyway, it wasn't the sort of thing one asked. No nasty physiological details. Especially where sex was concerned. Very Victorian. More so even than I realized before just this minute—it was a sad little family, or attempt at one, looking back. . . .''

"Yeah. Most I've seen have been.''

We sat in silence for a while, both thinking, presumably, of families and their sadness.

"So for all you know, this could very likely be something your mother just assumed herself? Not liking nasty physical facts?''

"It could have been that way. But it had the feeling of more; of a more definite fact, at least from hearsay. Like something she knew because Celia had told her, for instance. She wouldn't have been interested in any of the details, but just the result. If you see what I mean.''

"I know a doctor in Texas who owes me a favor. You don't remember, do you, who your sister's doctor was?''

"Not the obstetrician, no. But we had a fairly young family doctor then—the old one died. His name was Sorley. Jim, James Sorley. He might know—don't specialists always send reports back to the regular doctor?''

"Usually. I'll call my doctor friend and ask him to see what he can find out. Doctors are more willing to talk to each other than to anyone else.''

"You have a lot of friends.''

"Long life, virtuously lived.'' He smiled his crooked smile and handed me a fortune cookie. It said:

> He who prepares for the worst
> rarely regrets it.

O'Reagan's was:

> You have unusual equipment for
> success. Be sure to use it properly.

After we ate the sweet, tasteless cookies, I went over again in detail what I knew of the setup at the de-tox and Gentleman Malone's murder.

"Once the police connect it with Celia, I'll be a favorite suspect again," I concluded. "I benefited from her death, and I was right on the spot for this one. I could easily have done it during the time I said I went to the bathroom. Or just before the meeting.''

"Yeah," he said, "I thought of that." He looked at me with very cold gray eyes.

"Do you think I did it?'' I asked in alarm, feeling quite sick. Because if O'Reagan, who liked me, thought I might have killed Malone, I could imagine what Simmons, who didn't like me at all, was going to think when they found out about the connection between Celia and the drunk.

"Do you think I did it?'' I asked again.

"No," he said, "I don't.''

"Oh," I said and slowly let the breath out of my lungs. I hadn't realized until then that I'd been holding it. "I am certainly glad to hear *that*! Why don't you think so?"

"This and that," he replied easily. "You have an honest face. Let's figure out what we're going to do next so I can go home and get some sleep. You look like you could use some, too. I didn't tell you, but when I called to leave the message they said Simmons was in charge of the case now."

"Damn."

"At least he always was suspicious about your sister's death. This murder should clinch it for him."

"Yeah, and probably clinch me right along into jail, too," I said gloomily.

"They can't do that, don't worry."

"That's right. All they have, after all, is motive and opportunity. I shouldn't let a little thing like that worry me. I wish I hadn't left the meeting and gone to the ladies' room last night, though. Oh, well," I sighed and forced a smile. "As you say, this is sure to put Simmons hot on the trail of the old killer—I mean the old killing—which is what we want, after all."

"If he doesn't louse it up."

"By arresting me, for instance. I guess I'd better get busy on the Dunbar Oates business in the pitifully short amount of time I probably have left."

"All right. I'll try and find out if Sloan and his bride are going to be away from the house anytime soon. Any night, so I can have a look in that studio. At least."

"Want me to try and find out?"

"No. You concentrate on Oates."

"Well, find out, then—but do me a favor?"

"What's that?"

"I'd like to come with you. If you did get caught, with me, I could make up some implausible story about why we're there. They probably wouldn't believe me, but they probably wouldn't have us sent to San Quentin, either. Beatrice doesn't know you, and she's the one who'd be likely to see us; she said Henry never goes down there. It's his tribute to women's lib or something. Anyway, they're less likely to make a fuss if I'm with you."

"OK. I'll find out when they're going to be out, and if it can wait on you, it will. Not because I buy your reasoning."

"Thanks. I'll get you that key. And were you going to see

what you could find out about that Halff woman—whether if it was Beatrice that Henry was seeing, if they could've been meeting at her place? They must have been meeting someplace, right? If it was Beatrice . . .''

"Right. They could have had a cabin in the mountains—Sloan and whoever it was—rented in some other name; that's what I'd do. But in the beginning, it must have started somewhere; it couldn't be at his place, and if it was Beatrice it apparently wasn't at hers, so . . . I'll see what I can dig up with the Halff woman.''

"Pat?"

"Yeah?" He looked at me suspiciously, alerted perhaps by my use of his first name.

"There is one other little thing I didn't mention.''

"What's that?''

"Well—when Mark and the witch and I were first talking, actually it was to Mark that Malone first said, 'Haven't I seen you somewhere before?' ''

"And?''

"And,'' I went on reluctantly, wishing now that I hadn't decided to trust him with this, "Mark got a little upset, said he didn't know what Malone was talking about, and walked off. Then he came back after Malone left us.''

"You didn't tell the police this?''

"No. I wasn't going to tell you, either,'' I admitted, "but then I decided to trust that you wouldn't jump to any conclusions. I think Mark was probably just suffering from withdrawal and all that.''

"Could be,'' O'Reagan said noncommittally. "Thanks for telling me.''

"Well—we said partners. I was starting to feel a little guilty.''

We sat looking at each other without saying anything more for what seemed a long while. Finally, I broke the silence with another confidence of sorts. "And Pat?''

"What else?''

"I happen to have this gun.''

"Good for you.''

"A pistol. I kept it when I found it, going through Celia's things. I forgot to tell you about it. It was hidden in a cowboy boot. Memento of our Texas childhood.''

"Did she have a license for it?''

"I don't know; I didn't even know she had a gun. I didn't see a license in her papers. What would it have said?"

"San Francisco Police Department all over the place; you'd probably have noticed it. What would she be doing with a gun?"

"That's what I wondered. Maybe she was enraged about the other woman and was planning on shooting Henry—and his pushing her under the cable car was, therefore, just self-defense? Seriously, I'll get it—I stuck it in a ski boot."

I got the boot out of my closet and handed him the gun. He took it gingerly and opened it.

"I took the bullets out. That wasn't hard to figure out, only I wasn't sure about the safety switch."

"Catch," he corrected absentmindedly. "Covered hammer; nice for shooting from your coat pocket and small enough to fit there. Very handy. A thirty-eight, so it's big enough to hurt, too." He balanced the gun in the palm of his right hand, feeling the weight. "You shouldn't have kept it, you know. Serious offense to carry a weapon like this, and the fact that it isn't registered—at least to you—makes it worse. They're guys sitting in the big house right now for less than that."

He glared at me. I looked innocently back.

"But what I wanted to know was, is this the safety? Which way is on?"

"This, this way's on. I still say the best thing would be to get rid of it—if you want a gun, go buy one; get a permit."

"For now I'm just going to keep this one," I said stubbornly.

I started picking at the remains of the dinner. O'Reagan started in again, too. We were both using our fingers. I wasn't really hungry anymore but couldn't stop picking away at the food, just because it was there.

"Since you were there when Celia was hit by the cable car, why is it you didn't see Henry, or Dunbar, or whoever, if one of them was there?"

"Whoever it was would presumably have had the foresight to change their appearance. If it was premeditated. Or they could have taken out a contract with some of the hoods around town. But I doubt it; none of them travel in those circles. Sloan doesn't, anyway; I guess we don't know about Oates. Maybe your sister had a lover, if the marriage had gone bad. Maybe Oates?"

"I doubt that—they'd had a patroness-recipient relationship for an awfully long time to suddenly become lovers. Or even not suddenly. And I don't think Celia would have taken a lover. Too prim, or something. Of course, I might be wrong. The police didn't turn up any hint of one, did they?''

"No, and they looked. Hard.''

He got up from the table, stretched, picked up his coffee cup, and took it over to the sink. "Where's that key you promised me?''

I went through my desk drawers until I found the two keys that Henry had given me two years before and which I'd never returned. I took one off the ring, stuck it back in the drawer, and gave the other to O'Reagan.

"The lock may not be the same, but it was a new one then, and a good one—so hopefully they haven't changed it.''

"Thanks,'' he said, adding the key to the four or five on his own ring. "Time to go.''

"I'll go down with you, I want to take the dogs to the corner. . . . Diana! Orphan!'' They hadn't been out all day except for the postage stamp backyard and were ecstatic at the chance to get out. "Outside!'' I told them—their favorite word—and we all tumbled down the stairs together.

From the top of the hill the downtown city lights were bright-colored jewels in the crisp black night, gold and yellow and red. The stars were bright, too, high above; but lower down, over on the left half of town, chunks of fog, white against the black night, were drifting in among the golden skyscrapers. We parted at the corner.

When I got back upstairs, I put the tiny black pistol that looked to me so much like a toy or a movie prop back into the ski boot. I put the boot beside its mate, in the back of my spare closet, and went to bed and almost immediately to sleep.

I woke very early the next morning, which was unusual, clutching the fragments of some dreams I couldn't remember. Celia with a sewing machine. Stitch, stitch, stitch. Something about George Washington. Standing on his head? I lay very still, trying to keep my mind empty and lure the dreams back, but they wouldn't come. Finally, I gave up and started thinking about all the things O'Reagan and I had talked about the night before. Beatrice of hidden origins. Was it Henry who was sterile? In the dream fragment, Celia stitching on something pink and billowy and feminine. And George Washington standing on his head. I thought for a while about what that might signify, and I decided to do a little further research—in the high school yearbooks of Ronald Cremmens' hometown: Needles, I remembered, Needles, California. Down by the Mexican border, sort of. Simmons wouldn't like it, but then, Simmons wouldn't know.

I got up and packed a small canvas overnight bag.

TWENTY-SEVEN

I FIXED A BIG BREAKFAST AND THEN, LUCKILY, LINGERED OVER my coffee. Luckily, because the doorbell rang just about the time I'd otherwise have been walking out with my suitcase. When I went down to answer it, I found a tall policeman standing there. He didn't have on a uniform, but I could tell he was a cop all the same.

"Mrs. Margaret Elliott?"

"Yes?"

"I'm Ryan, San Francisco Police," he said, sticking out a big hand with something official-looking in it; presumably a police ID.

"Yes?" I said again, in a rather lady-of-the-manor tone.

"Captain Simmons asked me to bring you down to Headquarters. He wants to talk with you in connection with the stabbing in the de-tox Tuesday night."

"Am I under *arrest*?"

"No, ma'am, just routine, but he wants to have you down there."

"All right," I said. "I'll just go up and get my purse. How long do you think this'll take?"

"I don't know, ma'am."

I wished he would stop calling me ma'am.

I went upstairs and stuck the small suitcase I'd packed for Needles under the bed.

The cop, though plainclothes, had come in a police car. He opened the back door for me, slammed it shut behind me, and got in front with a uniformed driver. As we drove off, I wondered what my neighbors would think; I saw a couple of them peering eagerly out their windows. Then I noticed there weren't any handles on the inside of the doors in the back seat and stopped thinking about my neighbors.

The driver let us out in front of the big gray box that is police headquarters and drove off. The plainclothes cop took me directly to Simmons' office.

Two years didn't seem to have affected him much. The brown suit was a little more crumpled, maybe, the red-brown hair a bit longer and grayer, the bulge over the tip of the belt a little bigger. For all I knew, the fat brown cigar, constantly going out and being relit, might have been the same I'd last seen him with.

"Sorry to drag you out so early, Mrs. Elliot," he said, not sounding sorry at all. "But I wanted to get to you before you went off."

I felt a guilty lurch in my upper stomach, where some of my breakfast was still waiting to be digested, and wondered how he'd found out.

"Went off?" I managed.

"Went to work, or whatever you do. That's right, you don't work, do you? Inherited a lot of money from your sister—your *half* sister, that is—right?"

So he hadn't known I was going out of town; how could he have? And just as well, considering the mood he was in.

"I know very well that always made you mad, that hundred thousand dollars," I said as mildly as I could, "but what does that have to do with the stabbing of that poor drunk at City Hospital?"

"We'll *get* to that. And it didn't make me mad, just curious. Right now, I'd like to hear more about this orderly you claim you saw when you left that AA meeting."

"Are you arresting me? Or what? Aren't you supposed to warn me that whatever I say may be used against me? The way you're talking, maybe I should get a lawyer."

"You can get as many lawyers as you damn well please," he said, his face turning from red to purple. "That's up to you. However, this is just a little friendly questioning, being as how there's developed a possible connection between your *half* sister's supposed accident and this de-tox stabbing." His big brown eyes were narrowed to slits, watching to see how I would react.

I didn't say anything. Simmons didn't know that O'Reagan and I even knew each other, much less that we'd joined forces to look into Celia's death on our own. I didn't think it would be such a good idea to tell him at this point, either. For one thing, it might make it harder for O'Reagan to get information from the friends he still had in the department. So I had to act as if I didn't know any more than I had when I left the de-tox Tuesday night. I felt very nervous. I hadn't done anything wrong. But I didn't have a lot of confidence in our system of justice, either.

Finally, I remembered to ask, "What do you mean? What sort of connection? And wasn't Celia's death an accident—are you saying you were right, after all?"

"That's as may be," he answered loftily. "The fact is, this drunk who got it at the de-tox, Malone, was at the scene. When your sister got it."

God, I thought, he sounds like some war fanatic, or maybe a gangster; he got it, she got it . . .

"And so you think there's a connection? Why?"

"Why!" he exploded and turned to the other man in the room, also homicide, presumably, who hadn't said anything up until then. "God's oats and little canaries, she asks me 'why'?"—he mimicked my slight Southern accent; it's very slight, but in his version it got bigger.

"All right, lady, I'll spell it out for you. Your sister—*half* sister—got killed in unusual circumstances. Some would say suspicious. I would, for instance. She was very rich. Very, *very* rich. You benefited from her death; so did her husband; so did her son. Substantially."

"So did her daughter," I put in as he paused to relight the revolting soggy cigar, wondering if they'd thought of connecting that death, too, with Celia's. And which, unfortunately, wouldn't let me out, because of the will she'd started but never finished, naming me as one of the two beneficiaries.

"The daughter don't come into it. At least—"

I saw the thought dawning in his spaniel eyes, like the sun trying to come out through a thick fog and sort of halfway making it. Maybe I should have kept my mouth shut on that one.

He picked up one of his telephones and bellowed into it: "Get me the file on that Holmes assassination! Yesterday! Bring it here!" His face turned purple again. "No, you idiot! I didn't say the assassination was yesterday! Get it! Bring it!" He slammed the receiver down and returned his attention to me.

"She made a will, too—the daughter? Benefiting you? If I remember right, you wouldn't have to be limping along on any measly hundred grand if that had gone through, would you?"

"That's right," I said evenly. "But she didn't sign it; she mailed it to Houston with a couple of changes. And just for the record, I might as well say now that I didn't know anything about that will. Not that you'll believe me," I concluded bitterly. "And if you're going to keep on talking to me like this, I think I should have a lawyer."

"Keep your pants on. Let's just go over your statement here about Malone's murder. That's all I have you here for; I'm not arresting you. Yet. Just tell me everything you remember about Tuesday evening."

"I did. I made a long statement."

"That's right. And now do it again."

"All right. But you never did say exactly why you're so sure they're connected. Or you started to—why do you?"

"I can't believe you're that dumb. But here's the wrappings: Malone was a witness to your sister's death. So-called accident. Horseshit. And he turns up murdered—in a de-tox the day after he arrives, after talking with your sister's son, her husband—and you. Full cast. And what was it he was saying to you? Malone? Something abut seeing you somewhere before?"

"He said that to everybody. But OK, I see what you mean by a connection. You're not arresting me?"

"Not at present, sweetheart, not at present."

"All right. I'll tell you again about Tuesday night. I'd just as soon not be here all day."

I went over it again. Several times. The other detective whose name was Lowell, a quiet, gray little man who reminded me of a field mouse, asked a few quiet, gray questions from time to time. Although he kept in the background, I had the impression in the end that he was Simmons' superior, in rank as well as intelligence.

Finally they said I could leave.

"Don't go to Europe, sweetheart; we may want you again," were Simmons' parting words.

Which was fine with me. I wasn't planning on going to Europe.

TWENTY-EIGHT

THE UNIFORMED COP TOOK ME HOME AND DROVE OFF. I TOOK the change of clothes I'd packed out of the nice canvas case and stuffed them into a shoddy-looking backpack instead, with a clear plastic bag full of ceramics tools hanging out over the edge. I put out enough food and water for the dogs to last them about a month and took them out for a quick walk. I tried calling O'Reagan but got only his answering service. Then I put the backpack into my car and drove off. Nobody seemed to be around or paying any attention to me. I drove up to Fort Mason and went in and put plastic covers on the clay pieces I'd made the day before, so they wouldn't dry out completely and be unworkable when I got back.

I drove across town on Broadway and turned onto Highway 101 just on two o'clock. No one seemed to be following, and I knew I probably had a sense of my own importance greatly exaggerated by paranoia.

I stayed on 101 as far as Paso Robles, where it suddenly became very hot. Then I cut east, through huge bare hills baking slowly, over millions of years, toward some completion on too vast a scale to imagine. I was avoiding Interstate 5, stretching flat and straight and boring all the length of California's big central valley without a wrinkle. Just an exit every hour or so to the same five gas stations and the same two coffee shops they have at every exit of every freeway in the country—perhaps, by now, the world. It was patrolled by helicopters looking for speeders, and I figured if Simmons did decide for some reason to look for me, I'd be a dead duck on the Interstate. I had to get on it for the bit between Lost Hills and Rio Bravo, but so briefly I didn't have time to get really nervous.

I had to get on Interstate 40 in the middle of the Mojave

Desert, though: it's the only direct road there is from Barstow to Needles. Just after I got on it, a highway patrol car zoomed up from behind, lights flashing and siren howling. My heart gave an odd lurch and beat irregularly for quite a while after I pulled over and stopped. The cop, meanwhile, went zooming on by without even a glance in my direction, became a tiny speck in the immense distance, and then disappeared. I started off again, trying to think about the dinner I'd have when I got to Needles. I was suddenly very hungry, but I didn't want to stop to eat until I got there. Pancakes, perhaps, with lots of butter and fake maple syrup.

And all during that long drive I went over and over everything I knew about what O'Reagan called the cable car case. I thought a bit about O'Reagan, too, trying to define for myself a little more clearly the relationship that was developing between us. Business, mutual interests—yes. Friendship? A beginning, at least, maybe more than that; we'd liked each other from the start. And sexual attraction? Some of that, too. But I retained the feeling, intuition, whatever it had been, that I'd had at the Café Cantata that first night, that the focus of a relationship between O'Reagan and me wasn't going to be any simple matter of attraction followed promptly by bed. It was more complicated . . . it was going to be necessary to work out the business and the friendship parts . . . And then? That was not so clear. . . .

The approach to Needles from the west is a narrow valley through the mountains. It was very dark when I hit the long downgrade into town, about midnight, the mountains close on both sides darker than the star-filled dark of sky.

Needles
Pop. 4,051   Elev. 550

The green and white sign briefly picked up by my headlights looked old and careworn.

I took the West Broadway exit which promised motels and checked into a rundown-looking place on a side street. It was not so glittery and plastic as the ones on motel row, and its sign advertised "Room Phones" and "Quiet." It was quiet, too, at half-past midnight.

The usual thin, elderly man in a droopy, short-sleeved shirt and wilted trousers—both a little too big—gave me the key to number seven in exchange for twenty-four dollars. He had enough energy, maybe, for about half a person. He grudgingly agreed to reopen the switchboard, and I promised I'd be quick.

O'Reagan's answering service took down my name and the motel's phone number. Then I went back out for a quick and tasteless meal on motel row. They were out of the pancakes I'd been thinking about, so I settled for a four-dollar hamburger that tasted like straw or possibly cotton.

Back at the Cozy Rest I wanted to ask if O'Reagan had called back, but the tired man wasn't in the office. I thought he probably needed all the rest he could get.

Needles had looked pretty big coming downhill in the dark, but the wide spread of lights after the miles of desert emptiness was misleading. In the light of day, I could see how little there was to it. A bored young Chicano at the gas station next to the motel gave me directions to the one high school.

It was a cluster of five or six big buildings, three-storied, sand-colored structures of nondescript age and style, and a huge, new-looking gymnasium. There were no trees and no grass, so it was a bare and desolate-looking place. The library was on the bottom floor of the building next to the gym.

The librarian, a short woman in her thirties with flyaway, curly brown hair and alert gray eyes, looked curious when I asked about the yearbooks for fifteen to twenty years before but said merely, "We have them all the way back to forty-eight. Is there one particular one you want?"

"I'd like nineteen sixty-three to start"—that world be Ronald Cremmens' senior year—"no, make it sixty-two, sixty-three, and sixty-four. Then I may want some others later."

I sat down at an empty round table, metal, with a worn-looking Webster's dictionary in the center. Some boys at the next table were talking quietly. They looked about fourteen, scrawny, freckled, hungry. Their talk faded in and out of my reading.

"Kawasaki . . ."

The yearbook I started on was an artificial-white-leather volume with 1963 stamped across the front in gold. The title page said: "Mystic Maze—Needles—Home of the Mustangs. Dedicated to the friendly and willing merchants of Needles." Its purpose, I read on: "To share treasured memories . . . friendship and laughter, excitement and disappointment . . . gaiety and sadness . . ."

"They don't have any steering control," from one of the boys.

"Yes, they do."

"Just think if you're going too fast, hit the curb, and fly up into a tree!" from the third, longingly.

I flipped over to the senior-class pictures. The officers were featured in a full-page spread, sitting on and standing by a new white Ford convertible, new seventeen years before. Ronald Cremmens wasn't one of them. I found him easily enough, though, in the C's; Ronald Lesley Cremmens, looking not much different from the pictures printed in the newspapers two years before: bony head, glasses, the nondescript hair crew cut. Later it was longer, and he'd been starting to get bald.

God, he looked young! And—innocent, was it? Vulnerable? Well, he had certainly been that. But to what, precisely?

I looked through the rest of the senior pictures twice, but there was nobody named Beatrice Brown. I hadn't really expected that there would be, but I'd hoped. More disappointing, there was no picture of any female in the senior class who looked like she might be Beatrice under another name. I was assuming that she wasn't necessarily the age she said she was, but instead anywhere from Cremmens' age (five years older than she claimed) down to the age she said she was, thirty. Therefore, I checked the smaller pictures of juniors, sophomores, and freshmen. I even went down through the eighth and seventh graders, these preceded by a half-page spread of the class officers on bicycles. She wasn't there, as far as I could tell.

The motto of Ronald Cremmens' senior class was: "Make the most of what comes, and the least of what goes." I settled down to go through the rest of the book, especially the activities, to try and spot Beatrice or someone who might be Beatrice in those more informal photographs. I felt discouraged, almost certain that I'd taken a lot of trouble for a wild-goose chase.

Mystic Maze Coeds, the school-paper staff, student council, service club, FHA . . . no Beatrice that I could see.

"It was either a Harley or Indian, I swear to God!" from the neighboring table.

''Japan.''

''I don't see why they got in trouble for it. Kind of stupid.''

I read on: the G.A.A., which turned out to be the Girls' Athletic Association. No Beatrice. Concert and marching and junior high school bands . . .

''Yamaha.''

''Kawasaki.''

''I'd like to have that Y-two-one-two-five three-cylinder Yamaha three-fifty.''

Cheerleaders in miniskirts, majorettes in satin, and pompom girls in short jumpers. No Beatrice. The pep club: ''While our mighty team is fighting, we'll shout her praises to the sky!'' The team had son a little over half their games that year.

''God, this book's thick.''

''It's two books.''

''Harley Davidson . . .''

And on through activities '63: the senior-class trip to San Francisco; the sixteenth annual Marathon, complete with floats, a black Cadillac, and a princess; then, Queens of Homecoming and of Dreams. Still no one looked like a possible Beatrice.

Then I thought I spotted her. I wasn't sure at first, but the longer I looked the more I thought it might be her.

It was the section called Stage Craft: a rather close-up shot of three people on stage, interacting in some way. The play was called *Winter Money*. The hair and clothes looked forties or thirties. Which was helpful, because they weren't so dissimilar to the way Beatrice styled herself as an adult. The hair of the one I believed might be Beatrice was longish and frizzy—just the way she wore her hair now—and probably the reason I was able to spot her. If it was her.

I read the names beneath the picture: Bill Evans, Sally Overton, Jane Shingle.

Jane Shingle was Beatrice? Something about the whole *gestalt,* not just the hairdo, the features . . . but the total.

I sat back and took a deep breath. Jane Shingle.

''I'm afraid if I *read* anything, I'm going to just get sick.''

''Just sit down, then.''

Two girls were standing by the main desk, leafing through a small newspaper.

Jane Shingle. I wondered why she wasn't in the senior or

junior pictures and looked back to check the S's. No. I looked at the picture of the play again. A winter play—*Winter Money*. Maybe she'd started the year, then dropped out for some reason, or moved. Now I had a name to try to find out about. I hoped it wouldn't lead me to some middle-aged housewife or bank clerk. . . .

"The girls' team beat Parker."

"Is this *all* the paper? They don't even show what I did after—"

"The girls' team beat Parker, all right."

"What did I have on that day? Oh, my white pants . . ."

I looked on through the rest of the Stage Craft section and was rewared with another list of names under a group shot—the cast of *Carousel* taking a final bow. I would have recognized him from the tiny picture, but the name was there: Ronnie Cremmens.

Ronnie Cremmens, Jane Shingle. Both in plays that year.

I went quickly through the rest of the '63 book but found nothing further. Next, I wanted to look for Jane Shingle in the '62 volume, but the librarian hadn't given me that one, I noticed, so I went through '61. Nothing.

I went back to the '63 book and found what I was looking for in the list of teachers at the front. The stage arts teacher was one of the few females on the staff, a Miss Eulalia Henderson. She had also, it showed, been responsible for American and English literature, speech, and drama. Quite a load.

"Excuse me," I went up to the counter. The librarian got up from her table and came over. "You didn't give me the book for sixty-two."

"I'm afraid we don't have one. I don't know what's happened to it. I'm sorry."

"Would you have any idea how long it's been gone?"

"Not really. The only yearbook I've looked at lately is the one for my own class—sixty-nine. And these are the only copies for the earlier years. We only started having duplicates in seventy-two. Of course, there are people around town who'd have one, who were in that class—if it's important."

"Do you know of anyone, offhand?"

"Not offhand, no, but I'd be glad to find out for you. Madge," she called out to the girl who'd been afraid she'd get sick if she read anything, a willowy blonde of shining grooming. "Madge, what class was your mother in? Was it sixty-two?"

"*I* don't know," Madge responded. "D'ya want me to ask her?"

The librarian looked at me, and I nodded. "Please," she called back.

"Thanks. I'll check back with you later. I have another question."

"Sure, what?"

"In these plays they put on—this one, for instance, *Winter Money*, and then *Carousel* in the spring—would they usually be just the seniors? Or would the students in them be from several classes?"

"Well, they're always *mostly* seniors. But not all. They're cast by tryouts, and usually the seniors get the parts. But if someone younger comes along who's really good, they'll get it."

"Did you know a Miss Eulalia Henderson? She taught—"

"Heaven, yes!" she interrupted. "She taught English and drama here forever. She taught me."

"She doesn't still teach, I suppose?"

"Oh, no, she's been gone for, oh, ten years, anyway, maybe longer."

"Is she still alive? Does she still live here?"

"Oh, yes. She's in the Historical Society with me. She's very able still, even though pretty old. Did you want to see her about something?"

TWENTY-NINE

WELL-KEPT ONE-STORY HOUSES, VICTORIANS OF THE EIGHT-ies and nineties. Tall palm trees, medium-sized cotton-wood and pepper shade trees. Neatly trimmed lawns with flower-bordered walks, occasional scraggly vacant lots. Sleepy and quiet. It was a very old section of town and one I hadn't seen. Needles may be a terrible place in summer when the thermometer hits a hundred and twenty day after day. But that March the breeze was balmy and soothing, the bird songs sweet, the place altogether peaceful and appealing.

I parked my car in front of 234 Acoma Street, the address the librarian had given me for Miss Eulalia Henderson, and walked up the brushed dirt walk. It was bordered with a great variety of flowers, yellow and pink and red and blue, the kind my grandmother always planted at her country house in east Texas. I didn't know their names. The brass knocker, in the shape of a crescent moon, was shiny, but the door, which was white, could have used a fresh coat of paint.

I knocked. Nothing happened, so after a while I knocked again. It was about one o'clock in the afternoon, and I hoped I wasn't going to be disturbing the old lady's lunch. Or afternoon nap.

Then I heard steps coming, and a little old lady, much as I'd imagined her, opened the door. She'd not been young in the black and white photograph of seventeen years before, but the short curly hair was completely white now, and the bright eyes, which turned out to be blue, looked out on the world through thick glass lenses; the face was thinner and very, very wrinkled. She had on black old-lady shoes and thick brown support stockings, but in her thin gray cotton with its wide white collar she looked neat and cool.

"Yes?" she queried in a tentative old-lady's voice.

203

"Miss Henderson? The librarian at the high school, Margie Ramsey, gave me your address. . . ."

"Why, of course; how is Marjorie? Such a sweet girl. I used to see her at the Historical Society, but I'm afraid I've missed it lately. I've been ill."

"I'm sorry to hear that. I hope you're feeling better now?" She seemed a nice old lady, so naturally I hoped she was feeling better. And also I wanted her well enough to talk to me.

"Well, better, yes; thank you. Are you a friend of Marjorie's, Miss—?"

"Elliott," I said, holding out my hand, "Margaret Elliott. I'm a writer and was wanting to ask you some things . . ."

"Oh! A writer!" Her rather tired, grayish face lit up for a moment, and she smiled. She had a lovely smile; it seemed to express true pleasure, even delight. I felt a large thump of guilt. "Won't you come in?"

I followed her through a shallow white entrance hall, with a gateleg table holding a big old china pot full of some sort of thick ferns placed exactly in the center and a lot of different-sized photographs on the walls in black frames. She led me into a living room to the left and indicated a pale blue chair by a dark red couch. The furniture was old, shiny, dark mahogany; the walls, white. Like the door, they were a little dingy and could have used a coat of paint. But the white lace curtains, pulled back from open windows and letting the sunshine and the breeze come into the room, looked freshly laundered, almost new.

"Would you like something to drink? Some iced tea?"

"No, thank you—I hope I didn't disturb your lunch?"

"Oh, no, my dear, I always have lunch at eleven-thirty, eleven-thirty exactly, so that I'm finished by noon, you see. I was just taking a little rest—no, no—" she held a thin hand in front of her, palm facing me, to ward off my apologies—"it doesn't matter, not a bit. It's nice to have a visitor. What was it you wanted, dear; how can I help you? Is it something to do with the Historical Society?"

"No, it isn't that. I'm doing an article for my magazine, *Rolling Stone*," I lied. I was pretty sure she wouldn't ask to see any credentials, but I made a note to myself to ask O'Reagan to print me up some cards if I did much more of this sort of thing. Most people wouldn't be as trusting as Miss Eulalia Henderson.

"It's about the plane crash two years ago that killed Congressman Holmes—do you remember that? A student of yours was thought to be involved, Ronald Cremmens, although, of course, that was never proved. . . . He was a student of yours, wasn't he?"

"Ronnie? Yes, he was, and a very nice boy, too. I couldn't have been more surprised when I read about him in the papers. Although, as you say, nothing was proved. A nice boy—but perhaps a bit too easily swayed, a little insecure—a little *too* nice, perhaps!"

"Are there any particular times you remember that he was 'swayed'—maybe into something that wasn't quite right?"

"We-el, let me see. I had him in all my classes—I taught English, and I also taught drama and speech—and he was not a very good English student, I remember, although his grades were all right because he worked pretty hard. . . . He gave another student some answers on a test once, and, of course, that wasn't right. He was supposed to be good in science and math—which I guess he was, since that's the work he went into."

"What about drama?"

"He was quite good there; these shy ones often are, you know. In the real world they're self-conscious and awkward, but put them on a stage and they just blossom, sometimes. It's one of the really gratifying things about teaching drama, I've always thought."

"And he was one of those?"

"Oh, my, yes—he was all ankles and elbows until he had a part to play, and then he'd be positively transformed . . . he had real talent, I thought, real talent. I even talked with him once, I remember, about going to study in New York; his family had money. But, of course, they wanted a respectable life for him— science, mathematics, not the stage. A respectable life. Odd, the way it turned out, isn't it? One thinks of . . . nemesis. . . ." Her voice trailed off as she looked back over the years.

"Nemesis," I agreed, "or the appointment in Samarra. Although maybe if he'd gone to New York, he wouldn't have been acting the part of a revolutionary in California. I never thought he seemed the type."

"Oh, did you know Ronnie?"

"Oh, I meant from what I read in the papers at the time of his death."

We sat in silence. I was thinking of the scrawny, crew-cut kid who was bad at life but good on the stage, and the bundle of old clothes in a drainage ditch he became fifteen years later. . . .

"Do you remember a student named Jane Shingle? I'm also interested in her."

"Jane Shingle! Now, I was thinking about her just the other day—isn't that odd that you should mention her! Jane Shingle! Oh, yes, I remember Jane." She said nothing more for a few minutes. I waited.

"The daughter of a friend of mine is having trouble with her child—my friend's granddaughter, that is—and I was just thinking, if that girl doesn't watch out she'll end up just like Jane Shingle! Isn't that a coincidence, now; I probably hadn't thought of that girl more than once or twice in all these years until just the other day. . . . What is she doing now?"

"I don't know. I'm interested because I understood she was a special friend of Ronnie Cremmens?"

"I think they did go around together at one time, although she wasn't here that long. . . ."

"Maybe if you just tell me what you remember about her—she wasn't from Needles, then?"

"Oh, my, no; that family just came here when Jane was a junior, if I remember correctly. I had her for speech and drama then, and English, of course. I always wondered what became of her. Because she wasn't talented, like Ronnie, but she was ambitious. Sometimes that'll take a person a lot farther than talent will. And she was a hard worker—a very hard worker. That girl was just determined to make something of herself. But then she got in the trouble."

Miss Eulalia looked down at her thin hands, ringless, work-worn, seeing the trouble of all those years ago.

"She got pregnant, you mean?"

"Oh, no, dear—she got in trouble with the police!"

My heart suddenly paused, then threw in some extra beats to make up for the lapse.

"Trouble with the police?"

"Well, her family was very poor, you see, and she never really had nice clothes like most of the other girls did. They drank, you see, both of them, the parents. I know because they came to see me at school once about one of the other children. And I'm afraid it was quite unavoidable to conclude they'd both had quite a *lot* to drink—and it was only eleven o'clock in the morning! I always wondered what happened to that child, too—Jane's younger sister, that was—now, *she* was a nice person. Jane wasn't, not really. Although I did think she might go far in the world, with her ambition and her work habits.''

''Maybe she did,'' I said. ''What was the trouble with the police?''

''I'm sorry, I do tend to wander more than I used to; it's old age, I suppose. Well, as I was saying, Jane's family was poor—what we used to call in the South 'poor white trash,' you know—although the sister was a lovely girl. Anyway''—she took a deep breath and kind of pulled herself back from wandering off again—''anyway, the only money Jane ever had I suppose she worked for, and she had a job after school at Mr. Bob Bartell's insurance business; State Farm, it was. He was married to a cousin of mine. She came out here to visit me from Louisiana and they just fell in love. They're both dead now.''

''And Jane worked for him, your cousin's husband?''

''Yes, Jane worked there, after school. And then some of the money came up missing, quite a large amount, I'm afraid—and Jane just disappeared! So everyone was sure she'd taken it. But they never did find her, as far as I ever heard. No one ever saw her again for certain, although there was talk once someone had seen her on an airplane as a stewardess—now, who was that? I've forgotten. But it wasn't certain, anyway. You say you know her?''

I hesitated. ''It's possible I might know her under another name, but I'm not sure. The one I know, the woman I think might be Jane Shingle, has different-colored eyes—one green and one sort of hazely brown. Did you—''

''Jane did, too—why, Jane did, too! Not extremely different, mind you, but yes, distinctly different. I'd forgotten that!''

I felt supremely elated as I mentally ticked off my findings: someone who looked like Beatrice in general; had the right sort of different-colored eyes in particular; was a high school friend of Ronald Cremmens; and was a crook even then! Also possibly had worked as an airline stewardess . . . I wondered how O'Reagan was getting along in San Francisco. I felt very pleased with the prospect of telling him what I'd found out—very pleased with myself, in other words!

"What does she do, this woman you know? Is she an actress?"

"Not officially. She may be, privately—so to speak. Is that what she was intending, when you knew her? To be an actress?"

"Yes—and she was going to make it to the top if determination and work could do it, that one. She was interested in Hollywood rather than the legitimate theater—she was interested in money, you see. I mean, specially interested; more than most people, I think. But as I said, she didn't have real talent as an actress, not a big talent, anyway. I always thought she might end up, if she did succeed in the field, in some other area—production, perhaps. She was very good with scenery, as I remember, and costumes, things like that. A good organizer."

"What about makeup?"

"Yes, with makeup too. What is she doing now, this woman you know?"

"She's recently become a rich man's wife, for one thing. A *very* rich man. And she works as an occupational therapist. She may have done some acting or production or costume work—or all those—to achieve the marriage; I'm not sure. What else can you tell me about Jane and Ronnie Cremmens?"

"There's not much I can tell you about that, I'm afraid, dear. Jane came to town when she was a junior, the same as Ronald. I mean, they were in the same class."

"Where did she come from, do you remember?"

"No, I don't. Ronnie grew up here, of course. He and Jane were both in the junior play, Shakespeare it was that year, *As You Like It*. Somewhat," she added, after thinking it over, "modified. The next fall they were seniors, of course. I remember especially because that was the last year I taught stage arts. Then they brought someone new in—I was getting near retirement, and it was getting to be too much. I knew it was to be the last year, and so I paid particular attention. I savored it. Although"—she looked up from the wrinkled hands in whose direction she'd once more been reminiscing—"it was a relief, too; I hadn't realized how overworked I was until it was over. I still taught English for three more years, until I was sixty-five. But you're not interested in all that; excuse me. Sometimes I don't talk to anyone for days on end, and then it seems when I do get an audience, I'm just nonstop. It's embarrassing!"

"Don't be embarrassed on my account," I smiled. "I'm enjoying talking with you, Miss Henderson. Memories are interesting to me.''

"That's sweet of you, dear. Where was I? Are you sure you wouldn't like some tea? I would."

"Thank you, I'd like some, too. Can I help?"

"Well, come into the kitchen with me. You can't help, but we can talk while I prepare it.''

The kitchen was like the rest of the house: old, neat, clean, a little shabby. Two windows looked out into a bare and somewhat run-down backyard. I sat down at the small table beside them while Miss Henderson put on water, went back out the door and returned with two thin, pink-flowered cups and saucers and a matching teapot on a well-shined silver tray. In my mind I was starting to call her Miss Eulalia, but not out loud; we were not in the South, after all. . . .

"A regular tea party," I said, accepting the thin old cup offered by the thin old hand. "Thank you. This is lovely china."

"It was my mother's. It *is* such a pleasure, good china. They just don't make it like this any more; this is Haviland, and I think of all my possessions—my material possessions, that is—I've had the most pleasure from this china. So light.'' She lifted her cup and smiled.

"Now where was I, you were asking about something . . .'' She suddenly seemed tired. We'd been talking for over an hour and I had interrupted her nap, after all, so I thought I had better hurry, finish my tea, and go.

"You were telling me about Jane Shingle and Ronnie Cremmens being in the junior play together, or going together.''

"That's right. It was *As You Like It*; did I say that? And it was the next fall I had the idea they were perhaps going together. Jane was in the fall play, but Ronnie wasn't—his family was making him buckle down in the scholastic subjects, I think, to get into a good college. Although in the end he didn't go anywhere special. I was surprised, just somewhere local. I forget . . .''

"San Luis Obispo, the polytechnical state school.''

"Yes, that sounds right. Anyway, I saw them around together that fall, and then, after Christmas, I didn't see them together anymore. They'd seemed such an unlikely couple, you see, so I'd noticed. Then that money disappeared, and Jane did, too. Ronnie was in the spring play, the big senior play, but he'd only taken a small part. I remember he didn't seem very interested—sort of depressed. At the time, I wondered if it was because of Jane. And that boy never did have any close friends. . . ." Her voice dwindled off. She seemed suddenly to have run down, like an old clock that hadn't been wound in time.

"You look a little tired—and no wonder, with my interrupting your nap and then grilling you like this! Is there anything else you can think of, anything odd or unusual or that just seems to you worth mentioning?"

She gazed out the kitchen window, narrowed her eyes, shook her head slowly from side to side, and said, "No, I can't think of a thing."

"If you should happen to later," I said, getting my checkbook out of my purse and handing her a deposit slip, "here's my address and phone number—phone me collect, I'll be paid back by the magazine. I'm out of cards right now. And I'm very grateful to you for all the information and time and energy, and tea. And memories. Thank you so much." I smiled, liking her.

"You're very welcome, my dear."

She followed me to the front door and held it open for me.

"It has been most enjoyable for me, you know, your visit. And if I do think of anything, I will telephone. You may count on me."

Back at the school, the librarian had gotten hold of a '62 yearbook belonging to someone named Susie. I read some of the autographed messages at the beginning:

"To Susie, a swell girl, who has the toughest figure, as Don says." From Harold. "To a very nice girl with a wonderful personality that works like a magnet." From Don—the same one?

I turned to the page of junior pictures. There was Ronald Cremmens again, looking much the same as he had in the senior picture the next year, a little scrawnier, perhaps. Saring, Sedder, Shingle.

The face that looked back at me was Beatrice's, surely? Seventeen years younger, but not, apparently, particularly innocent even then.

THIRTY

WHEN I GOT BACK TO THE MOTEL, I TRIED TELEPHONING O'Reagan but got the service again. It was late for starting back to San Francisco, and I decided not to leave until morning. I took a long, hot bath, trying but failing to take my mind off Jane Shingle and Ronald Cremmens for a while. Then I lay down and tried to put myself in a state of deep relaxation but only partially succeeded, partly because I kept hoping that the telephone would ring and that it would be O'Reagan, and partly because I was hungry.

Finally I gave up, on both the relaxation and the phone call, got dressed, and drove back to the old part of town to a Mexican restaurant I'd noticed near Miss Eulalia Henderson's. The food was about a thousand times better and half the price of the motel-row quick food I'd had the night before. The tortillas were soft and hot and came with a side dish of halved limes, so that for a minute or two, smelling them, I could imagine I was in Mexico.

I tried reading the Needles High School paper I'd picked up in the library, but I couldn't keep my mind on it and switched to a paperback murder. I don't mind eating alone at home; in fact, I often prefer it, with something to read along with my dinner. But I don't like eating out alone; it's lonely. I hurried through the meal and was back at the motel by nine.

The tired proprietor, looking weaker than ever, said there were no messages. I tried O'Reagan again and again didn't get him. I told his service to have him call me anytime that night; I wanted to talk to him before I left the next morning. I realized then I was staying over that night mainly in case O'Reagan had any suggestions on further things to check out while I was down there.

The answering-service person took the message noncommittally, but I got the feeling she thought I was one of O'Reagan's cast-off girlfriends and that the chances of his calling me back were minimal. I thought about calling Simmons and telling him what I'd found out, but not for long. I wanted to talk to O'Reagan first.

I felt stirred up and speedy from my discovery of Jane Shingle. If she was Beatrice, the police should be able to confirm that. But I was tired of the fast, circular thoughts rolling around in my head, scurrying like rats, circling like buzzards over some rotten carcass. I like to do my thinking, such as it is, in the daytime, and I like to not think at all at night.

I picked up the paperback I'd started at dinner and tried to keep my mind on it. It was an early E. X. Ferrars and a good one, but my mind kept wandering away from her wandering widows, as she called them, back to that ex-widower Henry and his new bride. Jane Single? Jane Single? Jane Shingle?

And Lindy. And Lindy. If Beatrice was Jane and knew Cremmens, then she must have gotten that bomb from him and blown up the plane somehow. She'd been a stewardess. Maybe. If Beatrice was Jane. Or was it all Henry, or Dunbar? The thoughts kept circling; Celia, Lindy, Cremmens. A random ninety-something humans who happened to be on the plane with Lindy. Not to mention poor old Gentleman Malone, buried now in some pauper's grave.

Finally I put the book aside, turned off the light, and did some more relaxation exercises, which if they didn't stop the circling speculations at least slowed them down. "My right arm is heavy," I repeated, "my left arm is heavy . . ." Then I meditated on the color blue, and finally I slept.

In my dreams the high-up, gray planes were flying over, soundlessly, and there were some flashes of terrible white light. I lay on my back porch against the wall, huddled under a piece of old canvas. I hoped it would be enough to keep out the radiation, but I didn't think it would. I pulled the canvas tighter about me, all the same.

The only police I saw on the way back were interested in speeders, not murder suspects, and I arrived home without incident around seven Saturday evening. I returned the dogs' greetings with equal enthusiasm, dumped my backpack on the bed, and took the dogs out for a walk. When we got back, I ate some Swiss cheese and sourdough bread that was a little stale but all right toasted. Then I took a bath to clean off the highway and relax, but my mind kept buzzing. Then I called O'Reagan and talked again to his answering service. This time he'd left a message.

"He said to tell you he tried to call you back in Needles, but you'd already left. He said to tell you that your friends are going out tonight, and he's going out, too, around eight o'clock—that you'd know where?"

"Yes."

"And that you could meet him if you got back in time."

It was already after eight by then, so I hurriedly threw on some dark clothes, a pair of swoopy-legged black pants, and a heavy black sweater. Checking myself in the mirror, I thought I looked OK for breaking and entering—entering, anyway—except for my feet. I changed to dark socks and Birkenstock sandals, which are quiet. Finally, I added a dark wool cap and black leather gloves.

As an afterthought, I took Celia's gun out of the ski boot. Checking the safety, I decided it seemed nice and tight so that I needn't worry about its changing position accidentally. I stuck the gun down in the deep pocket of my pants, checked myself in the mirror again, and was pleased to see that not even a small bulge showed from the gun.

My stomach was feeling peculiar by then, and also the area above it, my solar plexus. I drove uptown to Celia's neighborhood and spotted O'Reagan's car on a side street, an old blue BMW with a distinguishing dent in the left rear fender.

It was almost nine by then and very dark out. There wasn't any moon, and there weren't any stars, either. The dark would be a help. It was windy, which was a good thing, too, because the trees were rustling around and the wind was making a lot of other strange noises, which gave me a better chance of getting to the cottage, and into it, without being noticed by any of the servants.

I cautiously took hold of the knob of the gate in the wall along the side of the house, which gets you to the cottage without having to go past either the house or the garage and servants' quarters. I turned it and it squealed loudly—just, I thought, like a pig being killed. I froze and thought of the pig I saw being killed, once, and hoped I'd never see another one.

After a while, not hearing any sounds of alarm, I squeezed through the opening that the squeal had made and then pulled the door shut fast. That minimized the length of the squeal, at least. After another little wait, hearing only the quiet, except for the wind noises, I walked quickly over to the cottage door.

Celia's house—I still think of it as hers, though it was Henry's by then, and now it is sold and strangers live there—was dark, a huge, ominous mass over to my left. The garage and servants' rooms were on the other side of the house and couldn't be seen from where I was, which meant they wouldn't be able to see me, either.

No signs of life in the cottage. But then, there wouldn't be. I took the second key Henry had given me from my left pocket, the pocket that didn't have the gun in it. I imagined it would be amusing to get in there quietly and surprise O'Reagan.

I stuck the key in the lock and slowly turned it. I could feel it moving, smoothly and silently. Slow-ly. And then, with a tiny click, it was free.

I let out the breath I'd been holding, turned the knob, and started opening the door slowly. It made no sound.

Lights were on inside. I could see a faint lightening of the darkness as soon as the door opened just a crack. I pushed the door open a little further and slipped into the small, windowless anteroom. I locked the door behind me. A crack of light showed from beneath the door opposite me, the one going into the studio. No light had shown outside, so the windows must have had some sort of blackout covering. I wondered why. Anyway, O'Reagan must have decided the light was safe. . . . I didn't hear anything.

I walked over to the studio door. The knob was on the right, and the door opened inward. I quietly turned the knob, then slowly pushed the door open and walked softly into the room.

"Freeze!" rapped out a strangely familiar voice, and it wasn't O'Reagan's.

"I mean it, *freeze*. Stop *right there* or you're a dead little bitch."

The voice, over to my left, was not loud, but there was no lack of menace in it for all that. Beatrice's voice. I recognized it without any trouble at all. Even though I'd not yet got to know her very well, or seen her very often . . .

I froze. I felt sick. I felt paralyzed.

"All right. Raise your hands above your head now, and *slowly* turn this way please, Maggie, dear."

She was waving a large gun—a very large gun; it looked like a cannon, in fact—back and forth between me and O'Reagan. He was sitting in a chair over against the wall, looking glum.

"What's all this? Who's that?" I tried.

"Shut up," she replied. "You know who this is; I've seen you together."

"I don't—"

"Shut up, I said. Go stand over there by your pal. That's right. Stop; that's close enough."

I looked at O'Reagan, and he looked back expressionlessly. Except for the decided air of dejection.

"Beatrice, what in the world—"

"Shut *up*, I said. I'm thinking."

I was sorry to hear that. I wondered how I might distract her—without getting shot, that is. It was an awfully big gun she was holding, was pointing now about equidistant—no favorites—between us.

I knew it would be as well to start thinking myself, but my brain didn't seem to be working too well. My senses were OK; I had all the appropriate feelings of fear and terror, and the sick feeling went from my chin down to my knees. My eyes took in the long, flowered silk dress she wore, automatically admiring the graceful, expensive lines of it, the brilliant blues and reds and yellows of the tiny perfect silk flowers.

Beatrice's two-color eyes glittered in the light which came from a big globe hanging down on her left. The big diamond engagement ring glittered, too, on the hand that held the gun. She must be left-handed, I thought feebly, and wondered if that would help. I didn't see that it would; the gun was quite steady, the left hand quite competent-looking. *Think,* I told myself, *think.*

"Well, Maggie, this may be a help. I'd been thinking about how to get you up here, and now you've come and volunteered."

She smiled, an automatic, social sort of smile that didn't reach her eyes.

"I wouldn't have chosen to have you both here at the same time—not alive, anyway—but I guess I'll just have to make do, and in the long run you've probably saved me a lot of trouble." She was speaking in a low, fast monotone. "And don't bother to deny the two of you have been snooping around, finding out things about me, prying into your stupid sister's demise, trying to prove that I did it. I saw you two coming out of the morgue the other night—and I saw *him*''—she waved the gun at O'Reagan—''at the inquest.''

"Inquest? I didn't know you were at the inquest.'' I decided the best thing for now would be to try flattering and admiring her cleverness until something more substantial occurred to me. Keep her talking—that's what they did in books, and sometimes it worked.

"The lady undoubtedly made a few alterations in her appearance,'' O'Reagan said, looking at Beatrice. "You did a good job. You used a different set of changes, I suppose, when you pushed Mrs. Sloan in front of the cable car? Which one were you? The blonde?''

"*I'm* Mrs. Sloan now, and don't you forget it. God knows I've earned it and I'm going to enjoy it, and no two-bit ex-dick or rich little bitch—''

"Tch, tch, such language for a prominent—''

"Shut up.'' It seemed to be her favorite phrase tonight.

"Were you the blonde, the floozy with the sunglasses?'' he persisted.

"Yes, I was. And it all went off perfectly until that stupid tramp practically ran me over and knocked my glasses off—it was a pleasure to stick the knife into that old bastard, let me tell you.''

"A mistake, however, in the long run,'' O'Reagan said mildly.

"Is Henry in on this?'' I asked. She shot me a disgusted look, and I added: "I'm just curious.''

"Henry? Of course he—is.'' She smiled again, with real amusement this time.

I couldn't tell whether or not to believe her.

Her smile broadened, but it was not cheering. "Maybe I'm lying, though. You can put your hands down now; just hang them there by your sides and don't move them around any. That's right.''

I did as she ordered and looked around the room. A small mouse ran across the top of a table for wedging clay, down at the far end of the room.

"Why the big black curtains over the windows? Or had you

planned this scene back when you were doing over the cottage?"
I asked.

"For film projection, stupid, or slides."

She waved the hand that wasn't holding the cannon over to
her right, indicating a big screen on the wall. At the other end
of the room, the wall with the door I'd come in through, a 16-
mm projector was set up.

"I didn't know you had anything to do with film," I said. "I
used to work—"

"Shut up."

Maybe if I got her talking about her crimes, she'd find the
subject more interesting. Maybe if she was doing the talking,
she wouldn't be forever saying shut up.

"She was just developing her plans for us, kind of thinking
out loud, when you came in, Maggie. If I followed correctly,
she'd decided if she killed me and then caused you to disappear,
permanently, then the cops would think you'd killed me—and all
the others—and then run off so you wouldn't be nabbed for the
crimes. She says they suspect you, anyway. But I think she's
having trouble working out the details."

"Where are you getting hung up?" I asked.

"Think you're pretty smart, don't you? All right. The thing
is, I have you right where I want you, Maggie, dear. I can cre-
mate you in my kiln"—she nodded her head back, over her right
shoulder—"and you'll disappear, all right. But there're a lot of
details I have to be careful to get right, to make it look like you
split. I'll have to get some clothes from your apartment, make
it obvious some are missing—take all the coats, for instance.
Better put those in the kiln, too . . . And you have dogs, you
said. I'll take them over to Oakland, that'll be a good place; no
one will pay any attention to a couple more stray, starving dogs
over there. I'll put them out separately—"

"They'll never go with you," I interrupted, furious. "They'll
bite you."

"I'm very good with animals. Shut up."

"How hot does that kiln go?"

"Hot enough, if I leave it going a couple days."

I had no idea how high a temperature was needed for cre-
mation. I'd never had any particular interest in it before.

"It won't get rid of everything," O'Reagan said. "There
would be some chunks of bone left."

"I can throw those away later; that's no problem. Be interesting to see how this affects my glazes. I'll have to put some very special pieces in, to remember you by."

She smiled that nauseating smile again; she really did look quite pleased and happy at the thought of adding O'Reagan and me to the glaze on some of her clay pots. There were a bunch of them, all sizes, on a long table along the wall behind her. Some of the vases were five or six feet high—showing good technical skill, but I didn't really care for the shapes. I'd be sorry to end up as a glaze on any of them. I saw the mouse that had earlier been on the wedging table, or another one, scurry down one side of the table behind Beatrice and then disappear from sight behind a pitcher.

"Some impressive work back there," I said.

"What are you going to do with the bones, if I may ask?" O'Reagan interjected.

"Throw them in some dumpster. In a paper bag. The cops won't be looking for anything like that. Sunset Scavenger will just grind them up with the rest of the garbage on Tuesday morning. No, that won't be any problem," she said again. "But I wanted *you*—what's your name? O'Reilly?"

"O'Reagan."

"O'Reagan, that's right. I'd wanted *you* dead in your own house. Or office, maybe, it wouldn't matter which. Before your girl friend got here, I could have got you over there on your own two feet somehow. Now, I don't know. You're too heavy to carry, and anyway, somebody'd be sure to see me."

She looked down at the big gun still held quite steadily in her left hand, the fourth finger sporting the glittering diamond. Keeping the gun on us, she backed over to the table that had her clay pieces on it, dragged a canvas director's chair out and back over toward us, and sat down on it. She sighed and rested the gun hand on her left thigh. She looked a little tired.

"Well, that's the main problem, Miss Priss," she said to me. "I want him dead, but I want the police to *know* he's dead—so when you disappear at the same time, they'll make the connection. So I can't just shoot him and burn him up in the kiln along with you. Pity."

"Yes, I see your problem," I said. "How to get his body away from here—he's so big, too."

"Right."

"I guess you were lying, weren't you, about Henry. Because if he was in on all of this, *he* could help you with the body. It might be too chancy to take it back to O'Reagan's house, but you and Henry could dump it in an alley easily enough—if you had him to help."

"Henry help?" She smiled. "You don't know the trouble I've gone to to keep that man out of this. What good would it have done, I ask you, to get rid of his rich bitch of a wife who he so nobly insisted on telling about us? And so nobly insisted on telling he wanted a divorce—so that I had to get rid of her in a hurry, before he lost out on all her money. What good would all that have done if he was hung for it?"

"None at all," I agreed.

"I carefully arrange everything, even though I have to hurry, for a time when he'll be three hundred miles away, and what does he do? He stays in town an extra day!"

"That would be aggravating," O'Reagan murmured.

"What you do need, though, Beatrice, is an accomplice, it seems to me—to help tidy up all these loose ends."

"Well, it won't be you, sweetheart. I wouldn't trust either of you under any circumstances, if that's what you're getting at. Just because I didn't go to some fancy Vassar College like you did, don't think I'm stupid."

"I don't think you're stupid."

"Shut up."

Back to that. I sighed.

"Isn't all this shooting going to be rather noisy?" O'Reagan asked in an easy, conversational tone. "It's bound to leave traces, also, if you do it here. Of course, they might never look here, but if they did . . . I can see the floor's all right," he continued, looking down at the shiny squares of dark red quarry tile. "You can just mop up the blood and wash it down the drain in one of those big tubs you have over there for your ceramics and burn the mop, I suppose, in the kiln. But that's a big gun you have there. Ever shot anyone with it?"

"What if I haven't?" she replied with a sneer, glaring at him.

"Well, if you haven't, then you probably don't realize what a mess it makes, a big gun like that. It'll splatter—things—traceable things—all over the walls. That brick is porous; you won't be able to get it all out. Probably mess up the curtains, too,'' he concluded, glancing over his shoulder at the heavy black drape just behind him.

She didn't say anything more, just continued to glare at him.

He went on: "Maybe we could make a deal—we think up a foolproof way to get rid of Sloan, and Maggie and I could do the job—she never liked him, anyway, you know. You'll be safe then because we can't tell the police any stories about you, having bumped off Sloan. And you'd have all that nice money, *all* of it. You might even give us a little of it for our trouble—''

"Don't be ridiculous,'' she interrupted. "You're not funny. Shut up. Something you said . . .'' She lifted her hand and pointed the gun between us more actively than she had before. "Got it!'' She smiled happily. "Thank you. I've figured it out; I knew I would. What I'll do is I'll kill her; then when I shoot you, I'll collect a nice big lot of your blood and stuff with some powder marks and then put both your bodies in the kiln, turn it on, and clean up the mess. Pardon me for thinking out loud in front of you like this''—she returned momentarily from her mental planning, flashing the social smile again—"but it can't be helped. Then, while you're cooking away in there, disappearing, I'll take the jar of blood and stuff over to your place and pour it on the carpet, or whatever—''

"Peruvian rugs—''

"Don't interrupt. Spread the stuff around, anyway, and make it look like someone tried to clean it up. So it's obvious you were shot and killed. That way they'll know there's a body, even though they'll never see it. They'll hunt all over the place for little bright-eyes here, but, of course, they won't find her. Eventually, the whole thing'll just dwindle away, one of the ninety-five percent of unsolved murders or whatever it is, and I won't have to be bothered with all this anymore. It's getting to be a pain in the ass,'' she concluded simply.

She looked from one to the other of us, a smile on her thin lips, her head high, as if waiting to be congratulated.

I thought, she's quite insane. But her plans were sounding all too workable now that she was getting the little details ironed out. I was afraid that she might start carrying them out at any moment and thought that I had better try to interject something fresh into our conversation before it got so stale and tiring for her that she ended it. I looked around the room for inspiration.

Projection screen . . . big, deep sinks for cleaning up after ceramics . . . slick tile floor . . . the long table with her greenware and bisqued clay pieces, some with glaze on . . . The mouse I'd seen earlier had been joined by another, and they were chasing each other, or something, quite near the edge, running back and forth around a tall, slender vase. . . .

"Yes," she said, still smiling, "that should do it, don't you think?"

"No, I don't," said O'Reagan emphatically. "For one thing—"

"Shut up."

"No, I don't, either," I said. "There are some things you don't know, that I've found out. That other people know now, too, or soon will—" I turned to O'Reagan and explained: "Simmons was out, so I left the information in a note; they said he'd be back sometime tonight."

"Sure you did, you lying little bitch," Beatrice said.

"Good," O'Reagan said. "They should be here soon then. I was getting—"

"Shut *up*, I said! What information, pray tell?" she asked, glaring at me, unconvinced, but, I thought, at least a bit worried. "What are you pretending to talk about?" she asked again, when I didn't answer.

"Well, all this money you have now"—I swept my arm out to indicate her person and the studio—"obviously you have as a result of killing Lindy, right?"

Her head slid forward like a rattlesnake's, her eyes as poisonous as any fangs.

"So," she asked in a voice I didn't like the sound of, quietly dangerous, "what about it?"

It was now or never.

"Just that your name isn't Beatrice, it's Jane—Jane Shingle! Teenage embezzler of the State Farm insurance funds—traceable old buddy of Ronnie Cremmens, back there in Needles!"

She looked shocked, all right. All the color drained from her face—it seemed instantly—and her thin lips dropped right open.

Behind her there was a small tinkling crash as the tall vase tottered over and smashed on the floor.

As she glanced back involuntarily, I yelled, "Simmons! Thank God!"

O'Reagan dodged to the floor and rolled as her head jerked

back toward the door. I grabbed the gun in my pocket, and then her gun went off.

O'Reagan was knocked against the wall. I heard a thud, then another as his heavy body fell to the floor.

I shoved the safety down as I pointed at her chest and started pulling the trigger. Big red splotches appeared on the front of her.

Then there was silence except for a clicking sound. Finally I realized the sound came from me, still pulling the trigger of the empty gun. I stopped.

Beatrice's gun was pointing down at the floor now, hanging from a lifeless-looking hand. The front of the thousand-dollar dress wasn't different colors now. It was all red.

The hand wasn't lifeless, though, because she lifted the gun and pointed it at me. But very slowly; she couldn't hold it upright, and I was out of the way of the shot when it came.

Blood was coming out of her mouth now, a thin stream from the corner of the thin lips that trickled down across a powdered cheek. I didn't know how many shots I'd fired, or how many times I'd hit her. But one of the shots must have got her in the lung, I thought stupidly, watching the blood running out the corner of her mouth.

The heavy gun dropped from the limp hand and hit the tile floor with a clatter.

I went over to where O'Reagan was lying on the floor. His face was a horrible gray color. There was blood all over the front of his dark sweater. Just like Beatrice.

I thought he was dead, and I thought, she's killed him, too. She's killed him, too.

But his eyes were closed, not open and sightless like hers, and he was breathing. A raggedy, horrible-sounding breathing, but it was life.

I went and kicked the gun away from Beatrice's limp-hanging hand in case she wasn't really dead, even though she looked that way, and could pick it up again. Then I went to the telephone and told the operator to get me emergency at Presbyterian Hospital, because they were the closest.

It was a red Princess phone, the same color as all the blood. With push-button dialing.

"Hurry," I said, "please hurry. The man is bleeding to death."

Then I called the police and told them to come on over, too, but in their case there wasn't any hurry.

I went over and knelt down on the floor beside O'Reagan, put his head straight, and put my hand under it for a pillow. I was afraid to move him anymore in case I made things worse. Then I got up, got a clean white towel from a rack by the sink, pulled his sweater up, and pressed the towel down where most of the blood seemed to be coming from. The towel didn't stay white long. The bleeding seemed to be slowing down, though. *Hurry*, I remember saying to myself over and over, hurry God please hurry. . . .

I held the towel down tightly and looked around the room, surveying the wreckage. Anything was better than looking at that gray face. . . .

One of my shots had hit one of Beatrice's huge, ugly vases. It was lying in several pieces on the floor, white, glaze-covered pieces near the small brown shards of unfired clay that had been the vase that saved my life. Knocked over, I supposed, by one of the mice. Great granddaughter, or great great great, perhaps, of the one I'd seen scurrying about the day I cleared the cottage of Celia's things. And not mentioned to Cook, since I'd always like mice . . . not like rats . . .

Beatrice—or Jane Shingle—was lying quite still, in the same position she'd fallen into after she'd last shot at me, in the blue director's chair. The different-colored eyes were staring at the ceiling. The Paris dress wasn't pretty anymore, bunched awkwardly as it was now over the sprawling body and covered with the stiffening blood. . . .

A thousand-dollar dress, I thought, and a fifty-thousand dollar ceramics studio. And about a hundred people had to die, so Jane Shingle could have them. She didn't have them long.

I heard the ambulance shrilling through the night, and for once I didn't hate the sound.

Hurry, I started muttering again, hurry, hurry. . . .

O'Reagan was looking worse, his face grayer, the breathing rougher. But at least he was still breathing.

I remembered I'd locked the door behind me, and got up and opened it.

"He's alive, take him first," I said, pointing to O'Reagan. "The woman's dead. I've called the police."

They seemed slow to me, but finally they had him on the

stretcher and out the door. As they went out, Henry came rushing into the room. He saw me first.

"Maggie! What—oh, my God, Beatrice! Beatrice! Darling, my God—"

He ran over and took her face in his hands, then knelt down beside the body and held it. He started crying, dry, rasping sobs.

I was still holding my empty gun. I'd put it down when I was trying to stop O'Reagan's bleeding, but I'd picked it up again at some point.

Henry turned a ravaged face to me and said, "I'll kill you for this, Maggie, if it's the last thing I do. I suppose that policeman was right and you killed Celia, too. Well, I don't mind about that, but I'll kill you for doing this to Beatrice. I swear it."

His eyes moved over to the gun Beatrice had held, now lying on the floor a few feet away, and he took one of his hands away from her dead face. I raised my gun and pointed it at him.

"Shut up, Henry. I'm tired. I didn't murder Celia. She did. Your precious Beatrice. Only her name wasn't really Beatrice, it was Jane. Jane Shingle. She changed it a long time ago over some minor crime she committed in high school—embezzling."

"You're lying, of course," he said. "You're lying. You're just trying to save your own neck and blame it all on her. Now that she's dead. The only woman I ever loved. I'll kill you."

"Oh, shut up," I said again. "The police are coming. They'll have to be the ones to straighten it all out; I'm too tired to argue."

"Drop the gun, Mrs. Elliott," said a voice from the doorway. I recognized the voice as Simmons'.

"Gladly," I said and did.

THIRTY-ONE

THE STRAIGHTENING-OUT TOOK A LITTLE TIME, THOUGH, AND meanwhile I had to spend a night and day in jail. I hadn't any proof that Beatrice was Jane Shingle, and while they would have let me go once they'd finally checked that out to its logical conclusion, the Cremmens' connection, that might have taken awhile. Particularly as Simmons didn't believe it.

Luckily, O'Reagan regained consciousness the next day for long enough to corroborate my story, including Beatrice's own admissions to us both.

O'Reagan had to spend several weeks in the hospital. He'd been shot in the right lung, and Beatrice's gun had made a pretty big hole in it. It was only because he got medical attention so quickly that he lived at all. So he considered that by shooting Beatrice I'd saved his life. I told him he didn't owe me anything for that, though, since I'd got him into the whole mess in the first place.

We were sitting in his hospital room one afternoon about two weeks after the big blowout, talking over some of the loose ends, when Simmons came in.

"How's it going?" he asked O'Reagan, and said to me with a somewhat shamefaced look, "Afternoon, Mrs. Elliott. There's some details of this Sloan business I'd like to get cleared up, if you're up to it, Pat? Good that you're here, too, Mrs. Elliott."

"Why not?" O'Reagan said. "Pull up a chair."

"I'm glad to see you're out of jail," Simmons said to me as he did so. "Why the hell didn't you tell me about all this Jane Shingle business before you went over there and nearly got yourselves killed?"

"Well, I thought about it, down in Needles. But our relationship was never very wonderful, yours and mine, and, anyway, I

225

wanted to talk to O'Reagan first. I thought he could talk to you better.''

"Also, she fancied a spot of breaking and entering," O'Reagan contributed. He was glad I'd saved his life, but he thought, too, that I should have gone to the police, that I'd taken too big a chance in going up there.

"Entering," I corrected, "with a key Henry had freely given me. Seriously—I'm afraid the whole affair was not quite real to me until I walked into that studio and saw Beatrice pointing that huge gun at me. Then it got real.''

"One thing I didn't get a chance to tell you, Maggie, and you, Jim," O'Reagan said. "I heard from my doctor friend in Texas. This came in the mail you brought over last night, Maggie. He got confirmation that Mrs. Sloan—the first one—couldn't have any more children after Lindy.''

"That's what got all this trouble started in the first place," I explained to Simmons, "only it took twenty years to . . . mature.''

"How do you mean?" Simmons asked.

"Well, I don't know what Henry's said," I answered, "but the doctor's information confirms what O'Reagan and I suspected, that Celia lied to Henry all those years, made him believe it was his fault that they didn't have children. Her idea of the female was pretty totally connected with the traditional things, like bearing children. She may even have come to believe it herself, eventually.''

"So?"

"Well, we think what happened was that Henry got restless and had an affair with Beatrice—and fell in love and she got pregnant, because he'd told her she didn't have to worry about birth control. At that point he must have realized Celia'd been lying all those years and was furious. And being the noble, moral sort, he told Celia all about the affair and insisted on a divorce. Which horrified Beatrice, of course, when he told her. She thought it'd be a lot nicer if Celia would die instead of getting divorced. One of the things she liked about Henry was his money—which, of course, was actually Celia's money. Lindy told me at the airport that her mother had originally been scheduled to fly back with her—back East for some board meeting. Reservations that had been made months earlier, by Henry.''

"At some point," O'Reagan picked up the narrative, "Beatrice had run into her old friend Cremmens and found out he was working on a special explosives project—it was his only claim to distinction, poor fellow. Probably she originally got the explosives from him to blow up the plane Mrs. Sloan was supposed to fly back East in after Christmas.''

"She had easy access to that information through Henry," I added. "But then she had to kill Celia sooner because Henry was on the verge of leaving her—and all that money. Cook told me she heard them talking divorce a few days before Celia was killed."

"Goddammit!" Simmons exploded. "I questioned that woman!"

"So Beatrice," I continued, "somehow got Celia to meet her down at the waterfront that morning. She dressed herself up, with a blond wig, big sunglasses, and appropriate clothes, as a floozy blonde so no one would ever connect her, Beatrice, with the cable car scene.

"And then that poor old wino nabbed your sister's purse, ran into Beatrice and knocked off her big sunglasses—so when she saw him two years later at the hospital, and he said he'd seen her before, she assumed he really remembered her from the cable car murder."

"I wonder," I said, "whether Beatrice just waited for some spontaneous chance to kill Celia, or whether she had it planned out ahead of time."

"Judging by what I saw of her," O'Reagan said grimly, "she probably had it all planned out. Although she was pretty good at improvising, too."

"And then it turned out that Mrs. Sloan had already changed her will in favor of her children, leaving Dr. Sloan with a few measly thousands and the house," Simmons contributed.

"Right. Instead of the millions she'd grown accustomed to the thought of," I said.

"So she put her rather good brain to work," O'Reagan went on with the outline, "and hit upon the idea of killing off one of the children. Since Sloan had legally adopted them, he would inherit."

"It may be that she tried to get rid of Mark, first," I told Simmons. "Lindy told me, again at the airport, that he'd been very sick from an overdose of sleeping pills—and that he didn't remember taking them."

"I never knew about that," Simmons said disgustedly.

"They weren't exactly advertising it," O'Reagan said dryly. "Beatrice could have had Sloan's keys copied—and then got in the house and slipped the pills into a bottle of whiskey next to Mark's bed; she knew he was a drunk and would be likely to drink most of it. But he didn't die—the tolerance of alcoholics to drugs is unpredictable—and she didn't dare try anything too soon again on him. Then, since Lindy was taking that plane back to school and Beatrice had the explosive handy, she was the next choice."

"Beatrice was the type who dislikes other women, anyway," I commented. "And Congressman Holmes being on that plane was a nice break for her. She whipped out the so-called California Coalition tape in a hurry, and no one really questioned it. Beatrice was probably a stewardess once, too, so she would have known the ropes—how to get the bomb on the plane."

"Yeah, we found the remainder of the stolen explosive—thank God!—hidden in that studio of hers," Simmons said. "Also, a piece of paper with a series of numbers that we finally figured out is the combination that opens the door to the stewardess' lounge at the airport."

"Maybe saving them for another try at Mark," I suggested. "Or perhaps she had some thoughts of becoming a rich widow, eventually. Although another plane crash would be too much coincidence to be safe, I'd think. But I do wonder if she'd eventually have got around to Mark again. You know, she named her son Alexander—master of the whole world, not just part of it. At the very least, I think she was trying to help Mark die off from his drinking. She kept telling him he could drink in moderation, just what every drunk wants to believe."

"How is Mark, by the way?" O'Reagan asked.

"He's got his health back from drying out. He's very young; his body can still snap back pretty fast. And he seems to be taking all this murder business pretty well. I mean, so far it hasn't sent him off on another binge. He never did get along with Henry, anyway—he'd known, by the way," I said to Simmons, "that his father had been having an affair before his mother was killed, but he never knew who with. I finally talked with him about it last week. Apparently at first he thought maybe his father *had* had something to do with Celia's death. His stepfather. That's why he was so angry and rude to him. Then later he decided maybe he was just being paranoid and dropped the idea.''

''And when they went to see the kid at the de-tox,'' Simmons said, ''the Malone guy recognized Mrs. Sloan—the new Mrs. Sloan—from the cable car scene. I really thought''—he turned to me—''that it was you he'd put the fix on.''

''I know.''

''Anyway,'' O'Reagan continued, ''everything had gone along according to plan, and Jane Shingle, alias Beatrice Brown, was smart and clever enough to wait two years to marry Sloan. She was finally sitting pretty when Malone came along.''

''And said, 'Haven't I seen you somewhere before?' I wonder if he really remembered her?'' I asked.

''We'll never know,'' O'Reagan said.

''Probably not,'' Simmons said. ''Anyway, she got rid of him. That was her first big mistake; it dug the whole thing up again.''

''O'Reagan said that, too,'' I said. ''But I'm not so sure. Do you think she could have got away with just denying it, if he accused her—put it all together somehow in that alcohol-raddled brain of his? The cable car accident killing Mark's mother, who was rich, and now that same woman was married to Mark's father?''

''She obviously didn't feel she could take the chance, anyway,'' O'Reagan agreed. ''So she hopped it up there that same night and killed him.''

''Probably dressed as that orderly,'' Simmons said. ''I thought you made him up, Mrs. Elliott.''

''And meanwhile, she saw me with a woman Henry said was Celia's childhood friend, Carlotta—and the same day Henry may have mentioned that Mary P. Lewis, Celia's best friend, had called him for my phone number. And that I'd gotten Cook's phone number the day before. She probably started then to wonder what I was up to.''

''And unfortunately,'' O'Reagan said, ''she was down at Headquarters with Sloan to sign their statements about the contact they'd had with Malone at the hospital—''

''And saw you and me coming out the door together.''

''That nearly cooked our goose, in the end,'' O'Reagan concluded.

''Thank goodness I happened to find that gun—'' I began, then broke off, avoiding Simmons' eye.

"I've decided to overlook that gun, considering everything." Simmons half smiled at me, though stiffly, like a man who doesn't smile much. I was glad to see him trying it out, though.

"No hard feelings, er . . ."

"No hard feelings."

I was liking Simmons a lot better since he'd made the mistake of arresting me. He was nicer when he was feeling a little humble.

"Besides," O'Reagan smiled at him, "we figure your goodwill will be a good thing to have in the business Maggie and I are setting up when I get out of here. . . ."

"Private eyes and ears," I ended sweetly.

ABOUT THE AUTHOR

ELIZABETH ATWOOD TAYLOR was born in San Antonio, Texas, and now lives in Rhode Island. Educated at Vassar and Bryn Mawr, she has worked as a film editor, a TV news reporter, a social worker, and an art therapist. She is also the author of MURDER AT VASSAR.